FOR A WILD WOMAN'S HEART

Ancient Songs
Book 3

LAURA STRICKLAND

ARE YOU SIGNED UP FOR DRAGONBLADE'S BLOG?

You'll get the latest news and information on exclusive giveaways, exclusive excerpts, coming releases, sales, free books, cover reveals and more.

Check out our complete list of authors, too!

No spam, no junk. That's a promise!

Sign Up Here

www.dragonbladepublishing.com

Dearest Reader;

Thank you for your support of a small press. At Dragonblade Publishing, we strive to bring you the highest quality Historical Romance from some of the best authors in the business. Without your support, there is no 'us', so we sincerely hope you adore these stories and find some new favorite authors along the way.

Happy Reading!

CEO, Dragonblade Publishing

ADDITIONAL DRAGONBLADE BOOKS BY AUTHOR LAURA STRICKLAND

Ancient Songs Series
For a Warrior's Heart (Book 1)
For an Exile's Heart (Book 2)
For a Wild Woman's Heart (Book 3)

The Three Sisters MacBeith Series
Keeper of the Gate (Book 1)
Keeper of the Hearth (Book 2)
Keeper of the Light (Book 3)

Do our ancestors journey with us
In the memories that we hold?
A hint of a tune,
A trill of breathless laughter,
A smile in a pair of eyes.
Sweet sorrow of things lost.
Is there a surer way for spirit to travel
Than via the echoes of what has been?

—Finlay the Bard

AT THE HALL of a Scottish chief deep in the western Highlands, a bard entertains those gathered, singing and telling tales while accompanying himself on the harp. He weaves his tales in praise of his host's ancestors, with a rare talent that keeps his listeners enthralled from the highest to the lowest. Amid the leaping torches and the flickering candles, there is magic encircling the great chamber this night.

He has told two tales of love lost and love found in far-off times. Surely his audience must have had their fill of his words and his music. But the hall still quivers with expectation. He is a skilled raconteur, and he knows his story full well.

His graceful fingers brush the strings, and a glimmer of bright notes pierces the air. So beautiful are they, he feels them as pain. His listeners catch a collective breath, and the great wheel that holds captive his heart makes a half turn. Blessed be those who hear my tale, he says in his voice like music. For to them will come the knowledge of the gods.

The third tale he tells begins:

Once long ago when Scotland was still full of magic, there was a princess. A Caledonian princess she was, born of the ancient people who walked this land before even our Celtic ancestors came, and her heart was a great prize. Listen now, while I sing ye a song for a wild woman's heart.

CHAPTER ONE

Western Scotland, the ninth century AD

THE STORM BROKE wild over the stones of the keep just at sunset, blowing in from the sea with sharp wind and lashings of rain. Deathan MacMurtray, hurrying in across the narrow bailey and up the steep steps to the walls, looked out on the heaving sea below the stretch of land where sat the stronghold. Naught could be seen but dark green waves and an ink-black sky.

A thousand attackers could lurk out there, and no one would know.

Not that he expected an attack. In this year of 843, Scotland was at peace, or at least so much as a land of warring clans and angry factions could be. Their new high king, Kenneth MacAlpin, had declared it so.

A wry smile, defying the misery of a face pelted by rain, touched Deathan's lips. Even here in the far reaches of the western Highlands it was said to be true, a united Scotland, all one. He knew his country, though, and the folk who inhabited it. If they could not find great matters over which to quarrel, they would find small ones.

A nation of restless hearts, it might be said.

Not allowing the weather to interrupt his duty, he paced the walls clear round, a dangerous exercise given the wet. Not until he'd assured himself all was safe did he relent and head inside, thoroughly drenched.

The keep—or some form of it—had stood for many years on this location at the edge of the sea. In the old days, it had been no more than a round house with a clutch of huts gathered around its skirts, protected by an encircling wall. His ancestors had fought to hold it against both their avaricious neighbors and the native tribes, they who called themselves Caledonians and others called Picts, or Blue Men.

Over the many generations, a fortified stone house had been built, a place where the clansfolk could shelter beneath the protection of their chief, the Murtray. And as prosperity had allowed, it had been expanded into the present keep.

They were not a wealthy clan, nor a poor one. Hard work kept their heads above water, and loyalty held them together.

Deathan loved every stone of the place with an unswerving devotion, and he would die defending it if he must.

Thunder rumbled overhead as he climbed yet another set of stairs to the house proper, through the arched entryway where one of the guards, Dannoch, stood wooden-faced. Unusual for that man, who loved to waylay anyone to talk. Perhaps the crashing thunder rendered conversation too difficult for him now.

It certainly kept Deathan from hearing the raised voices until he was well inside and approaching the upper hall where the family met, dined, and mostly dwelt. He paused abruptly at the entrance of the space, his senses going on alert.

A storm raged within the keep as well as without, or so it seemed.

It was not rare for Deathan's older brother, Rohr, and their father, the Chief MacMurtray, to disagree. Both strong-minded men and more alike than they would ever want to admit, they often refused to see eye to eye. But there was a threshold of discord they usually refused to cross. Rohr might challenge Da; he might even tease. Da might slap back verbally.

They seldom bellowed at one another.

But they did so now, both on their feet there in the hall, facing one another with heat and passion.

Deathan paused where he was, dripping water onto the flagstones. Overhead, thunder cracked so loud he could not hear the words being cried, as if the very elements sympathized with the men of Murtray.

He did not want or need this discord. Fresh in out of the wet, he wanted the heat of the fire and a mug of warm ale. A measure of peace as the stormy night drew down.

It seemed he would have none of it.

He eyed his father and brother, separated by a mere four paces or so, but by an incalculable distance. Their stance and appearance were so similar it looked uncanny, like a reflection disarranged by time. Both tall men with rangy builds. Da still held himself upright as befitted the warrior he had been. Rohr, though in his prime, could not quite dwarf his father.

Da's hair, once sandy brown, had early turned to silvery white. It formed a cloud around his head and shoulders from which his face looked stern, as one carved from stone. A wise leader he was, and a kindly one. Deathan had rarely seen him as enraged as he now appeared.

Rohr had hair the color of new-felled ash wood and eyes of blue, inherited from their mother. At the moment they glinted like the lightning that illuminated the windows, and flashed every bit as brightly.

The room brimmed with as much elemental power as did the world outside.

"What is it?" Deathan asked from the doorway. "What has happened?"

Neither of them heard him. Too busy arguing with each other or perhaps deafened by the storm, they raged on.

"Ye did no' think to tell me?" Rohr bellowed with none of the respect he surely owed his father. "No' before the messenger came to the door?"

Aye, there had been a messenger arrived this afternoon, so Deathan recalled. A single rider on a fine horse come from the east. He had marked the arrival but had been too busy to inquire after the man's business.

"I did no' think," Da roared back, "I had to bring to ye every small matter that came before me."

Rohr bellowed, "Small matter? Who could name changing the course o' my destiny as such?"

"We do as we maun in answer to duty, lad, and go where bidden. Did I no' raise ye knowing as much?"

Deathan blinked. His brother was not one to speak of destiny. Despite his bold and somewhat argumentative spirit, he tended to take things as given.

He would be given leadership of the clan some day—many years in the future, Deathan hoped. His father was, aye, still vigorous and not likely to surrender the reins soon.

"What is it?" he called again into the room. Thunder rumbled overhead once more, seeming to wring a response in echo from the very stones. Neither man acknowledged him.

"I should ha' been told o' this months ago!" Rohr hollered. "As soon as ever ye knew."

"'Twas no' months ago, but weeks I was mysel' informed. And what was to be done about it, save gi' obedience?"

Rohr threw up his hands. "Did ye no' think I would need to accustom my thoughts to such an—an intrusion?"

"I thought ye would obey as ye ought!"

"Aye." Rohr seethed. "'Tis wha' ye ha' always wanted fro' me—obedience. Nay of consideration nor feeling. Just blind obedience—"

"Lad, 'tis a decree from the king. How can the obedience owed be anything but blind?"

Deathan took several steps into the room. As the storm began to roll off over the dark hills, their voices grew louder. Would they disturb Mother where she lay?

"I will no' obey," Rohr said levelly.

Da's eyes flashed. "Ye will. If no' at my behest, then at that o' the king."

"Curse the king!"

Da drew himself up farther, impossibly tall. "List to wha' ye say! Am I to wash yer mouth out at the soap pot?"

Rohr took a step toward his father. "I should like to see ye try! I am no' a boy anymore, to accept yer discipline but a man grown."

"Ye be my son and sworn to me in fealty. So long as ye be under my roof—"

With sudden dignity, Rohr asked, "Do ye ask me to leave?"

"Wha'?" Da roared. "Would ye go?"

"I will tak' naught but my sword and my pony—those surely I ha' earned. And aye, I will go before I do yer mad bidding."

Da blinked. Deathan did not know if he believed the words Rohr spat at him or not.

Deathan did not even know if *he* believed.

The two men stared at one another, both breathing hard.

"Ye would no'," Da said, his voice a low throb. "Surrender yer home. Yer birthright. And to swerve a simple duty."

Rohr's lips curved bitterly. "'Tis no' simple. And ye should ha' told me, old man."

"What duty?" Deathan asked. What terrible thing could it be that made Rohr resist so hard?

Still they heeded him not. Rohr spun on his heel and, nearly walking through Deathan where he stood, marched out of the room, his eyes blank with fury.

Like the storm outside, he withdrew. That did not mean the disagreement had ended.

CHAPTER TWO

"DA, WHAT IS it? Wha' has happened?" Deathan moved to the fire, still dripping water from his hair and clothing. The most surprising thing about the battle that had just taken place, other than its sheer unexpectedness, was the fact that the two men would break it off with no winner, and no loser.

And with their raised voices, did they not think they would disturb Mother where she lay in her bed, in the next room? For Da and Rohr, rough men that they might be, and Deathan himself gave every due consideration to the woman they all adored. Mam had been sick a long time and bedridden these many weeks, too frail to be up on her feet. Deathan's older sister, Kearana, already wed and gone off with bairns of her own, had paid a visit only last month and wept in Deathan's arms before she departed again, afraid it would be the last time she would see Mam alive.

"I canna bear it. I canna," she had sobbed on his shoulder.

None of them could. Aene MacMurtray was a gentle, sometimes otherworldly woman nevertheless able to tame the men in her life with a look or touch. None of them could face the prospect of life without her, nor would they choose to upset her in any way.

This must be grave business, indeed.

Deathan kicked a log into the open fire and turned to face his father. "Wha' has happened?"

Herve MacMurtray dragged his fingers through his hair and

made a visible attempt to discipline his emotions. He cast Deathan a look before turning away. "Yer brother is gey upset."

"I could see that much. Why?"

"There is no choice in it. Why should he protest so much? 'Tis an honor, is it no', to tak' a bride o' the king's choosing."

Bride?

Before Deathan could speak, Da went on, "After all, it means we ha' the king's notice. He considers us among the strongest clans here in the western Highlands. And he wants his new country joined in peace. This—this is how he thinks to achieve it."

"What is?" A patient man, Deathan nevertheless grew weary with asking the same question.

Da turned to face him. His blue-green eyes, the same color as Deathan's own, looked weary in the wake of the quarrel, and deep lines bracketed his mouth.

When had he aged so? A vigorous man with a strong hold on the leadership of his clan, it had seemed to Deathan that Da would carry on forever. They might lose Mam, aye. But—

"Ye ken fine that the king, MacAlpin, has taken a Caledonian wife. To unite the country, so it can *be* a country, it was. And put an end at last to the warring."

"Aye." Since time out of mind, when Deathan's ancestors had first sailed from Ireland to stake their claims here in a kingdom they'd called Dalriada, they had fought the people already here. Those who called themselves Caledonian.

Now Kenneth MacAlpin thought to unite all into one country under the banner of Scotland.

Deathan had his doubts. He knew his countrymen. They might pay lip service to the king, but nay, that did not mean they would quit with fighting.

"Wha' has this to do wi' a *bride*, Da?"

Herve swung to face him. "The king has decreed that the strongest clans among us shall follow his example. That unions like his own should be formed throughout the land, uniting Gael and Caledonian. A young woman has been chosen and will travel here. To wed wi' your brother."

If someone had thumped Deathan hard on the chest, he could not be more surprised. He backed up and sat on a rug beside the fire.

A crowd of questions filled his mind. He chose one. "Why us?"

"As I say, 'tis an honor. The messenger who came last month—"

"Last month? And—ye did no' tell Rohr then?" Clearly his brother had been taken unawares, the source of at least some of his anger.

"Aye, well"—Herve frowned prodigiously—"'twas the height o' the training season and yer ma had only just taken to her bed. I thought there was no' sense in putting it to yer brother then."

"So ye announce it now?" Deathan's mind reeled.

"I had another messenger this day. The woman in question will arrive soon. For the wedding." Herve looked at Deathan implacably. "So I had to tell yer brother, did I no'?"

"Well—who is she, then? This bride."

A dreadful parody of a smile stretched Da's lips. "She is said to be a young woman and reputed to be bonny, so yer brother should no' complain too much, should he? She is a princess."

"Eh?"

"Among her own people. Royalty. And chosen to come to us. So ye can see—"

"Caledonian royalty?"

"Aye so"—Da frowned, thinking no doubt on Caledonians—"but of high standing all the same. Wha' could the king do but send her to a clan o' equally high standing?"

"Aye so," Deathan echoed his father. But they were not royal and had no blood connection to the king. There were a few figures of legend behind them—some great warrior near lost to the mists of time back in Ireland—and those who had founded their settlement here. Mostly hardworking people too stubborn to give up their lands. Worthy of admiration perhaps, but not necessarily worthy of…

A princess.

What would she be like, this young woman? Used to a high life of privilege and honor, to come to this oft-times rough place of rock and sea and sky. Would she consider it an honor?

"When will she arrive?"

Da shrugged. "Her party left home yesterday to mak' the journey. The messenger rode ahead so we might—prepare."

"I see," said Deathan, not sure he did.

"I had to tell yer brother," Da repeated. "'Tis a good thing for him, a direct connection wi' the king. He canna see that now. He will, in the future, when the union favors our fortunes."

Deathan said nothing. His father rushed on, "I can see the king's point o' view. There has been enough fighting, centuries o' it. If we are in truth to be a country, we must be one united."

Aye, mayhap, but Rohr must feel like his future, and all his choice in it, had just been stolen from him.

Deathan got to his feet.

"Where are ye goin'?" Da sked.

"To talk wi' my brother." Surely someone should.

THEY WERE NOT particularly close, for brothers. Though only a year and a half apart in age, they differed vastly in spirit—Rohr quick to declare his opinions, issue a challenge or flare to anger; Deathan far more apt to think before he spoke, to choose patience, and fall back on his duty.

Therein, mayhap, lay the difference in being raised to lead the clan and raised to support the man who would. Even though Deathan cared for this land with bottomless and selfless devotion, he would never be chief.

Did he envy his brother that place? He tried not to. He knew envy for a fruitless and destructive emotion.

Now he went with measured steps to his brother's chamber, tiptoeing past the door behind which his mother lay. A foolish effort, for if the raised voices had not disturbed her, nothing would.

The storm now rolled away eastward, the thunder fading to rumbles. Mayhap it had kept Mam from hearing the quarrel.

He found his brother in a wretched state, pacing his chamber like a caged wolf, tossing clothing and other items about, an expression that matched the trouble in his eyes.

"Wha' d'ye want?" Rohr barked when Deathan cracked the door and peered in.

"To speak wi' ye, just." Deathan slipped into the room and shut the door behind him. "And keep your voice down lest Mam hear."

Rohr ignored that. "He told ye? Da told ye?"

"Aye."

Rohr tossed his hands in the air. "A fine thing, is it no', for a man to have dropped upon him?"

Deathan did not know what to say. When his brother took this mood, he became deaf to reason. Still and all, reason must be employed.

"No' such a surprise, surely," he said.

"No' a surprise?" Rohr widened his lightning-blue eyes in a glare.

"Well, but ye knew ye must wed one day." A wonder that Rohr had escaped this long. As a man of a score and four years, and the future head of the clan, he might have any young woman of their acquaintance—or of those clans surrounding them. "There is the succession."

"Speaks a man whose future has no' just been decided for him." Rohr fairly spat the words. "Ye, the fortunate one."

"Fortunate?" If being second in everything could be considered so. If being the dutiful one who could only ever step into a role of prominence if the unimaginable happened and some evil befell the brother Deathan loved.

Aye, he loved Rohr. But by the powers, the bugger did prove difficult sometimes.

"Ye"—Rohr took a turn around the floor—"will be able to choose the woman ye wish to wed."

"Aye so, but Da might well ha' arranged a match for ye anyway."

"He would no'. I ha' already chosen my bride."

"What?" Deathan's eyes narrowed. "Who?" He could not recall his brother looking with especial favor on anyone. Though the lasses of the clan did follow him.

In droves.

"Caragh MacDroit." Rohr spoke the name like a curse, his vehemence the product of his anger.

"But—ye never showed favor to her. Or to anyone."

"How could I? 'Twould ha' set the tongues to wagging and brought all the fierce mothers out to argue for their bonny daughters. We kept it well secret. But I am in love wi' Caragh and ha' asked her to wed wi' me."

"Oh." It was all Deathan could manage.

"I was set to tell Da and Mam"—Rohr's face softened, speaking that name—"as soon as the season ended and the joining could be arranged."

Deathan thought on Caragh, but one of the lasses who continually trailed his brother. She was bonny, aye, with red-gold hair and a face like one of the goddesses from an ancient tale. Bards might sing of such a woman.

"I am sorry," he said. Indeed, this changed things, made the news Da had broken more difficult. "'Tis hard to bear. Perhaps if ye had told Da—"

"'Twould make no difference. This is a decree from the king that I maun marry some savage Caledonian tribeswoman from the interior—"

"I doubt she is a savage. Da says she is a princess."

A terrible smile stretched Rohr's lips, one akin to what

Deathan had so recently seen on his father's face. "They are all savages. They prick their skin wi' blue woad and mak' human sacrifices."

"I doubt that is true."

"Wha' d'ye know about it? The Caledonian version o' a princess will be some wild woman. Half tamed. Ye mark my words. Besides—"

Besides? Could this get any worse?

Rohr swung around and stared Deathan full in the eyes. "Caragh is carrying my child."

"Eh?"

"We did no' tell anyone—Caragh did not want to, before we were wed. But ye can see, the succession is already seen to, and I canna wed wi' this wild woman who comes."

For the second time that night, Deathan sank to a seat on the floor. "Ye maun tell Da. Ye maun tell him right away."

"When he is coming all over the high chief and throwing my fealty in my face?"

"Even so. Because the Caledonian woman comes at order o' the king, and will expect a bridegroom."

"Aye so. Ye wed wi' her, then!"

CHAPTER THREE

Darlei GLARED INTO the polished bronze disk that served her as a mirror before tossing it aside. She had no need to see her reflection. She knew the details of her appearance far too well and appreciated them little. The mirror was not essential among her belongings and should not take up room in the bag she packed.

She would take her bow. Arrows, to be sure, and her knife. A change of clothing and the things a woman needed in her pack that a man did not. A flask of ale. A few herbs in case she injured herself while in flight.

Circumstances were not ideal for leaving. Well, naught had been ideal since midsummer, when Father had told her of the agreement. The one that would send her to be the bride of a western chief.

A western Gaelic chief.

"It is not as if you have chosen a husband for yourself already," her father had said carelessly. "And it is past time you wed."

Yes, it was past time. She was twenty and should have a brace of babes by now. She'd had suitors, to be sure. A young woman of her status could not help but have suitors.

None of them had been…well, suitable. She had told Father that none was worthy.

"I am a princess," she'd declared. "Am I not?"

So she was. Her father was Caledonian royalty, one of a cluster of kings that had long ruled Alba's interior. She deserved, at the very least, a Caledonian prince.

That, however, was not the true reason she had failed to wed. She was waiting for—Och, she did not even know for what she waited. The right man, she supposed. One who made her heart lift, sent her weak at the knees. One who might make her surrender that which she guarded so fiercely within.

Her heart.

He had not appeared. Not by miracle or any other happenstance. And now a snare closed about her life. She journeyed to meet a husband she did not want, and would not accept.

"Are you sure about this?" Orle asked. Orle, her handmaiden turned dearest friend. The two of them had been together half a score years.

And now must part. Just as Darlei must give up her entire way of life.

She turned to face her companion. The tent had been pitched hastily alongside the trail last night, and for their purposes the two women had seen fit to light but one rushlight. By its dim radiance, Darlei could see the uncertainty in Orle's eyes.

"It is madness, this," Orle declared.

So it was. Darlei would have done better to leave from home, rather than flee this convoy with its attendant warriors. But yes, she would still disappear into the surrounding hills, near enough home to be familiar so she could find her way.

"Where will you go?" Orle asked. "What will you do for a home?"

Home. For a moment, Darlei's heart strained back to the high glen among the hills, the place where she'd grown. Never in her worst imaginings had she foreseen being forced to leave. By a heartless father and a feckless king.

Nay, but she could not say Father was heartless. He did what he believed best for the land he loved.

"If we show obedience to this new king," he had explained when he told Darlei of this match, "he will look upon us with favor, and we may be able to keep more o' our lands."

It was Father's reason for living, that. Holding on to their lands. Battling for them against the ages-old Gaelic invaders. Dying for them, if need be.

What was a mere marriage in the face of that?

She tossed her head. "What need have I of a home? I will live as I breathe, and range the land from hill to hill and loch to loch. I will be as the doe, who calls all the world hers."

"And who is brought down by the arrow. Your father will come after you, you know he will. He must save face before this chief to whom you are promised."

Yes. In her father's sight, promises were promises, and sacred. She would be causing him great embarrassment by leaving.

She would be saving her own life.

"That is why I must go now in the dead of the night when no one sees."

"The guards—"

"Will be talking together. I can move quietly enough to slip past them. A perfect night for it, with no moon."

"I will miss you." Tears brimmed in Orle's eyes.

"And I, you." A fierce hug. Only one, did Darlei allow herself. She could not imagine what lay ahead of her. Neither could she imagine a life wed to a western chief.

"You must be completely silent in this," she told her friend. "Father will question you, and most determinedly. Tell him only that I slipped away without your knowledge and you cannot guess where or when."

"Will he believe me?"

"Tell him you were sleeping when I left."

Orle wailed, "I can scarce bear not knowing whence you are bound." Agony filled her eyes.

"That is for the best, as I tell you. Father cannot get from you knowledge you do not hold."

Orle clutched at Darlei with tense hands. "Are you certain it would not be better just to go ahead with this marriage?"

"I am certain. Now lie down. Cover your head so you will not see me go."

The girl obeyed. Darlei shouldered her bow, picked up her pack, and slipped from the tent in utter silence.

Night met her, more deeply dark than even she expected. Cool air whispered against her cheek.

The air was rumbly, as if the gods quarreled at a distance. It might be well if the rain found her, making it hard for Father's men to follow. As it was, she could hear voices, deep male voices. As she predicted, the guards talked with one another.

The most difficult part of this endeavor would be getting her pony, Bradh, away with her, him being tied to a string line along with the others.

Silent as a shadow still, she moved to the rear of the camping place where the animals had been pegged. One good thing—the guards would not be on high alert for harm befalling them, so near yet to home.

The ponies seemed restless—no doubt due to that distant thunder—and several balked when she approached them. She shushed them between her teeth and stroked their manes and flanks.

"Quiet now."

Bradh snorted at her even as she slid her knife from the loop at her belt. She cut his line and, leading him on foot, started away.

The dark would hamper as well as shield her. Ordinarily, no one could catch her once she was up on the pony's back. But despite the way her heart pounded, this must be about stealth rather than speed.

If she could hear the guards' voices, they would be able to hear her movements.

In the distance away to the west, the storm growled more loudly. Bradh danced unhappily and she soothed him again.

"Come on."

She hoped Orle would not receive any punishment as a result of her actions. Father would be very angry. Would he believe

Orle's claims of ignorance?

Darlei had studied the terrain well before nightfall. The clearing among the trees where they had paused lay at the edge of thicker trees beyond. Her vision adjusted slowly to the deeper dark as she picked her way. Slowly, slowly, in defiance of her urgency.

The air grumbled around her as the storm moved in. It might be as well if the rain found her and offered them further cover.

Ears stretched for any outcry behind, she led the pony onward. If this endeavor were blessed, she would not be discovered missing till early morning, by when she would be far distant.

Would the gods bless her escape? Why would they wish to see her chained and confined in marriage to a man she could not love?

Rohr MacMurtray, he was called.

How did she know she could not love him, never having set eyes on him? He was a Gael, for one thing. She spoke his language only in the simplest form. Besides…

Besides, she did not know herself capable of that kind of love. Oh, she loved, to be sure. She loved Orle and her mother, back home, and Bradh, and even her father, in her way.

But to surrender her will and a large portion of her independence to a man, at cost to her heart? Nay, and nay.

For years now, she had watched her friends do just that. Turn so foolish with what Darlei could only term infatuation as to throw themselves away on some man who was no finer than he ought to be. Who sweated, and drank, and spat, and farted, and felt he could tell his woman what to do.

There was no man for Darlei, not like that, not in all the world—possibly not even the prince to whom she believed she was entitled. She would be cursed if she would lose her freedom to a Gael.

Thunder rolled again, much closer. The first drops of rain fell. At almost the same moment, she thought she heard a cry behind her.

Nay. Discovery could not come so soon.

On a rush of panic, she moved faster up the slope ahead of her, wending a way through the trees. She must cover some distance.

Before they came after her.

There was quite possibly not a finer tracker in all Caledonia than Father. Even in the dark. Even in the wet. Her heart strained within her chest. She must get away.

She must.

They came to a ridge of rock that dissected the trees, and she hesitated. The rocky spine stretched far in either direction. She could gain time by riding along it. Dangerous in the dark.

With very little hesitation, she mounted. Once upon her pony's back, she became one with the animal, their muscles and spirits aligned.

"Away," she told him softly, her ears reaching for sounds of pursuit.

The storm broke over them suddenly and with fury, a gift from the gods or something far less friendly. She felt Bradh's hooves slip on the wetted stone and clicked her tongue at him.

They needed to move from this exposed ridge back under cover of the trees.

Lightning struck close behind them and the pony took fright at the hideous noise and blinding light. He took off into the forest.

Darlei should have known then that her escape was doomed. For some reason, the gods had turned their favor against her. She could not possibly hear any sounds of pursuit, with the storm crashing all around.

Neither did she or the pony see the stream bank ahead. It bisected the wood, the trees all leading down, and Bradh fell into it without warning.

The horse stumbled. Darlei fell off, something she almost never did, and landed hard in rushing water. Flailing, she struggled up, her thoughts all for her pony and not herself.

"Bradh. Bradh!"

Her reaching hands landed on his wet coat. He, like her, was down in the water, flailing.

With a groan, she fumbled for his lead, her hands moving over his mane. He came up and she led him out of the stream.

Or tried to. The bank was too steep, the water rushing. The dark between flashes of lightning was too intense. She could see nothing.

Not till they scrambled up the bank at last did she realize the truth.

Bradh could take barely a step. Her pony was lame.

CHAPTER FOUR

FOR REASONS UNKNOWN to Darlei, the gods had doomed her escape. Brought this storm down upon her head. Put the steep stream bank in their path. Rendered her pony lame.

This, despite the fact that the same gods—those of blessed Caledonia—had favored her so often in the past. Favored her boldness and her daring. Smiled upon her exploits.

Not this night.

She stood there with the wild weather crashing all around her, Bradh's lead in her hand, and equally wild emotions pouring through her. Frustration and anger. Protest and denial.

Why would the gods want her to leave the home she loved and travel to the west? Almost as far west as a woman could go and yet be in Scotland. Why would they want her to wed with a stranger, a Gael at that?

It made no sense, and her heart rebelled. What was she to do now? Caught here with a lamed pony.

She could abandon him, she supposed, and move off on foot, but her heart protested doing that. Injured and possibly disoriented, would he find his way home?

Could she be so selfish?

Her bow and quiver had fallen during the crash. She had to slide back down the bank and search for them. She feared Bradh would take flight once she left him, but he was still there when she clawed her way up again, muddy and wet.

The pony's head drooped dispiritedly. She had not the heart

to leave him.

"Come, then."

She began leading him one careful step at a time, back the way they had come. Fortunately, they had come up the same side of the stream where they'd fallen, but it would be a long, slow journey.

Her mind simmered and steamed. If any good fortune remained to her, she might slip back into her tent before dawn—surely the light would come late in this weather—and pretend ignorance over Bradh's state.

But her luck had not been good this night.

The storm began to move off at length, and the night's darkness fled with it. Step by painful step, she led the pony. She could feel her own hurts now, bruises coming up all over her body.

None could rival the ache in her heart.

She heard them before she saw them—a party moving through the trees up ahead. Rough, impatient voices calling to one another. Her absence had been discovered.

The gods well and truly had abandoned her.

For the pony's sake, she stopped and waited for them to reach her. Yes, that was her father's voice. As the air began to lighten to gray, she caught sight of him down off his own pony and, no doubt, following her trail.

"There!" cried one of his men.

Father's head came up and he caught sight of her. She braced herself for what would come.

Anger filled his every line as he stalked toward her. A man of goodly height he was, built along graceful lines with brown hair like her own and a pair of canny, dark eyes now narrowed in annoyance. He wore his good cloak—thoroughly wetted—and a narrow bronze crown that denoted his status as a king. Long had their ancestors fought the Celtic invaders who pushed them back and back eastward, and stole their lands. So long as Darlei could remember, and years before that.

How could Father so betray his own, those who had fought

and died before him, and send her to wed with one of those invaders?

"Darlei!" he bellowed. "What have you done?" His voice echoed the distant thunder. His outrage came at her in a wave that found her even before he stepped up.

Those dark eyes examined her and moved over Bradh even before he demanded, "Explain yourself!"

Did he truly need an explanation? It must be clear, all of it, from the moment he had discovered her absence.

She lifted her chin. "I told you I did not want this marriage."

"So, what? You go creeping off in the night like a craven coward too weak to face her duty?"

That stung. "I am no coward."

"You might have fooled me. A woman of courage, you are not."

"Father—"

He raised his voice to a bellow. "A woman of courage accepts her future and her fate with strength and grace. A woman of courage would make me proud."

A veritable blow to the heart, that. Some of the anger drained from Darlei, but not all.

His quick gaze moved over her again. "Have you injured yourself?"

"Nay, but Bradh is hurt. We suffered a fall."

"So it is not enough you have betrayed me—you have ruined your good pony."

Betrayed? Now Darlei's eyes narrowed in an unconscious parody of his.

"I? Betray you?" It was he who had done that, giving her away at the orders of a presumptive king. "You have sold me into this marriage."

His fingers twitched as if they longed to give her a slap. "It was not of my choosing, which I have told you time after time, but that of a higher power."

"And who are we, to obey a Gaelic king?" she could not help

but retort.

"We are Caledonians and proud with it. The queen is one of our own. She speaks into her husband's ear. If we want a stake in this land, we must obey." His eyes flashed. "Is a marriage good enough for a queen not also good enough for you?"

She had nothing to say to that.

Father lowered his voice. "I should give you a good hiding, daughter. Perhaps that is what is required to tame you. But I would not put marks upon you when you go to your new husband. It appears you have already gathered bruises enough."

He turned and called over his shoulder to his men. "One of you, come and take this pony. Examine him for harm. The rest of you, back to the camping place."

The dawning sun came out, slanting through the trees. Just like Darlei's hopes of escape, the storm had faded into the distance.

IT SOON BECAME apparent that Darlei had done nothing but make things worse for herself. Not only was she bruised and battered with damaged clothing, but her father's man had determined Bradh was too sorely injured to go on.

Darlei would be forced to ride in the wagon with Orle, or go on foot.

Ah well, she was acquainted with consequences. From an early age, if her parents were to be believed, she had been strongheaded. Often wrongheaded, going about her own escapades and pursuing her desires with little thought for any harm that might ensue. In the past she'd been punished with lack of privileges, confinement, and, from time to time, even physical admonishments. None of it had proven particularly effective.

No punishment could match this. Being forced to walk to meet her ill fate.

"Mistress Darlei, why do you not ride with me?" Orle called from the ponderous wagon that also carried their baggage. "It pains me to watch you."

Darlei eyed her friend. To her knowledge, Orle had received none of her father's ire; he apparently accepted she'd had no part in what Darlei had done. A mere serving girl could not be expected to curb the will of a princess when Father could not.

Darlei felt grateful for that. Bad enough to go to her doom without her pony, who should have remained at their destination with her. Unthinkable to go without Orle.

"I am fine," she called back. A lie. She had bruises all down one side where her body had met the stones of the stream, and she must have landed first on her left shoulder, for it ached abominably. She did not want to admit it, though.

"Do not be foolish," Orle called back in the guise of friend rather than servant. "Morgal," she said to the young man who drove the cart, "please to stop so Princess Darlei can come aboard."

An amiable young man, Morgal did so. Darlei scrambled up, at a cost in pain.

"Are you bleeding anywhere?" Orle asked while Morgal tried to pretend he could not hear.

"Nay."

Darlei tried to get comfortable amid their various belongings. In addition to her possessions, the wagon also contained a small chest that held her marriage price.

Why she should have to pay a price while the unknown dog of a Gael toward whom she journeyed did not, she still failed to understand. All she knew was, the king had instituted the rules.

Or perhaps it had been the new queen.

Misery loved company, so it was said. As the queen had to wed with a Gael, so might she countenance dooming Darlei also.

"What happened?" Orle whispered. There had been no time for explanations when Father hauled Darlei back and she hastily changed her clothing. The men had been taking the tent down around them, almost.

Darlei shook her head. "It was an ill-fated venture."

"Please tell me you will not try again."

Darlei turned her head and looked into her friend's eyes, beheld great concern.

"Would you have me go meekly to my fate?"

"Nay, but—"

"Do not tell me you are eager to be banished to live among strangers."

"Nay, but—"

"Orle, my heart cannot accept this thing."

"I know." Orle bit her lip. "Yet I fear somehow you must."

Nay, and nay, and *nay*. Darlei carried Caledonia's wild heart within her. Whatever awaited her at the end of this journey, she would never surrender the bold woman she was.

CHAPTER FIVE

THE WEATHER CLEARED, turning warm and bonny, the gods breathing gently over the land. Autumn, when it turned fine this way, was Deathan's favorite time of year. He went out often hunting with his friends or just tramping the land in an effort to escape what lay at home.

Life in the keep had become intolerable.

He knew too much, that was the problem. Knew that the Caledonian princess was due to arrive at any time, depending on the weather and other vagaries of travel. She came with her father—a king, apparently, in his own right. With Mother so ill, Da called upon his seneschal to make preparations, and he, a man called Farchan, promptly turned the place on its head.

Deathan could not help but keep an eye on his brother, who continued to be moody and irascible, apt to quarrel with Da—or indeed, with anyone—at any time.

Deathan noticed now how often Rohr met with the lass, Caragh, seemingly by chance. She would stop by wherever he worked, usually in company with one of her friends, and they would exchange fervent, hushed words.

Once, the lass went away weeping.

As well she might. Soon enough, her condition must show, and she would not be able to name the father—a man who, indeed, waited by the day for the arrival of a woman destined to marry him.

Destiny, so it seemed, was a terrible hard thing. Better, so

Deathan decided, to live a quiet, ordinary life. To escape the notice of the gods entirely.

To be an unimportant second son.

The only person who seemed excited by the news of approaching events was Mother. Deathan stopped in to see her one morning before making his first round of the guard, to find her propped up on her bolsters, her face shining.

So long had it been since he'd seen her so, with a light in her eyes and some color in her face, that it put a check in his step as he crossed the floor to her bed.

Half the life had gone out of their world since she'd been confined to her bed. And watching her fade away had become a constant, mortal wound.

Now she reached for his hand even as he sat down beside her.

"Och, Deathan, is it no' exciting? I am to have a new daughter. And a princess!"

"Aye so." Deathan could not keep from smiling.

"What d'ye think she will be like? A Caledonian, aye—but verra grand, no doubt. D'ye think she will be beautiful?"

"Mayhap." Deathan tried to picture the woman and failed. Most the Caledonians he'd seen had been male, and many of those either rushing at him with blades in their hands, or lying dead or dying.

"Only imagine." Mother plucked at his fingers. "My descendants half Caledonian. Deathan, our world is changing."

"It is." He could only agree.

"'Tis a new land, this. One where enemies become blood kin." She spoke in the manner of a seer, almost. Was she so close to death that she could see beyond to what would come?

"I maun get up," she declared, "and help wi' the preparations. For such honored guests, all must be ready."

"Mam, nay. I believe all is in hand already. Everyone has been engaged in seeing to it."

"Aye, but the lady o' the house should stand to greet them when they arrive." She blinked her mild blue eyes at him. "I *am* still the lady o' the house."

"To be sure, ye are," Deathan reassured her with a clench of the heart.

"But this woman, this princess, will tak' my place." Mother's gaze held Deathan's persistently. "Once I am gone. Ye must see I ha' to be there to greet her. To guide her."

"Mam…" Deathan's throat closed so he could say no more.

"I want to be there at yer father's side when she arrives. Help me up."

Panic joined the grief in Deathan's heart. "Mam, I do no' think—" She had not been on her feet for more days than he could count.

"Ye do no' suppose me strong enough."

He did not. He kept from saying so. "Mam, I am certain your new daughter, when she arrives, will be more than pleased to come and greet ye here." If she had half a heart, she would.

"Aye so." Mother eased back against the bolsters, defeated. "And ye will come and tell me what she looks like, as soon as the party arrives, will ye no'? Every detail."

"Every detail," he agreed, and kissed her soft cheek.

He recalled that conversation later in the afternoon when the men on watch from the walls called out that a rider approached. Another messenger, he proved to be.

This one, unlike the previous from the king, proved to be a Caledonian.

He came swiftly, riding as one with his pony, his hair and the animal's tail both flying. Deathan, on the walls at the time, hurried down and so proved to be the first of the family to make contact.

The man was young, surely near Deathan's own age, and he was a sight. Long brown hair flowed about him in a cloud, and he stood—by the time Deathan reached him, having dismounted— heavily armed. Armed and covered with tattoos.

Moreover, he had an arrogant tilt to his chin and eyed the guard with what might have been measured hostility.

They eyed him back the same way, even though by then everyone in the clan knew what was to transpire. Caledonians in their midst.

Indeed, the news had spread like wildfire.

"I come from King Caerdoc," he declared in heavily accented Gaelic, his bright-hazel gaze settling on Deathan. "The wedding party approaches."

Wedding party.

"Aye so," Deathan said, his thoughts racing. "We stand ready to receive them."

The messenger's gaze flicked over him with some interest, warrior to warrior. In days not so long since, they might have met on the battlefield.

Now they were supposed to be countrymen.

"How far off is the party?"

"They follow me closely and will be here before sundown. Are you MacMurtray?"

"I am one o' them. Herve MacMurtray's son."

The messenger's eyebrows twitched. "The bridegroom?"

"Nay, I am his brother. Let one o' us tak' yer pony and care for him. And pray, let me offer ye our hospitality."

The man bared his teeth. "No one touches the pony but me. And I will ride back to inform King Caerdoc that you expect him."

"Very well so." Deathan shifted as Da came up to join him. "This," he told the messenger, "is Chief MacMurtray. Da, the party grows near."

The Caledonian inclined his head to Da in a lordly fashion. "Kind Caerdoc sends his greetings. He escorts his daughter in accordance with the MacAlpin's decree."

Heavily accented the man's Gaelic might be, but Deathan stood impressed all the same. He would not be able to communicate in the Caledonian tongue. Yet his people called these savages.

Would the princess also speak their tongue? How difficult for

Rohr, if she did not.

Da turned to Deathan. "Go and fetch your brother. He maun be here when his guests arrive. And ye, Master…?"

"Urfet." The messenger bared his teeth again. "I am cousin to the king."

"Aye so. Let me escort ye to our hall."

"Da, he wishes to ride back to his company."

Da looked uncomfortable. "'Tis no' necessary, that. We will welcome them in." He flapped a hand at Deathan. "Go. Go."

Deathan had no idea where to find Rohr. Given the way news flew about the place, he might reasonably expect Rohr to find him. He longed to go back up on the walls so he might catch a first glimpse of the party. Of the princess.

Only so he could inform Mother, of course.

He found Rohr just emerging from the midden. His brother looked green around the gills and had a hand pressed to his stomach.

Presumably he had already heard the news.

"Ye maun come at once," Deathan told him. "The party approaches."

"Already?" So Rohr had not heard. His apparent nerves stemmed from anticipation.

That gave Deathan pause. Bold and unflappable, his older brother tended to be. Near impossible to shake.

He stood shaken now.

"Come along," Rohr said disagreeably, taking out his ire, as so often, on the nearest target. "The nightmare begins."

CHAPTER SIX

DEATHAN WOULD STILL have preferred to go up on the walls, a place where his duties so often took him, to watch events unfold. Like a pageant, more or less, from which he was removed.

As, in truth, he was.

None of this was happening to him—the strangeness and immediacy of it all. The heavy weight of duty. The sacrifice and acceptance. For one of the first times in his life, he felt grateful he was not the firstborn.

Rohr hurried, dodging people still dashing around the keep, all of them staring, and headed for the front steps where Da waited. Some color had crept back to his face, but Deathan thought he still looked awfully grim, for a bridegroom.

Da stood with his advisors and the holy man, obviously re-lieved to see them. He stepped aside to offer Rohr a place, and Deathan fell in behind.

"They come," Da told Rohr uneasily.

Deathan wondered about the approaching party. How would they look? Deport themselves?

Rohr must have been wondering the same, for he leaned back toward Deathan and said, "Prepare for a throng o' savages."

Only, they were not. The party, when it appeared along a track now lined with clansfolk, looked rich and beautiful, like something described in an ancient tale of Erin, from whence Deathan's ancestors had come. On horseback they were, the messenger now having rejoined them, with what could only be the king at their head and a decorated wagon rumbling behind. Well clad and colorful, they flew banners and streamers that fluttered in the breeze.

The crowd began to murmur. Da stood like stone.

Deathan narrowed his eyes. Which was the princess? There—that must be she, surrounded by guards at every point. The only woman he could see.

She sat at the front of the wagon, wreathed in dignity. Head high, hands folded on her lap, and eyes gazing straight ahead at nothing. She wore a bronze-colored gown, and her hair hung down like a second cloak over her shoulders, brown and wavy and, aye, wild—though it appeared to be the only thing about her that was wild. She wore a thin bronze circlet upon her head.

A crown?

Aye, so it must be, for the man riding in front of the messenger wore one also. Indeed, Murtray received royalty.

If the Caledonian party had wished to make an impression, they succeeded. The crowd of many onlookers went silent in a wave at their approach. Rohr swore under his breath.

When the party reached the open gate and flowed through, when they crossed the bailey and paused at the bottom of the stone stairs, the silence became so complete that Deathan could hear the tinkle of tiny bells tied to their ponies' manes.

"Welcome!" Da stepped down the stairs and held out his hands. "Welcome to Murtray."

The messenger had already dismounted, alighting with that same lithe grace. He caught the king's bridle and bowed as he called out, "Caerdoc, King of the Caledonii."

Deathan tore his gaze from the princess to look at the king, even as the man swung down with an assessing glance for the keep. What did he think of the place? Impressive, with its strong walls? Rough and humble? Unworthy of his daughter?

He was middling tall and every bit as well dressed as the princess, with a similar mane of brown beneath his bronze circlet, and gray in his beard. A thin face, far haughtier than Deathan had expected. He turned to Da but did not smile.

Da bowed again. "Herve MacMurtray," he introduced himself. "We are"—a brief pause as Da sought a word—"honored by your presence."

Caerdoc bowed his head slightly. Not truly a bow.

Da turned to Rohr. "And this is my son, Rohr MacMurtray."

Rohr went down the steps. He had dressed in ordinary clothing, not knowing or not caring that the arrival would be today, and his hair hung unplaited and undressed. The color still came and went in his face.

Kind Caerdoc did not look impressed. He had a long, rather thin nose, and he employed it to gaze down at Rohr.

"My daughter, Princess Darlei."

Darlei.

The four Caledonian guards who had flanked the wagon dismounted and stood close as if—what, they expected someone here to do her harm?

A thought came into Deathan's head. *As if they expected her to flee.*

She disembarked from the wagon without any assistance from anyone, ignoring the hand the driver offered. On her feet she was tall, slim, and graceful. Her hair—och, but it was magnificent and shone in the sunlight. Her face—not so. If anyone could look less happy with the situation than Rohr, it was she.

Not a bonny face at first glance. Not soft enough to be called bonny. Like her father's, it was thin and carried an enormous amount of strength.

By all that was holy, though, Rohr should not dare complain.

Deathan switched his gaze to his brother, who now bowed to the woman he would wed.

"Welcome, welcome!" Da bowed again, not seeming to know what else to say. "All is in readiness for your stay."

The party filed into the keep. Deathan, who remained on the steps, moved back to afford the visitors room to pass.

She would pass right by him. On Rohr's arm.

He acknowledged, as she came up the stairs, that she did not appear a wild woman. Aye so, that hair was wild, barely disciplined, but the rest of her spewed dignity.

That was until she reached the step on which Deathan stood, turned her head, and looked directly at him.

Her eyes were silver. Not gray, as might be considered ordinary, but bright as two shards of armor. And they were wild, entirely wild, like those of a hawk confined, defying her comportment.

A feeling started at the root of Deathan's spine and crawled its way upward. Through his groin, through his belly and stomach, growing claws as it came, claws that eventually sank into his heart.

She hated them, did this princess. She hated them all.

THE FIRST DIFFICULTY came when Da again tried assigning someone to care for the Caledonians' ponies. They had reached the hall by then, just inside the arched doorway, and there came a flurry of displeasure.

The king spoke the Gaelic tongue, just like the messenger, Urfet—Deathan had almost failed to notice that. He had yet to hear the princess speak. But they now gabbed together in their own language, and it was the haughty messenger who stepped forward and said, "It is as I told you before, Chief MacMurtray. We will care for our own animals."

"But," Da protested, "I have lads standing by for but that purpose."

Urfet's eyes flashed. "No one touches our stock. None but our own hands."

It felt like a slap in the face. Whether it was meant so, Deathan could not tell. Another flurry occurred as the lads from the stables, who, indeed, stood by, mumbled among themselves.

Da said, "Verra well. Our lads will tell yours where to house yer beasts and lend what assistance they may."

Did Da appear nettled? Difficult to tell. Rohr did, though he stood unmoving with the princess's hand on his arm.

"The rest o' ye," Da continued, "please come in. Ye will wish to refresh yourselves after yer long journey."

The refreshments stood ready, a high table having been set across the top of the hall. The principals were led to it while the rest of the party thronged one of the side tables, all together.

King Caerdoc strode beside Da to a place at the center of the high table. Deathan, following, heard Da explain, "Forgive my wife being absent and unable to greet ye as she wished, King Caerdoc. She lies ill and much regrets missing this—er—joyous event."

"Ah." King Caerdoc directed a look at Da. "I am most sorry to hear this. My own queen stayed back at home."

Da nodded. "My wife, Aene, looks forward to meeting Princess Darlei, who will be her new daughter. Please, sit."

Caerdoc did, with the flair of a man taking a throne. His daughter sat beside him, and Deathan noticed his hand came out to circle her wrist for a moment.

A warning? Restraint?

Aye so, she looked like she could rip into them all, an affinity for Gaelic or no, and tell them what she thought of being here. She no more favored this match than did Rohr.

Deathan could not say how he knew that so well or why he should suppose he understood what lodged in the woman's heart. But he did.

Indeed, though he should sit on Da's other side at the high table, he took a place at one of the lower tables instead, among members of the household guard, where he could look on.

Where he could see her.

And his brother. For Rohr once more sat like a man stricken, never looking at nor speaking to his bride.

A woeful beginning.

CHAPTER SEVEN

THE FACES, ALL the staring faces. A sea of them turned toward Darlei, all holding avid expressions of curiosity, wonder, or condemnation. Their numbers increased as more and more people filed into the hall, and with each entry her spirit rebelled a little more strongly.

She could not bear it.

No woman could be expected to weather such a storm. The voices. The avid gazes marking her every move. The expectations.

She wanted to rise from her place at the table and flee. Not that it had served her well last time she'd made the attempt. And not that her father was likely to allow it. Already he had squeezed her hand in warning.

Everything she did here—each word and every exposed movement—reflected upon him. She could not shame him. *She could not.*

Yet nay, neither could she bear this. Rebellion took hold in her heart. There must be a way out of it. There must.

Oh, and her husband—the man destined to be her husband— he sat beside her now. Unspeaking, unmoving, stiff as if carved from stone.

No matter; one look at him had been enough to set her teeth on edge.

Not ill favored, nay, not if one liked men of his ilk. Which she did not. The men who in the common way attracted her were dark. Or red—not unusual among her people.

Rohr MacMurtray was fair. He had what she would consider a typically Gaelic face—broad in the forehead with eyes set wide beneath curving brows, like the carvings on their marker stones— and an unhappy line to his mouth. Well, she could not fault him for being unhappy. So was she.

He had hair the color of ripe grain, too dark to be called blond and too light to be brown. And freckles.

Like a little boy.

She could scarce imagine a man to attract her less. The very idea that she could be required to lie down with him—

Nay, do not think about that. She could come up with a means for escape before that happened.

And yet this did not look an easy place from which to escape. She raised her eyes to the stone walls—stout—and the rafters far overhead, topped with thatch. The place, a keep, they called it, had been built to shut enemies out.

It might also keep her in.

The doors—there were two of them out of the place, and she sat near neither. The closest, to one side, was traversed by a horde of women all bearing food and must lead to what passed here for a kitchen. The other wide door through which they'd entered lay at the far end of the hall. Score upon score of people between.

All staring.

It made her feel…well, desperate. It sent an impulse up her spine. To be alert for the fight, to stab, to kill if need be. To break free.

Yet she sat with her hands folded hoping it did not show.

Why could she not have been born a man? Then she would not be in this predicament. She could flounce around at liberty like the men of her party, and no one would question it. Except…

She stole another look at the man seated beside her. A man, yes, yet every bit as miserable as she. Where was *his* liberty?

Herve MacMurtray rose to his feet and the noise level in the chamber dropped. The Murtray, he was called here, so Father said, as if he were the only member of his clan of any significance. He had schooled her in such details, had Father, who did not want her to appear ignorant.

The Murtray was about to make a speech. She set herself to listen.

Though she was able to understand and speak the Gaelic language—Father had made certain of that also—it seemed arduous to listen. The Murtray spoke interminably about honor and the king—MacAlpin, he meant—and their duties to crown and country. Darlei knew all this. She rebelled at most of it.

Her endurance began to erode.

The faces before her blurred into an indeterminate sea. She avoided the stares, gazing into the middle distance, shut them away and imagined herself back home, riding through the meadows with the sun shining down on her head and the wind at her back.

All the avid faces narrowed to one, which quite unaccountably caught her attention.

He sat directly in front of her at the end of a board running in the other direction down the room. He should be listening to the Murtray, who was presumably his chief. He watched her, instead.

To be sure, everyone looked at her. He *watched*. There was a difference.

Through narrowed eyes, she frowned back at him.

A young man he was, no doubt one of the Murtray's warriors, for he had the look of a fighting man. He sat in his seat with his legs spread out—relaxed and yet not relaxed. Difficult to judge the Gaels by their clothing, but his appeared fine. Was he someone of importance?

Curious now, she inspected him further. Brown hair, light brown—the color a blond child's hair tended to turn as he grew. A face that was neither what she'd consider handsome or ill favored, with a strong nose that lent it character. His eyes…

Too much distance divided the two of them for her to see

their color, but they were nice eyes, set beneath level brows. And his mouth—wide, mobile. She had a sudden image of him using those lips to drop a kiss into the palm of her hand.

Now, why should she imagine such a thing? She had no desire for it. And he meant naught to her. He was no sort of man to catch her eye. And above all else, he was a Gael.

The Murtray finished his speech at last and sat down. Father rose and began to speak in turn. Darlei jerked her gaze away from the young man. She truly should listen.

Her gaze fluttered to Urfet, who had stationed himself beside the main door. He stood with his arms crossed over his chest and his head high, proud.

Now, Urfet was the sort of man to attract her. Graceful, strong, and competent, marked by tattoos and with that indefinable something that characterized Caledonian men. She had long followed him with her eyes, though she would die rather than let him know it, and in truth she certainly wanted naught to do with him or any other man.

She wanted her independence.

And Urfet had more women after him than any man should fairly wish. Only—why could it not be one such as he, if she had to wed, rather than the poor specimen who sat beside her?

Father spoke on of old battles and the new king. Darlei's gaze crept back to the young man sitting nearly at her feet.

A good place for him, she tried to tell herself. And now that she thought on it, surely she'd seen him outside, on her way in. But who was he?

No one special. The hall thronged with men, very similar men, one like the other.

Father finished his interminable speech and sat down. The women began circulating with the food.

"Did ye ha' a good journey?" the man beside her asked. Rohr. That was his name. She had best remember it.

It took her a moment to interpret what he said, her ear not accustomed to the tongue. She thought about the journey. Her attempted escape. Nay, it had not been a good journey.

She wondered what would happen if she told him, *I am already sick for home.*

"Yes," she said instead. And then, repeating it in his tongue, "Aye."

"Murtray is one o' the grandest holdings on the western coast," he said boastfully. "I suppose that is why the king chose us for," he concluded without conviction, "this honor."

Darlei considered all she might say, the polite things and the not so polite. She chose among them. "I gather you are as unhappy with this proposed union as I."

He stared at her, wide blue eyes gone wider, and a look of astonishment on his face. He had not expected honesty from her, nay.

She leaned toward him confidingly. "Mayhap if we work together, we can find a way to escape this unjust demand the king has made."

CHAPTER EIGHT

DEATHAN WATCHED THE Caledonian princess simply because he could not seem to do otherwise. She was not beautiful, nay, not in the ordinary way. Too much strength in that face. But there were beautiful things about her. That glorious hair, all wild and tumbled. The graceful way she moved. A body like a goddess from an ancient tale.

She fascinated him.

Well, that was not so unusual, was it? A royal party of Caledonians did not turn up at the keep every day. At least, not without knives and spears in their hands.

Now they drew their knives only to cut their meat. He was impressed by their manners and by the fact that they spoke his tongue.

She—Princess Darlei—produced a knife from her belt and cut her own meat, a service Rohr might well have offered to perform for her. He was meant to be looking after her, was Rohr. But, keeping a close eye on Rohr, Deathan could see his brother, usually all bold confidence, appeared cautious and careful. Cowed.

She put him off, did the princess. Not what he had expected, perhaps.

Would he fall for her? Abandon his lover who already carried his child and tumble into the princess's arms?

How could he help it?

That thought startled Deathan, so he turned his gaze away

from the two at the high table and concentrated on his food. Spoke to those around him.

Yet something made him look back again. The princess leaned toward Rohr and said something that brought the color to his face.

A strange reaction on the part of his brother. A very strange one.

The welcome feast went on and on, Da doing his best to make an impression. He and the Caledonian king spoke at length and most earnestly. Deathan began to see what perhaps King Kenneth had been trying to accomplish with this union—with these unions all over Scotland. Bring together people who otherwise might not have met except on the field of battle.

The princess and Rohr did not speak for long, and Rohr wore an expression like a man who had been kicked in the face. What had she said to him?

Her gaze fell upon him, Deathan, a few times, but she turned her eyes as swiftly away. She had plenty to look upon, did the woman who was to be—

His sister. As good as.

The realization started a sick feeling in his gut, a churning conviction of a wrong done. An odd familiarity, as if all this had happened before.

Only it had not.

He'd taken too much ale, that was it.

The evening moved on and the music began. Old Coll, his father's harper, had much skill in his hands, and his songs always affected Deathan most strongly. Stirred up unaccustomed feelings.

At last the party at the head table rose. Their guests had traveled far, he could almost hear Da say, and must be weary. They would be shown to their quarters.

When she came down from the head table, still with Rohr at her back, the princess passed close by Deathan. And they looked into one another's faces once again.

Aye, she had silvery eyes, bright silver, like a glass women used for primping. Like light on water or, more properly, the polished surface of a war shield.

She did not appear the slightest bit friendly or welcoming of his interest. And yet…

He felt precisely as if he'd been anchored by a rope and drawn toward her.

In reaction, he took a swift step backward, almost treading on his neighbor's feet, and bowed.

She did not so much as incline her head, and sailed by. Disdainful of him.

And yet…

There had been something. Glittering bright in the depths of those unusual eyes. Acknowledgment. Curiosity.

Recognition.

But how could that be? They did not know one another.

He quit the hall, but he did not go to his bed. Instead, he walked far up the shore, alone in the dark save for his feelings.

DARLEI DID NOT know what to make of her quarters. A prison, it looked like, all bound round with stone walls. A bed such as the westerners used instead of a sleeping bench, standing out into the room as if sleep—or some other act that might take place in a bed—was of primary importance.

Only one window.

She went to it immediately, ignoring Orle, who stood in the middle of the floor looking bewildered. Could she escape through the window? Given, she was terribly high in the building, but hurling herself to her death would, at this point, be preferable to her other choices.

The window was too narrow for her to fit.

"Darlei? Are you unwell?"

All at once, Darlei wanted to weep. She wanted to rage and scream and stamp her feet, and tear the room apart in protest of her fate.

Instead she stood staring at what little she could see of the outside world. Darkness. A few stars.

"Darlei?"

Emotion choked her throat so she could not speak. She turned from the slit window and looked at her friend.

"Oh!" Orla tossed aside the robe she'd been holding and hurried to embrace Darlei. "My dear one. Is he so terrible, this man you must marry?"

Darlei said nothing.

"Is he ugly? Old? Nasty?"

"None of those things."

"Well, then." Orle drew away far enough to look into Darlei's face. "It might be worse. Tell me of him."

"He—" Darlei tried to focus on the man she was to wed. Fair hair, freckles. A frowning face. Another image intruded instead— the man who had been seated near her feet.

He was not good looking either. Not the way Urfet was. Too foreign. Too Celtic.

When she'd left the hall, she had walked right by him, close. They had looked into one another's eyes. His were…

Curious. Nay, not as much as he appeared curious about her, though everyone here must be. But curiously unusual eyes in a man—neither blue nor green, something in between. Fringed with long, light brown lashes.

Very fine eyes.

Oh, and she must be tired if she had begun admiring the eyes of random strangers. She must be overwrought and overcome.

Orle still waited for an answer to her request. *Tell me of him.*

"He did not say much to me. I do not think he is impressed with his bride."

"Ah, well, you will become better acquainted, I do not doubt, before the wedding."

"I need to sleep." She'd done little of that during the journey, her anger and rebellion making it impossible. Now she felt she might drop where she stood.

"Yes, come. I have your robe ready."

With careful, gentle hands, Orle helped Darlei out of her fine gown and into her robe. Out of her shoes. Braided her hair for sleep.

"I am so glad you are here." Darlei hugged her. "Will you stay with me?"

"If you like."

They lay in the strange, high bed. Orle soon fell into a doze, but Darlei found she could not sleep after all.

"I am afraid, Orle," she said into the dim air of the room. It was a thing she rarely admitted, and she said it only because no one could hear. Caerdoc's bold daughter did not admit to being cowed or uncertain.

But…

Terrible as all this was, it would only get worse. She would have to wed the dull specimen she had met this day. Settle into a life here. The festivities over, Father would leave. All their folk, save Orle, would go home.

She would have to stay.

She feared if that happened, she would lose herself. Become a woman she was not and had never meant to be.

Because she could not imagine it. That man, for her husband. Raising children among strangers.

They would eventually no longer be strangers. That terrified her most of all. Because if she ceased to be Princess Darlei, if home became so distant that she no longer reached for it, who would she be?

She could not let that happen. Lying there with Orle breathing peacefully beside her, she vowed it. She must do all she could to keep her heart wild and Caledonian.

She must have dozed eventually, the weariness of body overtaking the agony of mind, for morning came with a trickle of gray light.

She lay with her forearm bent over her eyes and listened to Orle moving around the chamber, and sickness stirred in her gut.

Not sickness. *Dread.*

What would this day bring? Entertainments, no doubt. A whole raft of activities in which she would be expected to partake.

Back home, she liked mornings. She would rise early, dress herself, and go out to visit the ponies. She spared a thought for Bradh, whom she had injured and who she hoped was all right. She envied Bradh—he had been allowed to go home.

Home was a sizeable settlement in a small glen surrounded by steep mountains. His fortress, so Father always called it. Her tribe had been there a long time, fighting against the encroaching Gaels. Holding the western gate, as Father put it.

Was that why the king had given them the honor of this union? A kind of reward? A role in making Scotland one country?

Yet in her heart, it was not one country. She doubted it would ever be. And she did not appreciate being made the sacrifice.

Yet only a coward would lie here and refuse to face the day. And a coward, she would not be.

❦

CHAPTER NINE

"**S**O WHA' D'YE think of your bride?"

Da asked the question almost jovially, as if he thought Rohr should be overjoyed with the situation in which he found himself.

Deathan looked up sharply to catch his brother's response. The three of them were at breakfast in Da's quarters, the hall still being cleared of last night's feast.

Rohr looked like a ghost and as if he had not slept all night. Wandering the shore, perhaps, as Deathan had. Or visiting his lover?

"She is bonny, is she no'?" Da asked when Rohr did not speak at once.

"Bonny?" Rohr repeated as if he had never heard the word. "Nay, I should no' say so." His lips curved in a bitter smile. "No' at all to my taste."

"Well." Da appeared taken aback. "Ye must admit, she is no savage."

"I am no' certain about that."

"But—" Da frowned. "I ha' to say I was most impressed by the whole party. Their demeanor. The fine clothing."

"If ye suppose, Da, that lifts them from savagery, ye are verra much mistaken. As for the wench—did ye no' look into her eyes?"

Da put down the cup he had just picked up, and Deathan could see him fighting against his annoyance. "Rohr, are ye certain ye are no' just taking against them—against her—because ye do no' want the marriage? For to be truthful, I saw naught wrong in her."

"It is no' that." Rohr got to his feet and took a restless turn around the room. Would he tell Da the truth? That he was in love with someone else and that his lover carried his child?

"Son, we ha' been over all this. A decree fro' the king canna be disobeyed. And it might be far worse. She is young, healthy, and whatever ye say, no' ill favored. Once ye get to know her—"

"I will fall in love wi' her, is that it?"

"Not every match is for love. I was fortunate wi' your mother, aye. And I would have wished the same for ye. But many matches made for the sake o' an alliance do grow into love. That may well happen."

Rohr snorted and tossed the cup he held, fortunately empty, across the room.

"Come, finish eating your breakfast."

"I am going out." Rohr turned for the door.

"Ye will be here to entertain our guests." Da issued it as a command. "Ye will no' embarrass me by absenting yoursel'. We ha' events planned—"

Da spoke to the empty air. Rohr had gone.

Da's jaw grew tight as carved stone. In the past, when he got such a look, there had usually been some form of retaliation. Now he fought through the anger again and drew a breath.

"This grows more difficult than I anticipated. I had thought when he met the lass, he would become reconciled to it."

Deathan said nothing.

"So." Da sent him a somewhat challenging look. "What d'ye think o' yer new sister?"

Sister. The name grated on Deathan, all out of proportion. Like salt swiped across an open wound.

Once more, not waiting for an answer Da went on. "I was surprised in her, I will admit."

"She speaks our language."

"She has been educated. Far better than your own sister."

"I did no' ken that was customary among the Caledonians."

"It is not. She is a princess. I did not think her ill favored." An open-ended invitation to Deathan's opinion.

"Not did I." Beautiful hair. And those wild, warlike eyes. Carefully, Deathan said, "Mayhap Rohr favors a different sort o' lass altogether. Quiet and biddable."

"We do no' ken Princess Darlei is no' that."

Oh, Deathan knew. He knew.

"Rohr maun mak' up his mind to it. As ye would, aye, if 'twere ye?"

If it were he.

Da looked at Deathan with rare approval. "If only 'twere yoursel' set to wed the lass, I doubt I would ha' all this trouble."

If only.

DARLEI FORCED HERSELF to stand still and endure it as Orle helped her into yet another grand gown, remaining motionless as the woman dressed her hair, struggling with the near-impossible task of coaxing it into some form of obedience. Her hair at least seemed bent on retaining its wild character. Whether *she* would, here, remained at question.

She felt ill, stifled, as if fingers clutched her around the throat, cutting off her air. The big chamber, cool and dim, seemed far too removed from the life that might be glimpsed through the narrow window. One of the Murtray's servants dropped off their breakfast, which Orle neglected while struggling to perfect Darlei's appearance. A good thing, that she would not have to face all the company at breakfast. A bad thing, as she could not possibly eat.

Orle's efforts completed at last, Darlei crossed directly to the slit window, her hands stealing to her neck as if she would loosen a bond. Nothing there. The restrictions she felt were not physical ones.

Only, they were. For she would be kept here, would she not? Trapped in this place with no means of escape.

Cool autumn air poured through the window, though she still could not see much beyond a strip of sky. Despair hit her a terrific blow, and she clenched her hands to fists against the stone sill.

How had her life come to this? She had known, even if she refused to admit it, that Father would eventually choose a husband for her. She had thrust it from her mind, not having the same urge to wed as most young women. She had hoped—vaguely—her future husband would be a good man from one of the local tribes. A warrior, mayhap.

Like Urfet.

She might respect him. Perhaps be attracted to him, again like Urfet. Eventually become fond of him.

She did not expect love, as such. She did not know that she believed in it. Women fell victim to foolish infatuation, yes. She'd watched that happen often enough, and had watched it transform, over time, into either friendship or tolerance.

She had never anticipated this. An order from a king who was a Gael upending her life.

A husband at whom she would never have looked twice.

Or perhaps even once.

Her father would remind her she was a princess and would instruct her to behave as such, with dignity and acceptance. The trouble was, not only was she a princess, but Caledonian to the heart.

She did not want that to change. She did not want to become like these people here. Gaels.

Behind her, Orle laid aside her brushes. "Darlei?"

Darlei turned away from the window with its narrow illusion of freedom. "What did you think of the strange bed?" she asked her friend, employing a sharp edge of sarcasm. "I near thought I would suffocate."

Orle gave her a doubtful look. She had tried hard to be Darlei's strength since the news of the marriage had come down, and during the journey. Now she looked as low in spirit as Darlei felt.

Darlei had been thinking only of herself, but Orle too had lost all she knew and loved. She would stay here with Darlei when the rest of their party left. At least, Darlei prayed Orle would not refuse to stay, now that she saw what it was like here.

"Come," she told her woman more gently. "Let us eat some of this food. There are no doubt many activities planned for the day, and I must appear well and strong, that I may impress these self-important Gaels."

Not as a princess—nay, she did not care about that. But as a capable woman in her own right. One who did not need a man. One who did not need the husband being thrust upon her.

Let him prove he was worthy of her, not the other way round.

Despite her determination, she merely picked at the food, finding her stomach did not welcome it. This was odd fare, not like what she was used to at home. Yet another thing to which she would be expected to accustom herself. Halfway through the procedure, there came a scratch at the door. One of Father's guards stood there, and a whispered conversation with Orle took place.

"You are expected in your father's room. He wishes to escort you out."

Darlei puffed out a breath. "How do I look?"

"Magnificent," Orle assured her.

Darlei nodded. The fine clothing would have to serve as her armor. What would sustain her far better, though, was a hard and sharp attitude behind which she might conceal her fear and dread.

No one should guess her true feelings. With luck, no one would.

CHAPTER TEN

ARLEI'S FATHER INSPECTED her carefully, and seemed satisfied with what he saw. He had also dressed in his best and looked clear-eyed and merciless.

"Chief MacMurtray will wish to show off his holding today," he informed Darlei as he ate his breakfast, also delivered to his chamber. "You would do well to act impressed."

Flatter them, he meant, these trumped-up interlopers. Though Darlei supposed they could no longer be considered interlopers, after so many years on Scottish soil. Was that not the goal, in the ordering of these marriages? To make all one.

She nodded soberly. She could pretend to be impressed, though it would make her squirm inside.

"It is best for you to learn all you can about life here," Father went on, "since this way of living will be your own."

And was she never to return home? Back over the hills they had traveled and to the places she loved? Could she not serve a given sentence here before renouncing it all?

Nay, for there would be babes by then. Children. *His* children. She shuddered.

Father eyed her closely. No fool he—did he believe in her false calm?

"Daughter, tell me I can trust you."

"Trust me?"

"To accept your fate and behave as you aught this day."

Anger touched her, but she had her armor in place. "To be

sure, Father."

He appeared relieved. Then again, a measure of doubt still hovered in his eyes. "Come, we are to meet our hosts outside."

Darlei had no objection to getting out in the air. A crisp autumn morning it proved to be, and as she exited the keep at Father's side, trailed by Orle and Father's guards, she did her best to take it all in.

Beyond the wall, which encircled the keep itself along with a narrow strip of grass nearly beaten into mud, lay the settlement. A crowd of dwellings huddled like so many children up against the walls, as to a mother's skirts, they seemed too numerous to count. In one direction, hills rolled away to the distance, into infinity. Home. In the other direction...

The sea.

Darlei had never beheld the sea before yesterday, and then she'd been far too upset to appreciate the sight. Now her eyes feasted. A broad expanse, blue-gray beneath the pale morning sky, it drew her gaze and accelerated her heartbeat. If there were one thing here she might admire—

"King Caerdoc. Princess Darlei." Chief MacMurtray walked toward them, a fatuous smile on his face. With a sinking heart, Darlei saw Rohr at his shoulder.

"Good morning," Father said.

Murtray bowed. "I trust ye spent a comfortable night."

"We had all we required."

"I am that glad to hear it."

Struck by the falseness of this speech, Darlei eyed these two men who, in days gone by, might well have met on the battlefield while doing their best to kill one another.

Now they made stilted, hollow conversation. It was *all* hollow here, empty. Was that what bothered her so about it?

"We will be pleased to show ye the settlement today. But first, Princess Darlei"—Murtray turned to her and bowed again— "Rohr would like to take ye to make the acquaintance o' his mother."

"Ah," said Father before Darlei could speak. "Darlei would be most honored."

The mother was ill, Darlei recalled hearing last night. Too ill to leave her bed. She inclined her head at Rohr, who stepped forward.

"This way, mistress." He offered her his arm.

Did he not mean to address her as *princess*, then? For even if she became a member of this clan perforce, she would always remain that. Caledonian royalty to her bones.

That kept her head high and her feet steady as they stepped back into the keep.

"My mother is most anxious to meet ye," Rohr said as they went. He was a good bit taller than she, and the muscles of his arm felt like iron beneath her hand. "She is pleased to ha' another daughter."

"Ah. You have a sister, then?"

"Aye, older than me. She is wed and has been gone from us for some time."

"Do you have any other siblings?"

"Just my younger brother, Deathan."

"And if I may ask, what is the nature of your mother's illness?"

Rohr hesitated. "She was never particularly strong. Of late she suffers from pains in the joints that make it difficult for her to move."

Darlei stole a glance into his face. Shut down tight. But she caught the merest hint of a smile when he added, "Though she is shut awa' in her chamber, unable to rise, she is very much still the center o' life here at Murtray."

Darlei nodded. They had come to a broad door where Rohr hesitated again. Then he lifted the latch and swung the panel open.

A bright room, much better lit than the one Darlei had been given, with two windows and colorful furnishings. It was as if someone had determined to make the chamber as cheerful as possible for its occupant.

A woman—no doubt a servant—bustled around busily and turned her head to smile at them when they entered. In addition to the servant and the woman who lay in the bed, the room was occupied by a young man.

With a stab of surprise, Darlei recognized him as the man who'd been sitting directly across from her in the hall last night. Now he occupied a chair close beside the bed, his hand extended onto the counterpane. What was he doing here?

Even as he glanced up, her mind put it together. Was he the brother of whom Rohr had spoken? What was his name? Deathan.

Before she could decide for sure, he got to his feet.

"My brother, Deathan," Rohr said.

And the young man inclined his head at her. "Princess Darlei."

She nodded back, her gaze clinging to his for an instant before she looked at the woman in the bed.

All her assumptions, and some of her hard-held armor, flew out the nearest window.

In stark contrast to the rest of the room, Mistress MacMurtray looked pale and nearly colorless. Hair that must once have been somewhere near the color of her sons' had faded to soft gray. A face once round and no doubt pretty now bore lines carved by pain. Her eyes—they too looked faded, the same muted blue as the sky outside.

Yet she had a glow about her, a quiet grace, as if her suffering had worn her down to the sweetest components of her personality. Indeed, the smile she gave Darlei was rife with sweetness, and she held out a wasted hand.

"Daughter."

It was the warmest welcome Darlei had yet received, and she had to fight back her emotions. She went forward and took the seat Deathan had vacated.

The woman's fingers clutched her hand. Swollen the joints

were, and misshapen, her grip weak.

"I am Aene MacMurtray, yer new mother, if ye will let me be. I ken fine I am no' a stitch on yer own mother, who, my son tells me, did no' make one o' yer company. But I am here for ye, as she canna be."

Darlei deciphered this incredible statement with some difficulty. "Nay," she said, "my mother was not able to come. She needed to stay back and keep things running at home." Plus, as Darlei suspected, Mother, who did not approve of the match, had tired of arguing with Father about it.

"Aye, well, it will be a great comfort so to yer father, knowing she is there making sure all is well at home. I am no longer able to help Murtray as I used to do. Let me look at ye," she went on before Darlei could speak. "Aye, ye be a beauty, sure enough. Just as Deathan said."

Startled, Darlei shot a look at Rohr's brother. He had retreated no farther than the door where he stood watching.

Heat came to Darlei's face as she replied, "You are too kind."

"And are ye no' a clever lass as well, able to speak our tongue as ye do. I confess, I was concerned we would ha' trouble exchanging words together."

"You need not worry for that, mistress." Darlei's voice was soft and respectful. No one could be harsh with this woman.

"I hope ye will come often and talk wi' me. I ken fine a sick room is no place for a young lass full o' life. But I would love getting to know ye."

The young man beside the door spoke unexpectedly. His voice was deep and almost musical. "Mam was just telling me, she would like much to be at yer wedding."

Aene MacMurtray grimaced. "I would like naught better. But I would ha' to be carried, and would that no' put a damper on the occasion?"

"I do not think it would," Darlei said. "Indeed, it would be an honor having you there."

Those pale-blue eyes lit up. "D'ye think so?"

"We can make a grand thing o' it, Mam," said Rohr, getting into the spirit. "Decorate a litter for ye wi' flowers and whatnot."

Aene laughed. "I do not know about that." She patted Darlei's hand. "Sit now and talk wi' me. Tell me all about yer home."

To Darlei's own surprise, she did. Rohr stayed to listen but Deathan did not. He must have slipped out the door silently, because when Darlei looked around for him, he was gone.

"Ah now," Mistress MacMurtray said at last, "I will hold ye here no longer, lass. Get out into the fresh air. Rohr, wha' entertainments have ye planned for her today?"

Rohr, who still stood by, answered readily. "Father has some games planned, so I think. Races and archery contests."

Aene raised a brow at him. "A chance for ye to show off a wee bit, eh?"

Rohr did not smile as he might.

"Am I to join in these games?" Darlei asked him.

Mistress MacMurtray gave a soft laugh. "Nay, I do not doubt ye are meant to watch and admire." She added, "Lass, ye will come and see me again?"

"I should like that very much."

Darlei felt a whit better when she and Rohr left the chamber. A measure of ease had found her there, in the gentle woman's company.

But it died swiftly as Rohr led her away, and not another word for Darlei passed his lips.

One thing was indeed abundantly clear. Rohr wanted this marriage no more than she.

✦ ⸻ ❦ ⸻ ✦

CHAPTER ELEVEN

SAY WHAT YOU would about the folk of Murtray. They were hardworking. Loyal. Dour at times and suspicious of strangers. When all was said and done, they loved a good contest, and they showed up in droves for what their chief had planned today.

The weather, always capricious here along the coast, did not prove quite so accommodating. In Deathan's opinion, it looked like rain, but he thought it might hold off till later in the day, keeping to the offshore islands before suppertime.

Father had arranged a number of contests, mock combats, which Deathan considered potentially dangerous, given the participants were old enemies. A footrace and one on horseback. A friendly knife battle and an archery contest.

Most these had been set up in the area between the keep and the outer wall, though the races would be held in the field outside the gate. Deathan did not doubt Da intended for Rohr to win all and show up in the very best light.

Rohr no doubt expected the same. When it came to such matters, his confidence knew no bounds.

He was, after all, the future chief of a clan that held a place of prominence on this coast. Cherished by his parents, admired by his people. Expected to be the best of the best.

Deathan, not two years his junior, had learned early not to eclipse him. It was fine for him to be fleet of foot—just not more fleet of foot than Rohr. Oh, his mam was full of praise for him, but Da did not approve. Rohr was meant to be first in everything. By the age of eight or so, Deathan, no fool, noticed that if he bested his brother, Da got a look on his face like a man who'd taken a mouthful of sour heather ale.

So Deathan had learned. Always finish second or worse. Never show all of what he could do. It sometimes caused a bitter feeling. More bitter than his father's disapproval? Cursed if he could tell.

He told himself he would be content with his place. Second to his brother, the eventual war chief and defender of this place he loved so well. More, he sometimes thought, than Rohr loved it.

Content, aye.

But that had been before. Before he had laid eyes upon Princess Darlei.

He rarely wanted things for himself, especially the things his brother had. Aye, he'd trained himself better. But och, he wanted Darlei with a raw kind of longing utterly foreign to him. One that made him ache inside. That fair lit him up with desire.

Why should Rohr be gifted with such a treasure, rather than him? Beyond unfair, it was.

He lurked in the bailey lost among the members of the clan and watched while his father came out in company with King Caerdoc, the two conversing amiably. Two strong men, easy in their confidence—both subject to a higher law. The king's edict had to gall.

Caerdoc's party followed, and Deathan eyed them with speculation. Their guide—Urfet—might well prove a problem for Rohr. The man was impressive in every way. Deathan wondered what Rohr would make of him.

In truth, though, Deathan waited for but one person to appear—Princess Darlei.

He liked the way she'd been with his mother, soft and gentle, and would have lingered to watch, just for the pleasure of looking at her. The grace with which she'd leaned toward the bed. The line of her profile, strong and beautiful. The heavy brown hair, all woven and braided, hanging down her back.

But that had been a time meant for Rohr and Darlei to bond. Had they? Would they? Did Rohr have too much else standing in his way?

Deathan looked around for Caragh but did not see her. Then Darlei exited the main door of the keep and he forgot everything else.

She was no longer with Rohr—he did not know where his brother was—but in the company of another young Caledonian woman, one with still-darker hair. They spoke together quietly, unsmiling.

Father had ordered a tent set up against the wall of the keep where the women were expected to sit and observe. Princess Darlei did not go there but walked up to Urfet and began a conversation.

And Deathan could tell, even from a distance and just from the way she spoke to him, that the princess felt an attraction for the man. Her admiration was in her every line and gesture. Not surprising. Deathan wondered if she entreated Urfet to win the competitions for the pride of Caledonia.

Aye so, if Father offered this for a pleasurable pastime, it might well turn into something else entirely.

Father stepped up to the Caledonians and very politely invited the women to take places beneath the shelter of the pavilion, gesturing to it. Princess Darlei shook her head.

Where was Rohr?

Sweeping his gaze across the crowd, Deathan caught sight of his brother standing over against the wall. Speaking with Caragh.

The lass looked unhappy and, in truth, half frantic. Rohr clearly attempted to calm or comfort her, but he appeared equally upset.

Androch, the clan's current war chief, stepped up to Deathan. For an instant his gaze followed Deathan's before he looked away.

Rohr needed to be far more discreet if he wanted to keep his secret.

"Master Deathan, are ye planning to compete?"

Deathan shrugged. "No' sure." There was not much point, was there, if Rohr needed to win?

"I think ye could win the footrace," Androch said. "And possibly the pony race as well. And ye be a good eye wi' tossing a knife."

Deathan shrugged. "That man o' the Caledonians'"—he nodded at Urfet—"just might tak' it all."

"Aye, he is impressive. But I will wager still on ye. Master Deathan, if I might say—'tis time for ye to quit hiding yer abilities."

Deathan stared at the man in surprise.

"Och," Androch said, giving a rueful grimace, "I understand why ye do so. But ye maun be true to yoursel'. A man's first duty is to himself."

"We both know that is no' true. A man's first duty is to his clan. And naught is better for the clan than a strong chief."

"Aye so." Androch flicked another look at Rohr, who had now parted from his lover and made his way over to Da. "And mayhap your brother would prove himself stronger, if ye challenged him."

"That is no' what is expected o' me," Deathan said.

"Aye, but there is only so much a man can shove down his craw." Androch patted Deathan on the shoulder. "Go and compete."

He stepped away then, and Deathan wondered—if he did compete, would he impress Princess Darlei?

But it was no more his place to impress her than to best his brother.

How furious would Da be if he did best Rohr here before all the clan? Before the Caledonians.

He walked up to the group that included Da, King Caerdoc, Urfet, the princess, and now Rohr.

Father was speaking. "But Princess Darlei, we ha' a place specially prepared for ye from whence ye may observe all the contests."

"I was hoping," she said very politely, "I might rather take part."

All the men stared at her with varying expressions. Her father frowned; Da looked disbelieving, Rohr offended. Urfet favored her with a grin.

"I am sorry…" Da faltered. "I do no' think I understand. Ye wish to compete in—"

"The games. I am a fine rider. Tell them, Urfet." She turned to the man beside her.

"She is a fine rider," he said in very heavily accented Gaelic. "And a better archer."

"It is no' done," Rohr said. "Women do no' compete in such contests."

"Not here, perhaps." Darlei lifted her chin. "Where I come from, we have broader minds."

The inherent insult made the king's frown deepen. "Now, daughter—"

Very swiftly, and eyeing Rohr, Urfet said, "Surely you are not afraid to compete with a woman?"

Rohr's face went red. "'Tis no' seemly. A well-bred woman does no'—"

Da trod on his foot. He went silent.

"Ah, well," Darlei said sweetly. "Perhaps by your standards, I am not well bred. As well that you best me, then, and put me in my place."

The dare was outrageous, somehow more so because her voice remained polite and kind. But in her eyes…in her eyes Deathan glimpsed a wild woman.

What could Rohr say? He exchanged a glance with Da and choked back any further protestations.

Urfet began speaking very low in Darlei's ear, in their own tongue.

"Daughter," King Caerdoc said sharply, "it is rude to whisper in company."

"Yes, Father. Urfet just reminded me, my own pony is lame. I shall have to use another." And her gaze moved to Rohr's face. "I begin with a handicap, it seems."

CHAPTER TWELVE

Da's HAND CAME down upon Deathan's shoulder. The gesture mirrored that of Androch only moments before, yet could not be more unlike.

"Son, I do no' think ye should take part in the competitions."

Da did not look at him but gazed away across the turf to where the first of the races was set to begin. The footrace this was, in which Darlei would not compete.

"We want to show well, do we no'? To best the Caledonians?" Deathan questioned.

"Aye so," Da admitted.

"I ha' a good chance o' doing that."

"We want your brother to win."

Deathan felt that. It went through him like a blade to the heart, even after all this time. Would his father not be proud if he bested the Caledonian warriors? Only Rohr?

He said quietly, "I am no' certain Rohr can beat that front man o' theirs, Urfet."

Da sent him a sharp glance. "And ye think ye can?"

"I do."

"Aye then, do it. But if ye come up on your brother in the lead—"

Deathan pulled away from his father's hand. He did not care so much about being first. But perhaps Androch was right. There was only so much a man could cram down his craw.

"I know I can rely upon ye," Da said. "As yer mother always

tells me, we can count upon Deathan as on solid rock."

Thick as rock, was he? Scant praise, and the equivalent of admiring how well a man took a stab in the back.

Not till Da walked away did Deathan fully appreciate what his father's words meant. Da knew he could best Rohr. For all his apparent disfavor, he did. Else he would not feel it necessary to ask Deathan to hold back.

That caused some satisfaction. Not enough. With rebellion in his heart, he stepped forward and took his place in the line of runners.

They were to run down the length of the field where the ponies were exercised, around a small tree at the bottom of the field, and back again. Deathan hoped someone had been assigned to pick up the offerings the ponies left ahead of time.

He glanced at the tent, set on the elevated area up beside the keep. Princess Darlei was not there. Looking around, he saw her standing behind the starters.

She did not so much as glance at him, but his heart beat hard. Harder. *He could make her see him.*

A primitive urge it was, to want to win. To want to win in order to gain a woman's attention. An urge he denied far too often.

At the center of the line, the members of the Caledonian guard jostled and shoved one another playfully for position. Rohr was at the far end of the row, well separated from Deathan.

King Caerdoc stepped up, raised his arm, and brought it down with a shout.

They ran.

It took Deathan a moment or two of pounding over the turf to figure out what was going on. That this was not like any race they normally ran. Indeed, the jostling at the beginning should have told him.

The Caledonians pushed one another, tripped one another— or tried to—all while laughing and leaping free of the obstacles. They shoved the Gaels also, who did not react at all well.

One of them came at Deathan, and he dodged nimbly, leaping free. That was when he realized some of the Caledonian runners sacrificed their race to take out the competition. So their man, Urfet, could win.

Indeed, Urfet was well in the lead, striking across the green turf like a bolt of lightning. Lithe of limb and full of vigor, the man looked unstoppable.

Not on my ground, Deathan thought, and took off after him.

He had to dodge two more Caledonian runners. The rest could not catch him now. He and Urfet were way out in front.

They rounded the tree, Urfet making a neat loop of it, Deathan losing a few steps. He could no longer hear the onlookers hollering, so loud did the blood rush in his ears.

He passed Rohr heading the other way to round the tree.

Waiting for them was the crowd of Caledonian runners they would have to pass going the other way. They let Urfet through and looked to bar Deathan's way, but they did not, merely held out their arms and made good-natured faces, letting him pass.

He was right on Urfet's heels.

He could see his father and the king waiting. He could see Darlei.

Darlei.

He put down his head and ran.

For all that, he did not know he had won till he skidded to a halt in front of his father and King Caerdoc—with Urfet now at his heels.

Urfet slapped him on the back. "A good race!"

King Caerdoc beamed. "How close it was. But your man, Chief MacMurtray, won."

"I am his son," Deathan said.

No one heard him. Rohr came running up, face red with either effort or anger, and spat in Urfet's face, "That was no' fair! Wha' kind o' race is it where the runners attack one another?"

Urfet's expression went from congratulatory to cold. "It is our way," he said, "to try to trip one another. All in fun."

"It is cheating!" Rohr stepped up. "I would ha' won but for it."

"As your brother did?" Urfet gestured at Deathan. He at least had heard him identify himself.

It was the wrong thing to say if he wanted to allay Rohr's anger. Deathan thought he did not.

"It is cheating, and ye will pay for it!"

Princess Darlei appeared and inserted herself between Rohr and Urfet. It brought her so close to Deathan that he could smell the fragrance coming off her hair.

"It is our way," she told Rohr, "in friendly competition." Her eyes glowed wild silver. "If you have a difficulty with that—"

Rohr backed down, but Deathan could see it cost him. Cost him in pride and self-discipline.

"As ye say, princess."

"A misunderstanding only." King Caerdoc stepped forward. "We are not used to one another's ways."

"Indeed." Da did not look at all happy. His gaze slid over Deathan as if he did not exist.

But Princess Darlei turned to him. "Congratulations. You ran well."

All the reward he could fairly ask.

DARLEI GAZED INTO the face of the man who stood before her. He who had beaten her hero, Urfet, in the race. Wild emotions pumped through her. Annoyance, yes, that Urfet had not won, though Urfet himself did not seem upset by the loss and, indeed, at least a Caledonian had not been last. Disquiet with her bridegroom and his ill-tempered acceptance of his defeat.

Deathan MacMurtray—the victor—returned her look in full from his curiously colored eyes, which held an equally curious expression, one she could not quite identify.

His skin glowed with moisture; his chest still rose and fell from exertion. His hair, loosed during the run, tumbled down his back. Unlike earlier in the muted light of his mother's chamber, she could see it was indeed a shade darker than his brother's, and made up of half a score colors from golden to brown.

No more the type of man she preferred than his brother, especially standing there next to Urfet. And yet—something about him made it difficult to look away.

By all that was holy, he could run.

She looked him in the eye and asked loudly for Master Rohr's benefit, "Do you have any objections to how the race was run? After all, you managed to win despite our supposed *cheating*."

Everyone there stared at her, and then at Deathan.

A glint of some emotion entered his eyes. Curiosity, mayhap. Or appreciation. Mischief?

He inclined his head. "Princess Darlei, I won by pure luck, I am sure."

"Nay. You won by effort. Let none here deny it." What incredible eyes the man had. Fringed by brown lashes longer than her own.

She looked at Rohr. "Surely you are pleased with your brother's victory."

Rohr's expression turned sour. "To be sure, my brother ne'er ceases to surprise me."

Oh, but Darlei despised this man.

Chief MacMurtray said quickly, "Why do we no' move on to the pony races?"

"Yes." Darlei put herself forward. "In which I will compete."

"Daughter—" her father began.

"As," Darlei smoothly overrode him, "I always do at home." Would he deny her here before these strangers, and try to exert his authority? Cause another embarrassment?

"Princess Darlei," Urfet said softly, and with a note of laughter in his voice, "rides better than most our men."

"'Tis no' appropriate," Rohr said. "Mistress, please go and sit in the tent where ye will no' get hurt."

"Hurt?" She stepped up to him, not bothering to hide the disparagement in her eyes when she looked into his face. "I am not afraid of an injury. Are you?"

Rohr looked angry enough to spit, but he glanced to his father the chief.

"To be sure, ye may compete," Chief MacMurtray said, "wi' yer father's permission. We are honored."

"I would like to offer Princess Darlei my mount," Urfet said, "since hers had to be returned back home."

Darlei stared at him. His mount was a wild-headed creature that took all his skill to handle.

He winked at her. As they started away, he spoke into her ear in their own tongue. "You wish to win, do you not?"

Oh, she did.

CHAPTER THIRTEEN

A S THE PONIES were led out across the green sward, the sun came out. Darlei could see a bank of clouds far over the ocean, and the sky had been churning with light and darkness all the while. Now radiance, however brief it might be, illuminated the scene.

It showed Urfet leading his wild beast across to Darlei. He would sit out this contest, which surely he might have won, in order to offer her a victory.

She could not squander the opportunity.

Without hesitation or undue modesty, she hiked up her skirts, tying them high. Across the way she could see Rohr leading out his own mount, a light-coated pony that looked very fine.

Yes, would not the son of the chief have the best?

And there—her bridegroom's brother, who also intended to ride, his pony chestnut brown with a black mane.

They made a fine picture coming across the green turf, the sun in Deathan's hair.

Rohr marched up to Darlei and Urfet. "Can we expect your riders to bump and shove us aside here too? So long as I am fairly warned."

Darlei answered him. "We would not so endanger our animals."

He tossed his head and moved off to the starting line.

"Beat the bastard," Urfet said in their own tongue, and boosted her up on the back of his pony. "You know you can."

"Yes." She did.

They formed a ragged line where a post had been set in the ground. Chief MacMurtray gave instructions. They would make two circuits of the field, passing the post without stopping on the first. The pony to pass the post the second time was winner.

There would, as Darlei saw when she nudged Urfet's mount, Cai, into line with her knees, be a certain amount of jockeying for room. Eight mounts started—four Gaels and four Caledonians. She found herself next to Deathan. He sat his pony well, with unthinking grace.

She need not fear being bumped by him. She did not understand quite how she knew that. She just did.

He slanted her a glance before the chief gave the signal. Cai gathered himself beneath her and ran.

For one terrible moment, she thought she would not be able to control him. Far too strong for her, he was. Far too wild, barely disciplined. Then some corresponding wildness deep within her stirred and arose. She cried to the animal.

"Go. Go!"

Deathan MacMurtray had got out ahead of her, as had one of their own men. Deathan gave her a glance as she passed him and saw him lean into his mount. He meant to give her a run for the victory.

She stretched herself along Cai's back, hair fluttering, bare skin of her thighs against his rough, shaggy coat.

They flew.

She almost lost control of Cai again at the bottom of the field when they rounded the tree. Perhaps she did lose control. It did not matter, for by then she and the pony were one. Cai made the turn, turf flying from his hooves, and she hollered for joy.

She had passed their own man and was out in front when they gained the post for the first time and turned again. The faces of the onlookers blurred. They dashed on.

Who was behind her? All of them! But who was closest? She

tried to look, but her streaming hair prevented it.

No matter. Her heart had now joined with Cai's. His magnificent wildness was her own. No one could catch them.

As they approached the post to win, she caught a glimpse of brown to her left. Brown, and a stream of gold. Deathan—he was catching them.

She stretched herself higher on Cai's neck and called to him in her own tongue.

"Faster. For Caledonia."

They thundered past the post and several strides beyond. It took all Darlei's strength to halt the pony.

Deathan drew up beside her. He was smiling, and admiration shone in his eyes.

"A fine race, princess. I congratulate ye."

She nodded regally, then turned back to her father and the chief.

Urfet took Cai's lead from her and helped her down, smiling broadly. "Well done."

"He nearly caught me there at the end."

"Nay, he never had a chance. Now go face your furious bridegroom."

Yes, Urfet had taken a dislike to Rohr MacMurtray and wished only to annoy him. He led Cai away, still smiling.

Darlei turned to the waiting party.

Rohr looked more than annoyed. He appeared enraged. Where had he finished in the race?

He handed his pony off to a lad and gave Darlei a scathing look.

"Pray, mistress, lower your skirts."

Ignoring him, skirts still kilted up, she turned to the chief.

"An astounding ride, princess," he had the grace to tell her. "I maun say I have never seen the like."

"Lower your skirts, daughter," Father said softly in their own tongue.

She did, moving without haste. Did she embarrass him? But

the men here had to learn she was not like their women.

Or any other woman.

Chief MacMurtray said, "'Tis safe to assume, princess, ye will no' wish to compete in the next contest—a combat wi' knives."

She could if she chose. But after a glance at her father, she lifted her chin.

"Certainly not."

DEATHAN LED HIS pony away toward the sheds, barely able to feel the ground beneath his feet. He still floated on the remnants of the chase. Himself, chasing Princess Darlei.

Had there ever been such a woman?

Rohr came up beside him, scowling deeply. "Ye blocked my way," he said.

"Eh?" Deathan glanced across at him. Rohr had already sent his mount off with one of the lads and jogged after Deathan, apparently just to complain.

"Ye blocked me there at the start," he accused. "I could no' get clear awa'."

Deathan stopped walking. He often took a place behind his brother, aye, since Rohr had been born to be at the front. He would not stand unjustly accused.

"Impossible. We started at opposite ends o' the line."

"Aye, but"—Rohr's face went red—"when we cleared the pack, ye got out in front o' me and prevented me getting by."

Deathan narrowed his eyes. Rohr might have ridden around him. *Only he could not.*

"At the very least," Rohr carped, "ye might ha' beat her."

"I did try. She rides like the wind."

"A shameful performance! Everyone there saw her legs. I think she and that guide o' theirs—Urfet—cooked it up between them. 'Twas his pony, and I saw them whispering together."

"No doubt." Deathan suggested mildly, "Their pride required a win—as did ours."

"The two o' them are likely lovers. I wonder if he has had her." Rohr tossed his head. "She is likely no' even unbreeched."

Deathan stared, too appalled for words. It took some gall for Rohr to make such an accusation with his own lover and unborn child at his back.

He started moving again. "A word o' advice, brother."

"From ye?"

"Do no' destroy your marriage before it has begun." She was extraordinary, was Darlei. Any man should be grateful to wed with her.

"Wha d'ye know o' it?" Rohr turned back. "Do no' compete in the next round. Stay and groom yer pony."

Deathan did not compete in the next contest, nay, but not because his mount required his attention. One of the lads was more than happy to take that duty.

He went to watch instead. The contest—meant to be friend-ly—was held in the bailey, and the princess had a seat in the tent with her woman beside her.

Deathan edged into the back where he could watch her as well as the competition.

Several of the Caledonians were competing, including Urfet. It should have been clear from the first footrace that these men threw themselves into competition whole. No one expected blood to be drawn.

Deathan could tell by his brother's expression how badly Rohr wanted to win. As future chief, he should be best among the many.

He could also tell by the glow in Urfet's eye that the fellow meant to prevent it.

It came down to the two of them in the end. The last two standing who had not been disarmed.

The two Caledonian women watched closely, their heads together. No doubt speaking in their own tongue. The competitors circled, circled, half crouched. The spark in Urfet's eye made Deathan wonder if the man toyed with Rohr or if—

The flurry came quickly and to exclamations from the crowd. The goal was for one man to disarm the other, but when the encounter ended, it was with a rush of blood.

Down Urfet's arm.

Da, also seated and watching, surged to his feet. King Caerdoc followed more slowly. The Caledonians edged in. Would it come to blows?

But nay, for Urfet made nothing of it. He smiled and shook his arm—the skin of which Rohr had laid open with his blade.

Da quickly waved the healer forward, but Urfet wagged his head and said something to Rohr.

Congratulating him?

It was not a clean win. But the Caledonians, seeming to fight—and play—hard, made nothing of it.

Princess Darlei, though, jumped to her feet, looking as if she wanted to go to Urfet. Her companion urged her back.

Was Rohr right? Could there be something between the two?

It should not matter to Deathan either way, save that what he'd said to his brother was true. It would be a shame for his marriage to be doomed before it began.

CHAPTER FOURTEEN

RAIN CAME SWEEPING in from over the sea before the archery contest concluded, chasing them all inside. Darlei would have liked to stand outside and watch the clouds lower over the sea, absorb the magnificent power of the rain striking the water, for she had never seen the like. But apparently among the many things women here did not do was stand out in the rain.

A relief, withal, to have the competition ended. It had not gone well for her intended bridegroom, other than his one questionable victory, and he was not in a good mood.

Having seen that, and indeed, having seen more of the man, Darlei could not like him.

She hated to admit that to herself, it being one of the last things her mother had warned her about before they parted.

Daughter, I know you are unhappy about being sent away, but give this a chance. Give him *a chance. Your future happiness depends upon it.*

Good and fair advice but impossible to follow. Nay, she had not wanted to be sent here like a sacrifice. Not only did she dislike the man to whom she'd been sent, she did not respect him.

She did not know how to overcome that. She supposed if she tried hard enough, she might look past the fact that she was not attracted to Rohr MacMurtray. For she was not. A woman did not strictly have to be attracted to her husband, though it would unquestionably be far better if she were.

But Rohr was a small-minded and bad-tempered man who so

far had done little but whinge and frown.

He had not won the pony race, and everyone there from his people to her own had known he felt the loss. She had wanted very badly to compete in the archery competition, for she knew very well she was a dead-eye shot. But due to the rain, that had not taken place.

Even before the rain canceled the competition, Father had taken her aside. "Daughter, it does not seem that the young ladies here participate in the men's games. I know what a good shot you are. But why not let it go?"

Let her bridegroom win, he'd meant.

Rohr should have had a good chance. Urfet would not have competed due to his wounded arm. And for some reason, Rohr's brother—Deathan—also stood down. But Rohr had not been ahead and looked set to lose to another of the Caledonian warriors when the rain came down.

She could hear it on the roof of the hall even now as she sat beside the despicable man, who still wore a scowl on his face. And that said something about the power of the elements, for the roof was high and built strong.

Something about the power of it resonated with her. This place she might grow to like. Its people?

Never.

She looked about for Deathan, absent this night from the table below her. He had taken a place at the end of her own table. She leaned forward to steal a look at him.

No more the sort of man to attract her than his brother. And yet...

There was something about him. The way he moved, mayhap. The way he looked at her.

His smile.

He had a singular smile, did Deathan MacMurtray. A shy thing, and perhaps guarded, it made an appearance but rarely, and transformed him when it did.

He, at least, was a warrior—something she instinctively did

respect. He had done well in the competitions. Taken losing to her well. He did not sit beside her brooding like a small boy.

By the gods, if she had to marry, she wanted to wed a man, not a child.

She did not speak to Rohr and he did not speak to her. Food was brought and presented, dish after dish. The rain pounded down. The onlookers stared.

Darlei supposed she should make an effort to speak to Rohr for appearance's sake. But she just did not care.

How was she to endure this life? Curse the king. And curse Rohr MacMurtray.

The dishes were cleared, and an old man appeared to entertain them. He brought a harp and accompanied himself as he told stories and sang, his aged voice beautiful despite a few cracks.

As Darlei listened, she relaxed. Many things she might abhor about the Gaels' world. Their music, though, was not among those things.

Upon the thought, she looked up across the hall and found a man standing to the rear. Deathan had abandoned his place at the table and stood against the wall.

Watching her.

She tried to convince herself that was not his purpose—that he had perhaps gone there the better to listen, for he seemed as enthralled with the music as she. But nay, his gaze rested unwavering upon her, and whenever she lifted her eyes to his face, it quickened.

Never had any man anywhere looked at her so. It made her pulse speed unaccountably, and had her upright in her seat, as if drawn by strings.

Rohr did glance at her then. He still had not spoken more than a word or two, and now as he followed her gaze to the rear wall, she dropped her eyes hastily.

The last thing she needed was this man, who could not stand a slight or a loss catching her looking at his brother.

A thought came stealing into her mind. Why, oh why, could

not Deathan be her intended husband instead?

MASTER COLL'S MUSIC wove a spell, and Deathan fell whole into it, leaving his place at the table, the better to listen. He could still hear the rain falling. The notes of the old man's harp somehow blended with the sound of it, wove a spell to hold the company.

What would it be like, Deathan wondered, to possess the power to evoke such emotions in others? But in truth, mayhap at least part of what Deathan felt stemmed from another source.

She sat beside Rohr at the head table as if upon a throne, brown head high, some of her thick, heavy hair now dampened by the rain. Features like stone. Only the silver eyes glittered, alive with a soul-deep wildness.

Just as if some untamed creature from the far reaches of Scotland, a fox mayhap, had showed up at their gates and come inside to take part in the festivities, sit at their table, grace them with its presence. For all its apparent composure, still wild.

An odd fancy, he admitted. He seemed full of fancies about this woman he did not know. He needed to leave off with it.

Coll, the harper, told a lengthy and winding tale about one of their long-ago ancestors, Adair MacMurtray, it was, who had come out of Ireland and stayed to help grow this settlement. The bard's music skipped and danced, emphasizing the words, and the chorus went, "A warrior he was who fought for love. I will find ye always, so he vowed, below or above."

A life lived for the sake of love, Deathan thought. Could aught be finer? But what sort of man might deserve a love so strong? Surely not an overlooked second son.

Surely not him.

Darlei raised her silvery eyes again and found him, fastened upon him. Connected with him in a way that founded fire deep within, stoked it in his belly and sent it through him in a flood.

He wanted her.

Not so strange. Whatever Rohr seemed to think, she was beautiful, with her strong, graceful body and those proud, somehow canny features. He was not in the habit of desiring women—he had no time for it. In this instance, he had no choice. The desire just came.

She was to be his brother's wife. His sister, as good as. If ever anything in life could be wrong, it was that.

Frustration crawled up his throat and near choked him. It seemed an old, familiar sensation.

He needed to get away out of this, escape the spell of the music. Despite the rain and despite the way he felt when Princess Darlei looked at him.

He should step outside, let the cold rain wash him down. Perhaps quench this fire.

Yet he stood where he was until Coll's tale ended, the sweetness of the final notes fair piercing his heart. Not until then did he drag his gaze away from the young woman at the high table and watch the servants begin to circle the hall again, refilling cups one last time.

With the entertainment done, the evening would soon end. Princess Darlei would withdraw to her room.

To her bed.

By all that was holy in the heavens, what was he to do with this desire?

Sure enough, Da was rising at his place, making a speech about what an honor it had been having their Caledonian neighbors share this day in friendship.

King Caerdoc looked gratified. Rohr looked pained. Darlei looked carefully blank.

"In three days," Da concluded, "we shall hold a wedding that will heal old wounds and begin a new age in our land."

Three days. Three days only did Deathan have to approach her, speak to her, get to know her.

Before she became his brother's wife.

━━━◆━━━

CHAPTER FIFTEEN

"WELL, AND DAUGHTER, have you resigned yourself to this marriage? Young Rohr—he has much to recommend him, does he not?" Father asked.

Darlei turned from her seat in front of the glass—a large, very grand glass placed in her chamber to no doubt impress her—and looked at him.

He'd come to her room early while Orle still helped her dress, and seemed most terribly uneasy. He could not keep still and kept stealing hard glances at her.

She had not slept well, troubled by odd dreams. Last night's music had played through her mind, stirring up echoes of other songs. She'd almost felt as if her own fingers danced upon the harp strings.

Foolishness. She was a woman who rode ponies and shot arrows, not one who played delicate music.

She'd also dreamed of...a man. Nay, he was not Deathan MacMurtray—a bit surprising, since he had been so bright in her mind. Another man this had been, with a mane of long brown hair and green-specked gray eyes.

She wondered suddenly if Deathan's eyes had specks of green in them, up close. Up very close.

"What do you think of the bridegroom?" she asked Father instead of answering his question.

Orle's hands, busy upon her hair, froze.

Father stopped pacing around the room. "As I say, he is not

so bad. Could be worse."

How?

"That is not much of a recommendation," she said flatly. Her anger over this—being forced to this marriage—had hardened into something that surpassed mere distress.

Father sent her another sharp look. "He is of a good age and not ill favored. I am certain that once you get to know him—"

"He no more desires this marriage than do I. he barely speaks to me."

"Do you speak to him? Do you make yourself gracious and charming?"

Darlei turned from the mirror to face her father. "I do not wish to *make* myself anything. I am the woman I am."

"In this instance, daughter, I fear you must try to be accommodating. There are expectations. You—"

Again she interrupted him, something unthinkable back home. "In a few days you—you and all the company, save Orle—will go home. Abandon me here among strangers." To her horror, tears came to her eyes.

"Daughter, I am sorry. It cannot be helped. I came here this morning for that very reason. Let today be better. Go forth into it open and accepting."

"Accept my fate, you mean?" Her lips tightened.

"Yes. I entreat you to this for your own good."

"You would have me ingratiate myself with a man who does not want me." She thought fleetingly of Deathan, standing by the rear wall of the hall. Watching her.

"As you do not want him. His father means to speak with him also. The sooner you make up your mind, the better for all."

"I see." Darlei rose to her feet.

"We are entering a new age. A new Scotland. Old hostilities must be laid aside."

"Tell that to my bridegroom. He behaves like a small boy kicking his feet because his toy has been withheld. He is jealous of Urfet and angry he did not win those competitions. I cannot respect him."

Grief came to her father's eyes. "I regret hearing that. Respect means much to you, as I know very well."

"Rohr MacMurtray does not respect me. Not anything about me." Her chin jerked up.

"I am hoping that will change as he grows to know you. But, daughter, you will not help yourself by acting aloof and hard. Is there nothing here you like?"

"The sea. And"—another bright image of Deathan flooded her mind—"Mistress MacMurtray is sweet and kind."

Father's face softened. "Make yourself a good daughter to her, then."

Indeed, if she felt a prisoner, how much worse for that gentle woman confined to her bed?

Last night's rain had cleared, so Darlei and Orle, having shared breakfast in Darlei's chamber, went outside for the first time on their own. Only they were not on their own.

The clansfolk were everywhere hurrying about their business. They stared. And they bowed to her, but with very little warmth in their eyes.

She was the savage princess from Caledonia's heart. The bride who had won the pony race. So foreign she might have stepped down out of the clouds.

But she had a destination.

The sea beckoned to her. With Orle at her side, she picked her way down the stony path that led to the shore.

A lovely day, yes, all the rain clouds chased by a lively wind blowing inland from the west. The sky had turned deep blue with streamers like the tail of a pony, and the sea—even deeper blue—mirrored it with white combers that swept majestically to break over the gray rocks. Darlei lost her breath when she reached that place, the spray making showers of radiance, and stood on one of the rocks, unmoving.

She might stand forever so.

Far out in the blue water she could see other lands, which

surprised her. She had not known there were other lands west of the sea. Oh, there was Ireland, but that was farther south.

In the ancient days, so one of her teachers had told her, the Celtic peoples believed in a land far to the west called Tír na nÓg where their fallen heroes went after death.

Could what she saw be that land? Nay, surely not.

There were people on the shore, but they all stood aside from her, watching—still watching. Even when she stepped onto a higher rock where the spray broke at her very feet.

"Darlei," Orle, who'd remained behind her, called. "Is it safe?"

"Surely. Step up here with me."

"I do not believe we should."

They spoke in their own tongue, and the people on the shore began to mutter.

"Darlei, do not fall."

"I will not."

She teetered a bit, but it was only at the impetus of the wind.

"She is going to jump!" cried one of the men on the shore.

Suddenly, someone leaped onto the rock beside her. She turned with a smile, thinking Orle had found her courage. "It is magnifi—"

Not Orle. Deathan MacMurtray stood there, alarm filling his eyes.

"Princess! Careful, I pray."

He seized her elbow, and they stood that way for several heartbeats, gazing into one another's face while the waves broke over their feet. She felt…

But there were no words for what she felt, no words in all the world.

In the clear light, his eyes were blue, aye, dark blue like the water out beyond the rocks, but with green specks in them. Like the flecks on a gemstone.

She had never seen such eyes.

"I am not going to jump," she told him.

"I never thought so. But the rocks are wet. Ye could slip."

"I but wanted to feel the power of it all. It is magnificent."

"Aye so." He did not look away from her at the water. "'Tis."

They stood close, likely far too close. She could feel the heat of his body. She could catch the scent of him even over the salt spray.

She had never smelled anything so good.

But people were watching, and she supposed she had already earned a reputation as the wild Caledonian princess.

"You may—" she began.

A wave broke over them, wetting them both to the waist.

She smiled at him in delight, unable to help it. And it became immediately intimate, even though they stood out here in the open, the focus of so many eyes.

"—help me down," she concluded.

She thought he would lead her by the hand. Lend the strength of his arm, mayhap. Instead he released his grip on her elbow and swept her up off the flooded rock.

Into his arms.

He did it so easily, she lost all her breath. When he turned and leaped down off the rock right to Orle's side, she lost all hope of breathing.

He set her down quickly, far too quickly for her liking.

Oh, by all the holy powers of the earth and the sky.

"Ye maun be careful, princess. The sea can reach up and snatch ye right off a place like that. Can ye swim?"

"I have done in the lochs back home."

"Such still waters are naught to the sea. There are currents beneath the surface, and the waves are far more powerful than they appear." Fixing her with those incredible eyes of his, he said earnestly, "We would no' want to lose someone so precious as yoursel'."

He thought her precious.

At least, he said he did. He might be a flatterer. They had plenty of those back home.

But nay, this man did not flatter. This man possessed a heart both steadfast and true. How she knew so, she could not say.

She just did.

CHAPTER SIXTEEN

IT MIGHT HAVE been a repeat of the quarrel Deathan had overheard only days ago. The same raised voices. The same words, when he walked into the chamber. Only this took place in bright daylight with no storm rumbling overhead.

That made it worse somehow, for the thunder was not there to drown out the anger.

The hall was, fortunately, mostly empty at the moment, the servants having cleared away last night's feast and gone. But it was not what might be called a private place to have a disagreement.

"Whisht!" he cried when he came in, staring from his father to his brother and back again. "I can hear ye outside, almost."

Da blinked. He reached out and clasped a hand on Rohr's shoulder in a gesture of warning and demand.

"Did anyone hear?" he asked Deathan.

"Nay, I do no' think so. But anyone could come in here, besides me. What is amiss?"

But he knew. Aye, he knew.

Before answering, Da drew his two sons to the rear of the hall and through a curtained doorway to what had become his private quarters. He had stopped sharing a room with Mam some time ago, saying he disturbed her fragile rest.

Deathan wondered if his father merely could not bear to witness Mam's suffering.

"This fool," Da said, lowering his voice to an angry growl,

"says the wedding will no' take place. He refuses to marry the princess."

"I will no' marry the princess," Rohr repeated.

Deathan's heart leaped painfully. If the woman did not become his sister—

"He will defy his king!" Da said, still employing a subdued roar. "And shame me."

Rohr gritted his teeth. Once again, the two of them looked so much alike, they appeared near images of one another separated only by years. "'Tis no' my intention to shame ye. I would ne'er do. But the woman, the princess—ye ha' seen her. A savage clad in fine clothing. She does no' understand, even, how to deport hersel' and comes pushing forward at every opportunity."

Aye, Deathan had seen her. A woman like to no other.

"She is scarce a woman at all!"

Ah, but she was. Deathan could testify to that after having lifted her from the rock where she'd appeared to teeter so dangerously. He doubted she would have fallen. He had but used it for an excuse to get his hands on her.

And when he had…

Something had come alive in him. Some desire he did not know how to control.

"That is unfair," Da said, speaking some of the words in Deathan's head. "Ye scarce know the lass. Is this yer pride talking, Rohr? Because ye did no' win any o' the competitions?"

Rohr went from bone white to hectic red. "They cheated."

"Their ways may be different to ours, but I canna say they cheated. Much learning must be done. I daresay that is the wisdom behind King Kenneth's decision—"

"Wisdom?" Rohr fair shouted it. "*Wisdom?*"

"Hush!"

Rohr lowered his voice but said, "I did no' come to ye for to argue it all again. I am telling ye, I will no' marry her. Having seen her, I will no'. Let that be an end to it."

"That canna be an end!" Da howled. "'Tis an order o' the

king—"

"Then I will go to the king," Rohr declared. "Seek audience wi' him. Declare this canna be done."

Both his companions stared at him.

In true distress now, Murtray cried, "Son, ye canna do that. D'ye think ye are important enough to gain audience wi' the king?"

"I am no' important enough to face the man, ye say? Yet he can ruin my life wi' an order?"

"Tell him, Rohr," Deathan heard himself say quietly.

Both men stared at him again. A new expression bloomed in Rohr's eyes.

"Wha'?" Da asked.

"Tell Da the true reason ye will no' marry the princess."

"Silence, Deathan—"

"Go on. It has to come out eventually. 'Tis no' a thing can be hidden for long."

For an instant, rage looked at him from Rohr's eyes. Then betrayal and chagrin. *Ye will pay for this*, that look promised.

But Rohr turned to his father, drew himself up visibly, and said, "I am in love wi' someone else."

If he thought he could end it there, he was very much mistaken.

Da lifted his brows and took a moment before he said, "That is most unfortunate, son. I am afraid it does no' alter wha' must be. Who is she?"

"Caragh MacDroit."

Da's gaze softened. "Aye, a bonny lass."

"I ha' told her, weeks ago, I would wed wi' her."

"I fear she will ha' to be disappointed."

"She is carrying my child."

That knocked Da back on his heels, so much so he stumbled to the nearest chair and sat down.

"Are ye certain?" he asked Rohr then.

"She is certain, which is what matters."

"Nay, I mean are ye certain 'tis yours?"

Rohr flushed again. "It can be no one else's. She is in love wi' me!"

Da shot a look at Deathan that said much his lips did not. He gave a heavy sigh. "Ye will ha' to provide for the lass, to be sure, and for the bairn. Still and all, it maun be kept quiet—"

"I will provide for her by marrying her."

"Son, ye canna."

"The child is my heir. That duty is already fulfilled."

"If 'tis a wee lad. The powers grant it is a lass, and saves us all a lot o' grief."

Rohr squared himself. "Ye ask me to put Caragh aside? To break my promise to her?"

"Better than breaking faith wi' the king."

"And marrying instead that—that—"

"Careful of wha' ye call yer future wife," Da said.

"I will no'."

Da rose back to his feet. "Ye will."

"And wha' am I to tell Caragh?"

"Tell her ye love her, if ye will. I ken fine a man canna always choose where he places his heart. But there is nay choice in this duty, and at times duty maun come before love."

Rohr swore low and bitterly.

"List to me, son." Da sounded a whit more sympathetic. "There is naught to say ye canna see Caragh on the side. Later. Once ye ha' wed the princess and some time has passed. Once Darlei has your babe in her belly."

"Ye bid him prove untrue? To the princess?" Deathan asked, the words torn from him.

"It happens," Da said regretfully.

"And she is no' a princess," Rohr growled, "save as those savages have set her up to be. Wha' do I owe her, compared to what I owe Caragh?"

Nothing, Deathan supposed. For true commitment stemmed from the heart.

"Caragh will insist on marriage," Rohr declared. "Because o' the babe."

"A marriage can be arranged for her." Da said. "One o' our clansmen, perhaps a widower—"

Rohr's eyes narrowed. "Ye would ha' me stand aside and see her marry someone else?"

A hard fate, indeed.

"Your wedding wi' Princess Darlei is to tak' place tomorrow," Father said. "What if I meet wi' King Caerdoc, suggest it should be put off a few more days." He made a face. "To be sure, that means we will ha' the Caledonians here a that much longer. They are to leave directly after the ceremony."

Rohr stared at him. "Wha' good will a few more days do?"

"'Twill gi' ye time to speak to yer young woman. That she may resign hersel' to what must be."

"I will not see her wed off to someone else."

"'Twould be easier, Rohr, if the child has a father as he grows."

"He will ha' a father. And an inheritance."

"No' a legitimate one."

Deathan thought Rohr might burst into flame at that.

"Pray," Da said again, "the child is a lass. And above all else"—he drew a breath—"above all else, King Caerdoc canna be allowed to hear o' this. D'ye understand me? No' at any cost. Nor the princess hersel'. Now go ye fro' me. Give me a chance to think wha' I am to say to Caerdoc, to win ye a few more days."

"A few more days," Rohr muttered as he and Deathan left the tiny chamber. "Wha' good will that do?" He turned his eyes on his brother. "And ye! I trusted ye no' to tell him wha' ye knew."

"'Tis better out and known."

"He does no' care that his own grandchild will be set aside in favor of a pup got on a vixen."

Deathan parted his lips to speak, but Rohr hurried on, "I should take Caragh and leave, is what I should do."

Deathan's heart leaped again, still more painfully. "And go

where?"

"Anywhere. The world is wide."

"Surrender your inheritance here?" *Leave it for me?*

Rohr narrowed his eyes at that. "Mayhap Caragh and I, wi' the child, could return after a time. Once the Caledonians have gone and the king has forgotten us." He fixed a glare to Deathan. "The place would still be mine."

Aye, as—so it seemed—was everything of value.

━━━━◆⟨⟩◆━━━━

CHAPTER SEVENTEEN

D ARLEI FEARED THE worst when her father called her to him later that afternoon. Some scolding, she supposed, for an unperceived misstep, all too perceived by their hosts. A further upbraiding for her behavior.

Instead, he told her that the wedding—her dreaded and misguided wedding—was to be delayed.

"Some matter relating to the health of the groom's mother, so I perceive," Father said.

"Mistress MacMurtray?" That did cause Darlei some dismay. "Has she taken a turn for the worse?" She should not care. Anything that put off the marriage was welcome to her. But she found she had developed a fondness for Mistress MacMurtray.

"I do not know," Father told her frankly. "She is unwell but, it seems, wishes to gather enough strength to be at the wedding."

"Oh, I see."

"So we shall be staying a few days longer before we depart." Father frowned. "I hope all is well with your mother at home."

"Mother will manage wonderfully. She is a strong woman."

Father lifted a brow. "You do not have to tell me so. I found that out as soon as I married her."

Indeed, that marriage had been arranged, her mother born of a neighboring Caledonian tribe. But they had grown to care for one another.

Hence her mother's entreaty—*give it time.*

Well, she had a few more days. A reprieve.

93

It had been a good day. She and Orle had spent part of it watching their men, including Urfet, tussling at games and informal contests with some of Murtray's warriors. Deathan had not been there, but she had enjoyed marking Urfet's prowess.

And in the afternoon they'd sat out on the hillside in the sunshine with that glorious seascape spread out in front of them, while the master harper, Coll, played for the company.

She had felt close to content. Almost happy. More so now with her wedding sentence temporarily lifted.

"What should we do to celebrate?" she asked when she left her father and shared the news with Orle outside.

"*Should* you celebrate?" Orle asked cautiously. She had spent a woeful amount of time earlier eyeing not their own men, but certain among the Gaels. Could she truly be attracted to any of them?

Of course, if Orle were to stay here with Darlei, she would eventually marry a Gael—were she to wed at all.

Darlei wanted to visit Mistress MacMurtray and make certain she was not unwell, but that might be better left for morning.

"I feel I must. I know what we shall do. There is a trail that runs along the shore. Let us explore that."

"Should we?" Orle asked again. "After what happened this morning?"

"This is to be my home. Surely I have leave to explore it."

Orle appeared dubious. She ran off, though, to change her slippers, which she did not want ruined.

Darlei, who gave not a care to her slippers, refused to wait.

The residents of the settlement once more watched her as she made her way down to the shore. It was the same back home. Everyone knew where the princess was and what she was doing, at most any time. But there she could escape. Take Bradh and go for a wild ride. Hike by herself into the forest.

What did these foolish people think she was going to do? Cast herself into the sea?

It was an idea.

Perhaps an ultimate course of action, later on, when she found herself wed to a stranger. After her father left, abandoning her here. When she discovered she could not endure taking Rohr MacMurtray to her bed. Bearing his children.

A thought came into her head: it would be cowardly of a Caledonian princess, taking her own life. But a kind of last hope to tuck away, yes.

A path led away in both directions from the trail that ended down at the sea. When Darlei reached it she stood looking. To her right, the path led to a series of sheds, and she could see people working.

She turned left.

She would walk but a short way beyond the curious eyes and wait for Orle to catch her up.

But oh, being alone here—with the waves sucking and clawing at the shingle, the sky endlessly blue, and the seabirds wheeling above—brought her back to life. A different sort of *wild* than when she ran off on her own back home, but healing all the same. She drew a salty breath and felt her anger, fear, and distress abate.

Perhaps she could endure this after all.

Her feet found their own way in and out of the foam. The tension left her shoulders. The rolling of the waves on the stones was like music.

Deep in her mind she heard someone say, *We are like these two stones, aye? Together on the shore for a time—*

It took her a moment to grasp that the quick pat-patter meeting her ears was not part of her thoughts, or a movement of the clattering stones. She turned to look back.

The strong sunlight half blinded her, so she saw only an approaching shape. A man, it was, loping toward her.

She wanted to run also, away from him up along the shore. But he came far too swiftly, and once he neared enough for her to see his face, she no longer wanted to flee.

He looked a beautiful sight, his body all in motion, strides swift and graceful, hair lit by the sun. Something clenched her heart, hard. As if her past ran to her and her future both.

This moment, it will change everything.

She stood with her feet in the foam and the hem of her gown wet when he reached her. He wore a look of concern on his face.

"Princess, wha' are ye doing here? Are ye lost?"

"I do not believe so."

"Ye should no' go walking out on your own."

"Why not?"

"Some harm might befall ye."

She gave him a long look. Tall, with those graceful, long limbs. Dressed casually in a rough tunic and plain kilt with well-worn hide boots. Hair loose streaming over his shoulders in an ashen-colored mane, with threads of gold and even copper in it.

Those eyes.

So intense was his stare, she had to look away from it. "Good thing you are here then, Master Deathan, is it not?" She resumed walking. He came at her side. "So I am not alone."

A curious thing—she could feel his emotions. They surged inside him precisely the way the waves did, at her feet. High and wild one moment, gentler the next. How did it come to be he who had found her?

"Does yer woman ken where ye be?"

"She has gone back to change her shoes."

He looked down at her feet.

She added, "I do not care for mine."

"D'ye no' think ye should wait for her?"

Oh, but she liked his voice. Deep and somehow, well, satisfying, it reached right inside her. He was not the sort of man to attract her in the ordinary way, being a Gael, but by all that was holy, he did attract her.

"I do not like waiting. Or taking time to change my shoes."

"I see." Was that a note of amusement she heard? "I suppose ye ha' so many pairs ye can just replace them as ye need."

"Pairs?"

"O' slippers."

"'Tis not that. Though I have ruined a good many over the years. I just keep wearing them till they come to pieces."

"Most practical."

She stole a look at him. "Are you laughing at me?"

"Och, to be sure, nay, I would no' dare."

"What do you think of me, then? Am I the savage princess determined to have her way?"

"I think a thousand things o' ye. Far too much to say." He drew a breath. "No' that ye be savage. I think ye do enjoy having yer way. Which o' us does not?"

"Where does this path lead, Master Deathan?"

"Nowhere much. Just up along the rocks and then eventually it peters out. Ye can climb on, if ye wish, to a headland. The view fro' there is grand, but ye will no' have a path."

His accent was wonderful and danced in her ears.

"No fit place to escape, then?"

He slanted a look at her. "Is that wha' ye wish? To escape?"

"Oh, yes."

He gave that some thought while they walked side by side, their feet hitting the path in time.

The rhythm to another song, she thought. One he and she made together.

"I suppose that makes sense," he said at last. "But 'twould do ye no good, would it? For if ye left and ran, how would ye live, off on your own?"

She glanced back—to see how far they had come, she told herself, though it gave her a good excuse to eye him again. Large as life and right here beside her.

"I do not know what I would do besides not wed wi' your brother."

"Aye so." That seemed to bring heavy thoughts down on him.

"The wedding has been put off," she said.

"Aye, for but a few days."

"Do you know why?"

"I do." He shot her a look. "I canna say."

"Father claims it is because your mother wishes to attend the joining and needs to gain strength."

"That may be what my father told him, aye."

"It is not true?"

He hesitated and shook his head.

"There is a mystery in it," she said. "Still, I should be grateful. Your lady mother is not worse?"

"She is not."

"I am glad. I like her very much."

Did his hand brush hers? If so, it was but a fleeting touch and as swiftly gone.

She stopped walking. Took one look back. No sign of Orle. No one and nothing followed them.

She looked at the man beside her, who had also paused. Suddenly she wanted to touch him, wanted it so much she ached. The desire burgeoned inside her from a place so deep, she scarce recognized it.

She scarce recognized him. But he mattered to her. *He did.*

"Tell me of yourself, Master Deathan."

Those beautiful eyes of his examined her face, touched the corners of her mouth, her brow. "There is no' much to tell. I am a second son. I mak' myself useful as I may."

"What will you inherit, of this place?"

He shrugged. "Naught."

"But you love it, do you not?"

"I love it most deeply." He glanced at the sea, the land, the sky. "More than I could ever say."

"And who is to decide you are not worthier of inheriting it than your brother?" Their eyes met, held for a long instant. *Or of marrying me,* her heart whispered.

"Fate says it." His lips twisted. "Destiny."

"Ah. Destiny can be a cruel goddess." To keep from reaching for his hand, she resumed walking. "Talk to me of this place you love."

He did.

CHAPTER EIGHTEEN

DEATHAN RARELY SPOKE so much or for so long. In company with his father and brother, he was expected to listen and hold his opinions. With Ma, he was comforting. In company with his friends, he was stoic, rarely expressing his feelings. With members of the guard, whom he directed, he was brief and to the point.

Now he talked, poured out words about this place he loved. The things he valued, and why. He spoke of his family's deep roots here that stretched back hundreds of years to the Celtic chiefs who had journeyed from Ireland to seize homes in a new land.

"My ancestor, Adair MacMurtray, so 'tis told," he related, "gained this holding by way o' love."

"Love?" Darlei repeated.

"Aye. Love for his wife and her grandsire whose holding it was, and who accepted him as his own. 'Tis said he chose Alba, and Alba chose him."

"Love," Princess Darlei said, "seems a powerful thing. I have never experienced it. Oh, I love my family to be sure. But not—"

She seemed to stick there.

Deathan said, "I understand. Love o' the heart. For one person."

She flashed a look at him from those silvery eyes. "Yes."

"Nor have I experienced that. Yet," he admitted.

"Perhaps it is not for everyone. Because though my friends

have fallen victim to the love of husband and family, I have never even been tempted."

"Mayhap ye were meant for something else."

"Destiny, again? She spread her hands. "But for what? Not this."

Did she mind so much walking with him? Talking with him, being with him? She saw herself only in a trap.

"I am sure ye will miss yer home. But again, ye may fall in love wi' this place one day."

They had reached the end of the path. It fell apart in a welter of stones and a rise that led upward.

"Let us climb," she said impetuously. "I want to see from the height."

"We truly should go back, princess. They will think ye lost and be worrying."

"I care not what they think." She scrambled on up the slope. Deathan leaped ahead of her.

"Let me go first."

"Why?" Slightly flushed, she glared at him. "Are there dragons you shall have to batter out of the way for me?"

"I hope not." He allowed his gaze to linger on her face. "I am no' wearing my sword."

The climb was stiff but worth it. At the last, he offered her his hand. The instant their fingers met, he felt... But nay, there were no words for what he felt inside, and his stunned mind did not try for them.

But he did not leave go of her hand, and when they reached the cliff top and looked out, they stood linked.

"Oh, magnificent," she breathed.

It was. From here, one could see the far distances of the sea, and mark how restless it was, ever-moving like a man's mind. Like the blood in his veins. The islands crouched low, the dragons all sleeping, so he did not have to battle them. He would not need his sword after all.

"It seems one can see forever."

"Aye." He drew her closer to him, and she made no protest, merely stood with her side pressing against his.

"Why did your ancestors not build their holding up here? Back home, we choose high ground."

"The storms. Ye will no' credit it on a day such as this, but in winter the waves come up and turn all to ice."

"I would love to see that."

"Perhaps ye will."

She ignored that as if it were a thing she could not contemplate.

"What lies beyond those islands, over the water?"

"Well, Ireland lies to the south. Beyond that—men have long wondered. The old tales said 'twas the land of the ever-blessed. *Tír na nÓg.*"

"I have heard that name. Why is it called ever-blessed?"

"Those who died winged away there, to feast and play music and remain forever young."

"Ah." That seemed to strike her. He saw the thoughts move in her eyes. "I can understand why they thought so. If ever such a place of promise might exist, 'twould lie where the sun goes to bed. I wonder—" Abruptly she paused.

"What d'ye wonder?" he asked with true curiosity. This woman fascinated him, all of her, not the least the workings of her mind.

"Why such a place should not truly exist. A kind of reward for all we endure here. Life is so hard, the choices we make—and are denied making—so painful and costly. And all that comes at the end is death."

Deathan gazed at her in dismay. For someone of her youth— surely not above a score of years—and station to stand there in all her beauty and express such pain seemed an abomination.

"Surely," he said, "life is no' all bad. There are rewards along the way."

Her lips curved bitterly. Her gaze remained on the horizon. "I have been given away to a stranger by a king I do not acknowledge. Can you show me the reward in that? I confess, I would rather fly away searching for that far place until my strength gave out and I fell into the sea."

Deathan wanted to comfort her. His heart did, and it strained his being terribly. But what had he to offer this woman? No promises. Only, perhaps, desire.

"We canna gi' up on life," he said, "however hard it becomes. Because we ne'er know what may happen tomorrow, when that blessed sun rises once again."

DARLEI TURNED TO face the man beside her, dragging her gaze at last from the far horizon. Their hands remained linked—his felt calloused and strong and warm, and she did not want to surrender it. In a curious way, it grounded her, kept her, yes, from flying off to die in the sea.

There must be something to live for. Could it be him?

Those two thoughts warred in her mind as she gazed into his eyes.

Those eyes of his—of a sudden she realized they were not unlike the sea. Deep, deep blue with flecks of green and glints of light that appeared in accordance with his thoughts. Or when he smiled.

A protective sort of spirit, this man had. He took it upon himself to look after others. He did not want her to despair.

How she knew that, she could not say. She just did.

Could he be her refuge? Her Tír na nÓg? A woman could scarce ask for more.

"I wish," she said softly, "that somewhat better awaited me tomorrow. I cannot quite believe it."

"Ye will make friends here," he proposed, "and find the comforts ye need."

"Will I?"

"Am I no' the first o' them? I pray ye will let me be."

Friend, or comfort?

A thousand things, she might have said. The words might come pouring out just as his had, when he spoke of his love for this place. Yet merely standing here with him this way felt suddenly so intimate, she could speak not at all.

What had a cruel fate brought her? Possibly his company.

A call sounded along the path that traced the shore. Darlei and Deathan both turned their heads to look back. Three members of the guard, followed by Orle, puffed their way along at top speed.

"Master Deathan?" the first of them called.

Deathan surrendered Darlei's hand with alacrity. She felt the loss of his warmth, his vibrancy, to her bones.

"Och," he said, "we are in for it now. They are no' happy wi' us."

Indeed, as Darlei turned to start back down the rise, she could see her father also hurrying. And Chief MacMurtray.

Deathan did not lend her his hand on the way down. She picked her own way carefully, even as he went before her to meet the first of the guards. They began an earnest conversation.

"Darlei!" Father caught up. His face was dark with displeasure, his eyes accusing. "What are you about?"

He spoke in their own tongue, and Chief MacMurtray, stopping beside them, gave an inquiring look.

"King Caerdoc, ye can see she is quite unharmed." He then turned on his son and began to berate him. "Wha' were ye thinking, going off this way wi'out a word? The princess's guard thought her lost."

Darlei drew a breath and stepped forward to Deathan's side. Calling on all her dignity, she said, "Chief MacMurtray, I cannot allow you to blame your son because I went astray. I took it in my head to see what lay up this track. And, indeed, had he not run after me, who knows what dangers may have befallen me? Would you fault him for looking after a guest?"

Chief MacMurtray stared at her. His eyes were blue just like his other son, Rohr's, but with none of the green flecks. Quite clearly, he did not know what to say, but he choked back his anger.

"To be sure, princess."

She jerked her chin up. "If you will blame anyone, blame me."

"Nay, but there is no blame in it. Yer woman merely came running. We did not ken where ye went and feared the worst."

And what was the worst? That she might have run off? That she meant to cast herself into the sea? That she might take the hand of a man who made her feel—

But she still had no words for that.

She looked at Orle, who mouthed in their own tongue, *I am sorry.*

Father stepped up and said smoothly, "We are, to be sure, grateful to Master Deathan. My daughter is headstrong—a fault she must strive to overcome."

Darlei lifted her chin higher. "This is to be my home. Am I not at leave to walk about here?"

"Not until ye are better acquainted, princess, wi' the lie o' it and its dangers," said Murtray.

She turned on him. "And how am I to become acquainted, if I am held on a lead?"

"Darlei," said Father sharply, "you will keep a respectful tongue in your head."

"No' at all," Murtray said. He looked about rather wildly. "Mayhap Rohr or—or, aye, Deathan may be your guide. Aye, Deathan?"

For the briefest instant, her gaze met Deathan's.

"Aye, Father," he said.

With that, Darlei could be content.

CHAPTER NINETEEN

ANOTHER ENDLESS SUPPER during which Darlei sat beside her bridegroom at the head table, sunk in gloom. Rohr did make some effort to speak to her. He talked of the wealth and riches of the holding—bragged on it, in truth. The trouble was, he did not allow her to comment, merely droned on and on, displaying no interest in her responses or opinions.

He had no interest in her. As if to prove it, he did not look at her even once.

Once or twice she did assay a thought, he spoke right over her. A recitation, it was, more than a conversation.

The evening had one or two compensations. Murtray's harper came out to play. Old Coll showered his listeners with beauty, the clear, fragile notes from his harp weaving a sure spell. If Darlei closed her eyes, she could almost imagine herself on the cliff top once more, gazing into eternity.

Holding Deathan MacMurtray's hand.

And that brought her to the second of her compensations. He had smiled at her. Deathan had.

It happened when they entered the hall, before he went to his place at the other end of the same table where she sat. After that, she was not able to see him, but she held the memory of that smile to her while she thought about him.

Thought about the way he looked tonight. Dressed in a green tunic that picked up the color in his eyes and with the wealth of his hair mostly braided—yes, her one glimpse had showed her all that. He wore a medallion at his throat—his strong, tanned throat.

She thought of his hand that she'd held. Wondered how it would feel if he touched her body with his warm, calloused hands.

Wished he would.

What was happening to her? She never entertained such thoughts.

He is to be my brother.

That reminder brought such sorrow to her mind, she could scarce endure it. An old ache, it seemed, and deeply rooted. But why should she feel that way?

She barely knew the man. How could so many emotions connect her to him?

The bard began to sing a sad, soft song of love and longing. Darlei closed her eyes again as Coll's sweet voice transported her. Away from this table. Away from this hall. To another place entirely.

She stood in the forest, the tall trees that surrounded her casting their own evening shade. A man stood at one side of her, and a tall, lean, gray hound at the other. Enduring a hard journey, they were, and yet her heart—her heart lacked for nothing.

She looked at the man. A stranger. *Not a stranger.* Tall and lean, he had brown hair and gray eyes specked with green.

The sight of him made her heart swell and her emotions rise unbearably. He was about to speak to her when—

"You will need to learn our ways, and no mistake. That way, ye will no' make—well, unseemly blunders. I do no' ken how it is among yer folk, but here our women tak' a step back and do no' speak out o' turn. They ha' influence, to be sure. My own mam does. And yet—"

The spell that had been woven shattered. Darlei opened her eyes and looked at the man beside her with loathing.

"You are mistaken in me," she said.

Rohr goggled at her. She could only guess at the ferocity of her stare, based on the wildness of her feelings.

"Eh?" he said.

"You are mistaken, Master Rohr, if you think I can ever be put in a box or otherwise shut away to speak only when you permit it. I am a princess, do not forget."

Low and angrily, he replied, "A princess who is to be my *wife*. Whether or no' either o' us likes it. Ye will learn yer place."

"Nay, *you* will learn my place, which will never be behind you."

She was upset that he had ruined the spell, that fragile thing she'd almost had in her grasp, and angry he should speak so to her.

Father glanced at her warningly and several heads turned. The big room had gone quiet in respect for the bard, and their words carried.

"Daughter," Father grunted.

"Listen to the music, pray," Darlei told Rohr, but it was too late. Her pleasure was ruined and Master Coll finished playing soon after.

On the whole, so she decided, she preferred it when Rohr did not speak to her at all.

She puzzled over it later when in her bed. Not Rohr's words—those she understood. She began to realize the kind of man he was. But she puzzled over the glimpse she'd had of the man standing beside her in the forest.

So real had he seemed. So very dear to her. How could he be mere imagining? Naught more than a part of the spell woven by the music?

He could not. Her feelings for him had been too real, too vital. She clung to the thought of him, held as tightly as she did to the memory of Deathan MacMurtray's smile, while she fell asleep. Her sole comfort in a difficult world.

She and Orle had become accustomed to taking their breakfast in their own chambers, the hall being always in disarray from the previous night's feasting. That next morning, Darlei wanted nothing to eat and told Orle, who nibbled at a barley cake, "I am going out to take the air."

Orle dropped her cake hastily. "Hold for but a moment, and I will come with you."

"No need."

"*Darlei*"—Orle popped up like a bunny from its burrow—"there is every need after what happened yesterday."

Darlei gave an impatient sigh. Intolerable, being hedged round this way. "I will stand right outside. I want only to breathe in the morning."

"I will come."

Orle had not yet dressed her own hair nor Darlei's. She snatched up a shawl and followed her mistress out.

The morning felt cool and carried a definite whiff of autumn. Back home, Darlei loved this time of year, when the colors of the leaves changed and the very ground grew crisp beneath her feet. She loved the scents that blew in from the far hills and the way the year pared itself down, preparing to die—year after year died, and always in the spring was reborn again. Was it so for people also? Did life follow life, and might one, perhaps under a spell of music, catch a glimpse of a time that had come before?

"Daughter, what are you about?"

She jumped when her father spoke. He had emerged from the keep with Urfet at his shoulder.

"Naught, Father. I wanted only to see the morning."

He fixed her with a stern look. "You will not wander off on your own again."

"To be sure not."

"Chief MacMurtray is taking a party of us hunting this morning."

Darlei lit up. "Wonderful! I may come?"

"I am afraid not. This is a party of men only."

"But at home, I always accompany you."

Almost gently, he said, "You are no longer at home, daughter. Best to make up your mind to it."

"Father, that is a thing I do not believe I can do."

"Best try. Your future happiness relies upon it. I am certain there will be compensations. Children, for instance. You might best lay aside your wild ways in favor of motherhood."

She did not want to lay aside her wild ways, and she most certainly did not want to bear Rohr MacMurtray's children.

She tipped up her chin. "I mean to visit Mistress MacMurtray this morning. I will just take the air first. Good hunting, Father."

Her father did not argue it. Urfet gave her a knowing look and a wink before the men walked away.

"Darlei," Orle said, "mayhap it would be better to be more…accepting and less defiant. It will make things easier, surely."

"Yes, Orle. No doubt it would. But easier is not always better."

Easier might well cost Darlei her spirit.

They paced sedately around the settlement, taking in the sights. A large place to be sure, and a busy one. Everyone seemed to have a task, and to be engaged in it.

The sea…

Well, if ever there were to be a compensation for what Darlei could only call her imprisonment, it must be that. It called to her. Lifted her. Made her long to go wandering again.

Something about its eternal, restless movement matched what lay inside of her.

Could she ever be still?

She stood several moments watching that seascape, marking the clouds far out over the water.

The hunting venture would end in rain.

But for all its magnificence, the sea was not what she'd come out hoping to glimpse.

Only one figure could satisfy the urging of her heart.

Yet she saw him nowhere. Not with the hunting party that formed up with their ponies just inside the curtain wall. Did he not accompany them, then?

Not in front of the hall or on any of the paths she could see. Not on the shore.

Frustrated and disappointed, she turned to go back inside. That was when she spotted her quarry high up on the inner wall, keeping watch over the country beyond.

Was he, then, in charge of the men? Maintaining the watch to make certain all was safe?

The eternal warrior, perhaps. Strong and vigilant. A man to whom a woman could entrust her heart.

He looked down, and their gazes met. For an instant all the bustle and all the uncertainty faded away.

He did not smile, and nor did she. Too serious, this. Far too vital.

Only slightly comforted and far from meek, she went back inside the keep.

⸺ ❦ ⸺

CHAPTER TWENTY

IT FELT LIKE the kiss of lightning, being touched by Princess Darlei's gaze.

Deathan had come out early to make sure the men had their instructions and to watch the hunting party away. He did not go with them, but Rohr did, at Da's insistence—no doubt in an effort to ingratiate himself with his betrothed's father.

Best they leave early, for they would have rain before long.

Deathan told himself he did not mind being excluded from the group and being left behind to see to the boring details of life at the keep. And for the most part, he did not. So used to it was he that he turned to those duties for refuge.

The glimpse of Princess Darlei helped. She was still here, and so was he.

He needed to examine what he felt for her. The leap that came to his heart every time he caught sight of her. The power of being in her presence. The way it had felt yesterday up on the cliff top, holding her hand.

As if his fingers had been yearning always for hers.

She is to be my brother's wife.

He stood with both hands resting on the stones of the wall even after she went inside the keep, those words echoing in his head, swiftly followed by others.

He could not bear it. He could not allow it to happen.

Och, but what had he to say in the matter? The king had made the order. Both men involved—his father and hers—

followed that order. Even Rohr could not prevent it.

How did Deathan think *he* could?

And yet the connection grew inside him and gained strength each time he saw her, every time he thought of her.

She should belong to no one, save him.

Grimly now, he nodded at the last of the men on watch and ran down the narrow stone steps to the front door.

She had already gone in, and he stood for a moment where she had, as if he thought he might catch the echoes of her being.

Madness, all of it, a painful kind of madness that hurt his heart.

He would keep himself busy this day, he resolved as he went inside. Occupy his mind, make the time pass. Keep too busy to think of her—aye, that was the only thing to do. First he would stop to see his mother, then off to supervise training.

He opened Mam's door softly and stopped as if he'd run into a stone wall.

Princess Darlei was there ahead of him.

She sat beside Mam's bed, leaning forward gracefully with her hand on the coverlet, the two women smiling at one another. Mam's smile spread to Deathan as she acknowledged him.

"Deathan, son, come awa' in."

"I—" He looked at Darlei. "'Tis no' a good time."

Mam ignored that and told Darlei confidingly, "Deathan always stops to see me before he begins his day. He is the very best o' sons."

"I do not doubt it," Darlei said. Her gaze fastened to Deathan's, and aye, the feelings all came rushing as they had out on the wall. The ache, the madness.

The desire.

"I can come back," he said stupidly.

"Nay, if you wish time alone with your mother, I will leave." Darlei got to her feet. "I would not spoil your visit."

Mam laughed, a thing so rare these days it made Deathan blink. A weak laugh, to be sure, but still hers of old, sweet and tripping.

"Is there a reason the both o' ye may no' be here wi' me?"

This time the glance Deathan and Darlei exchanged was fleeting. She looked away first.

"Come, Deathan." Mam held out her hand.

He went in and sat on the edge of Mam's bed, which took him very close indeed to Princess Darlei.

She sat back down and folded her hands.

"How d'ye feel today, Mam?"

"A little better. I had a good night and took some sleep."

"That is well." Far too often, pain kept her awake.

"I am excited to learn more o' my new daughter." She smiled at Darlei. "Pray, tell me o' life in yer father's kingdom. Was it much different to here?"

"Yes, yes it was." Darlei's gaze stole back to Deathan. "But I would not take up Master Deathan's time—"

"I am content to listen."

More than content to hear her voice, with its accent like music. To watch the light come and go in her face as she mentioned events from her childhood. To catch flickers of a smile meant for Mam, which nevertheless spilled over onto him.

To have an excuse to run his gaze down the length of her hair, touch upon the lift of her bosom. Follow her hands.

He had held that hand—the left one—in his. He longed to touch it again, to drop a kiss into the palm.

This was not like him. He never fell victim to this sort of attraction, that left him feeling like he'd been run over by a team of ponies. He did not know what to do with the feelings. So he sat. Watched her. Listened. Fell deeper into these waters that had opened beneath them.

She spoke to his mother, aye, but she included him, glanced often at him. Her childhood sounded fascinating, and her love for her home rang like a bell. When she finished, Mam said what Deathan was thinking.

"It must be so hard for ye to leave all that and come awa'

here."

Emotions warred in Darlei's face. Pride that said she did not want to admit anything hinting at weakness. Honesty. She nodded. "It is hard, thinking I may never see any of it again."

"But surely ye will travel home now that the country is one and united. No more warring. Ye will be free to come and go."

Darlei looked at Deathan, her silver eyes rueful and sad. But she said only, "Yes, mistress. So I am sure." She rose to her feet and clasped Mam's hands. "I must leave you. Thank you for your kindness."

"My dear, ye be always welcome here wi' me."

Deathan sprang to his feet as Darlei made to move past him, and was at the door ahead of her. In opening it, he could catch her scent. The fragrance that came off her hair.

"Master Deathan," she said courteously as she moved past him. And then, very low, so none but he could hear, "I will visit your mother first thing every morning."

"Ah. As will I." He bowed.

A chance for them to see one another. One built into the day. *Like a promise.*

He wanted the promise of this woman's company, and to give her promises. He longed for it. Wished to pledge himself, his heart, his life.

That shocked him so much, he stood like one struck as she left.

"She is a sweet lass," Mam said then. "Kind of her to come and see me. Now come, son, and tell me o' yer day."

There was little to tell other than that he feared he'd lost his heart.

After his visit with Mam, and still without breakfast, he went back up on the walls, paced them with a restlessness he could not deny. Eyed the land for danger—but aye, Mam was right. From whence would danger come, now, with the country all one?

He watched the clouds build up on the sea and imagined rain pounding down. *A small, quiet sleeping place. A woman in his arms.*

Not Darlei. Or was she? *He kissed her as if he needed the taste of her more than breathing. They made love, and it claimed him.*

It changed him.

He shook himself loose of the dream, one that beset him on his feet, and tried to think.

Tried to think of reasons to be near Princess Darlei. Means and excuses for being in her company. Mam had given him one.

He needed far more.

⸻ ❦ ⸻

CHAPTER TWENTY-ONE

T HE HUNTING PARTY came home at nightfall, soaking wet. Darlei happened to see them from the front steps as they came riding in through the gates looking disgruntled and carrying little game.

She and Orle had spent much of the long afternoon listening to Master Coll play upon his harp in the hall beside a good fire. The rain had sent damp creeping through the keep. Autumn now came in earnest.

She half hoped Deathan might come in to hear the impromptu concert, but he had not. Duties to which he must see, so she supposed.

Her next glimpse of him would be at supper. Indeed, Master Coll had been chased out now so the servants could set up for that meal, as if they knew their master headed home.

She would go mad here with nothing to do. With nothing to think about save her impending marriage.

To the wrong man.

Ah, and from whence had come that thought? She frowned. It had been there all the while.

"Let us go." Orle laid a hand on her arm. "Before they come in."

Very wise. Darlei did not want to be caught here by Father. By Rohr.

"Let us go up to the little room Mistress MacMurtray bade you use," Orle suggested. "It will be warm there."

"Yes." Mistress MacMurtray had a small chamber she no longer used, due to her infirmity. She had instructed her woman to keep a fire there, and offered the refuge to Darlei that very morning.

"I used to spend my days there, and do my weaving. It will be your haven now."

The lingering sadness in the woman's eyes had struck Darlei to the heart. Did she suppose she would never again rise from her bed?

The chamber was indeed small, a mere nook a few steps from Mistress MacMurtray's bedchamber, with but a single window. But the fire warmed it, and Darlei took a seat on a low bench, grateful for that.

Orle had been suffering all day from headache, no doubt brought on by the rain. Once in the tiny room, Darlei sent her off to lie down. "So that you will feel better by suppertime."

Orle looked torn. "I do not like to leave you alone."

"I will be content here."

But with Orle gone, Darlei did begin to feel restless. The room, so quiet and with the rain dashing against the stones, seemed to hem her in.

How many future days would she spend here like this? Orle could not be always at her side. Indeed, sweet-natured and pretty as she was, Darlei did not doubt that Orle would soon marry some brawny member of the guard.

Deathan MacMurtray's guard.

And begin having babes of her own.

Darlei would not deny her that. Certainly not for the sake of her own loneliness. She might bond with Mistress MacMurtray, but—

She paused as her ears caught a string of sounds above the rain. Orle, returning? Nay.

Someone—two someones were having a conversation. A quite fervent one.

The door to the little chamber stood open a crack as Orle had left it. Darlei moved away from the window with its drumming rain and over behind the panel to listen.

She knew one of those voices, surely?

Master Rohr. Master Rohr, it was, with a woman.

She would not ordinarily try to overhear. Nay, she would not. In this case, she needed all the knowledge she could obtain.

The woman—the young woman—was very upset. So much so that she did not keep her voice as low as she might. A woman pushed past endurance, she sounded, and Darlei felt a flash of sympathy.

Indeed, the first words Darlei heard from her were, "But Rohr, wha' am I to do?"

"I canna be seen talking wi' ye here," he told her harshly, dismissively, which just ramped up Darlei's curiosity.

What *was* this?

"Nay," the woman cried, her voice trembling, "ye will no' deal wi' me. Ye will no' give me answers, even though—"

"Caragh," he growled, "I ha' given ye an answer."

"No' one I can accept."

"There is naught to be done. My hands are tied. Och, dunna weep."

His voice softened a bit on the last two words.

Darlei just *had* to see. Body flattened against the door panel, she peered around.

They stood as close together as any two could be in the otherwise deserted hallway, obviously believing themselves alone. He dripped with wet, but she had hold of him, gripping both his forearms.

A pretty girl. A very pretty girl with hair of red gold falling in ringlets and a heart-shaped face, now twisted in misery. Darlei had seen her round the place before. With Rohr?

"I trusted ye!" the girl told Rohr plaintively. "I lay down wi' ye."

What ho!

"Now that somewhat has come o' it—"

What had come of it? What usually did. Well, and was this not a nasty snarl in an already-tangled thread?

"It canna be helped. D'ye no' think I would get myself out o' marriage wi' that savage wench if I could? There is no way out. Caragh, dearest"—now he almost caressed her name—"I would ha' wed ye if I could."

Darlei's heart throbbed. She caught her breath. Rohr would not like to know that she had heard. But so wrapped up in one another were they, neither of the couple so much as glanced at the door of the room Rohr no doubt believed stood unused.

"Ye still must." Caragh's voice throbbed with emotion. "I carry the heir to the clan, the Murtray who will follow ye."

"If the bairn be a boy," he cautioned her.

"It is a boy. Could a man o' yer virility gi' me aught less?"

Well… Darlei thought.

"Ye maun tell yer father the truth," the girl urged.

Rohr went silent for a weighty moment before he said, "Caragh, love, he knows."

"What? Ye told him?"

"I did. It does no' matter. The marriage is by order o' the king. Even my father canna prevent it."

"Does he no' care that I carry his grandson and heir?"

"I believe he does. He will no' defy the king."

"Och! Then marry her." Caragh's voice had turned sharp and vicious. She lowered it a bit so Darlei had to strain her ears. "Marry her if ye must, and then make sure she does no' survive."

"Wha'?"

"Kill her. Make it look like an accident, if ye will. Then ye can wed wi' me."

All Darlei's incipient sympathy for the woman died swift and hard.

Rohr said nothing.

"Why d'ye hesitate?" Caragh demanded in a fierce whisper.

"'Tis murder."

"So? Ye do no' have soft feelings for her, do ye? Ye do no' care about her?"

"Ha' I no' told ye so? I detest her. But Caragh—"

"Otherwise ye will be tied to her forever."

"God forbid."

"Then—"

"Caragh, there is no honor in murder."

Darlei's chest hurt from holding her breath.

"Not murder, surely," Caragh suggested insistently, "so much as extermination. Ye ha' said yon Caledonians are naught but vermin."

Darlei's cheeks flushed with anger. *That nasty-tongued she-viper—*

"Still and all."

"Wed wi' her as ye must. Then rid yoursel' o' her. Whose child would ye rather raise? Hers or mine?"

"Yours." The answer came quick. "List, I canna talk wi' ye here."

"Later, then? The usual place."

They parted. Darlei pressed against the wall, sure they must see her now, that Rohr might notice and glance into the firelit room.

But he walked past. Bound for his own chamber to change his wet clothes, no doubt.

Unmoving, Darlei squeezed her eyes shut. What to do now? Caragh was carrying Rohr's child and wanted her dead.

She must tell someone. Father. He would back off from the marriage.

Or would he? Could he, yet?

Father might perhaps approach King Kenneth, inform him how things stood, that there was another woman—and child— already in the way of a worthy match. The king could reconsider his order.

She could go home.

Her eyes flew open. Still she could not breathe.

To be sure, she *wanted* to go home, wanted it more than

anything.

But what of Deathan?

An image of him invaded her mind. Tall and somber, with that mane of honey-brown hair. Those green-specked sea-blue eyes, and the smile that came so gravely to them.

Something grew between them. Like a frond of bracken just unfolding in the spring, it barely knew as yet what it needed to be.

But the roots, the roots went deep.

She could not imagine what to do. But she unpropped herself from the wall and went back to her seat by the fire.

When Orle returned, saying she felt better and bringing her spindle, Darlei told nothing of what she'd overheard, even though it was all she could think on.

Best she keep Master Rohr's secret a while, till she decided what best to do with it.

CHAPTER TWENTY-TWO

D ARLEI CARRIED A knife to supper in the hall. Not the small blade, this, that she used to cut her meat, but the good, stout blade she carried when she went out anywhere at home. Because a woman never knew when she would need to defend herself. Or when her betrothed would decide she was just too inconvenient.

But Rohr, once more seated beside her, might have been carved from wood for all the notice he took of her. Even when she sought to engage him by asking after his success at hunting, he did little more than flick a glance at her and grunt, all pretense at civility flown.

Wholly distracted, he was, by what had happened earlier. By whether or not he wanted her dead.

Darlei's knowledge about him and Caragh was a weapon in itself, if a dangerous one. It offered her a measure of power she'd been sorely lacking.

The rain continued to fall so hard that she could hear it through the stout roof and over the noise that filled the hall. The great fire in the center of the room refused to draw in the heavy air, and smoke hung against the rafters, stinging Darlei's eyes and flavoring her meat.

Her mood was not improved by the fact that she'd caught naught more than a glimpse of Deathan. At first she'd thought he had absented himself from supper, but he came in late, dripping wet, and took his seat at the far end of the table without so much as glancing her way.

The man looked good wetted down, so he did. She sat beside her silent future husband, picking at her food while she played out a series of shocking fantasies in her mind.

Stripping the wet clothing from Deathan's body. Touching what lay beneath. The skin of his chest, alive with muscle. His lean belly and lower, lower still. The gleam in his eyes when she laid hold of him. The sheer, hot weight between her fingers, strong and smooth and—

But how could she know how he would feel between her hands? She had never touched him there. She had never touched any man that way.

Had never wanted to.

Now she sat at supper playing at being a proper princess while she went hot at the very thought of Deathan.

Was this desire? This raw, primitive urge that had her imagining how he'd feel and wondering how he'd taste? No wonder women got into trouble. No wonder Caragh had.

Caragh wanted her dead.

She twitched, and, beside her, Rohr jerked also, as if he paid attention to her after all.

And if this was desire, why Deathan MacMurtray? He was not the sort of man to turn her head. He certainly was not Urfet. He simply *was*.

That supper seemed interminable. Not even a scattering of songs from Master Coll served to lighten spirits much, and when they filed out, the mood could only be considered subdued.

As Darlei and Orle returned to their chamber, Darlei found herself wondering: could she exist on half measures? The hope of catching a glimpse of her husband's brother? The chance of a smile?

Nay. She would starve on such a diet. Wither and die.

Then a thought burst upon her mind like a rising sun. She had a chance of seeing him at his mother's bedside, come morning.

It proved enough to get her through the night.

DEATHAN WENT TO his mother's chamber early, as was his habit, to check on her before he began his duties of the day. Despite himself, he felt a surge of disappointment at finding Mam alone but for her serving woman, who gave him a smile and promptly hurried out.

Too early for Princess Darlei, mayhap. He should have done a round of the walls first, as he had the other day, in the hope they might, aye, meet here.

He gave Mam a wide smile and told her, "Good morn. Ye are looking well."

She did, in truth, with a bit of color in her face and a sparkle in her eyes. He bent over the bed to kiss her cheek.

"I feel stronger," she answered. "I am going to try to get up today."

He backed off a step. "What?"

She smiled shyly. "I so wish to attend your brother's wedding. And I would prefer not to be carried like—like a babe."

"Aye so, but—" A sudden fear assailed him, that of something going wrong, of losing her. This gentle woman who filled such a great place in his life. "Wha' does the healer say?"

"Och, him."

"Aye, him." Deathan could not help but smile.

"He does no' think it will harm me to try. Then again, I do no' think he believes I will succeed."

"Ah, well, ye ha' chosen a fine day for it. All last night's rain is flown and 'tis a glorious morning. If ye would like me to lend an arm—"

The door of the chamber whispered open. Princess Darlei slipped in. Deathan immediately lost all his breath and half his wits.

How was it she could do that to him? Without a word. With but a smile, and even though the first of those she gave to his mam before him.

"Good morn, Mistress MacMurtray. Oh, am I intruding?"

"Not at all, my dear. Come in."

Mam held out her hand and Darlei stepped forward to take it, which again brought her very close to Deathan. So close he could once more catch the scent off her hair—herbs?—and see the shadows her lashes cast on her cheeks when she blinked.

"I was just telling Deathan that today I mean to make an attempt to leave this bed."

"Do you?" Darlei's eyes widened, surprise quickly followed by concern. "Should you?"

"Sit. Sit." Mam patted the edge of the bed and Darlei perched on it. Deathan took the seat alongside, which had their knees nearly touching. "I am determined to attend your wedding. And I would prefer not to be carried, as I was just telling Deathan. Thanks be, I have more time now that 'tis been delayed." Sudden worry invaded her eyes. "I hope no' on my account."

"I do not believe so, mistress," Darlei said uncertainly. "I hope you will be most careful not to injure yourself."

"Ye be sweet to worry for me. 'Twill go slowly, no doubt. I will get up today, try to take a few steps tomorrow. Deathan will be here to help me."

"Well then, I do not doubt you will be in good hands." Darlei cast Deathan a smile that stole his breath again.

He wondered how she did it, managed to present herself in a lovely gown with her hair all dressed and her manner polite, yet still carry the spirit of a wild woman in her eyes. It attracted him in ways he could neither control nor explain.

They spoke for a while quietly about the day ahead until Mam's woman came back in with her breakfast.

"I must go." Darlei got to her feet.

"As must I."

"Deathan—come back after ye ha' assigned the men," Mam

said. "The healer will be here by then."

"Aye so, I will." He kissed his mother's cheek once more. When he turned, Darlei waited at the door.

"I must speak with you," she murmured as he opened the chamber door for her. "Alone."

They stepped out into the corridor together.

"Is somewhat amiss?"

For an instant she looked torn. Then her gaze met his and she steadied. "Yes. I think so."

"At noontime, then. Meet me out front of the hall. I do no' doubt Mam will be well tired out by then."

She nodded. Slipped away on soundless feet.

He need only live till noontime, to be with her again.

THE SETTLEMENT TEEMED with life when Darlei slipped out to meet Deathan. Small boats were far out on the water, and folk hurried past on various errands. A group of men that included both Rohr and Urfet worked with a number of ponies in the field.

The day could not be more different from yesterday, bright and beautiful, with the sun striking sparks off the water.

Darlei stood drinking it all in before someone slipped into place beside her.

She knew him without looking. Knew him by feel.

All morning long, she'd questioned her desire to confide in him. Chased round and round with it. Was he the proper person to tell?

Mayhap not, but she trusted him instinctively, she did. And she could not say that about many of those around her. She could not trust even her father to act in her best interest, in this matter.

She turned to Deathan with a smile. "Have you been with your lady mother all this time? How went her efforts to rise?"

His expression went grave. He often looked so, quiet and

serious. Only when he looked at her did he come to life.

"It did not go as well as she hoped, or perhaps imagined. She is very weak. The will is there, but 'tis a long while since she has left that bed."

"I am sorry to hear it."

He nodded.

"May we walk? I do no' wish anyone to overhear what I must say."

"Aye. Down to the shore?"

"Please."

She wanted to take his hand. Wanted it so much she ached. But there were people all around, and she did not wish to attract notice. So she folded her hands at her waist, an act of self-discipline.

"I must confess, princess, you have my curiosity at a pitch. Wha' does this concern?"

"Your brother." She barely spoke the words, so he had to bend his head to her and listen.

"My—"

"Wait. Wait until we reach the shore."

A bright day, and no mistake. Darlei had to narrow her eyes as she watched the boats bouncing on the waves. White horses danced as far out as she could see.

He waited with that patience that seemed so much a part of him till they reached the shore, where the sound of the waves might cover whatever she wanted to say.

"Now," he prompted her.

And she said without looking at him, "I believe your brother wishes to murder me."

CHAPTER TWENTY-THREE

DEATHAN EYED THE woman beside him, who looked not at him but continued to gaze out to sea, as if she had not just spoken the last words he expected to hear.

Her profile was strong, strong. That stubborn, pointed chin and the nose that was perhaps a bit too robust to grace the countenance of a woman.

She looked deadly serious.

"What?" he asked, hushed. "I think I canna ha' heard ye right."

"You did."

She drew a breath, trying to master her emotions or perhaps seeking words. His was not her mother tongue, after all.

"Last evening after supper I heard Rohr talking to a young woman, in the corridor outside your mother's small solar. They did not know I was there."

Oh. Deathan blinked rapidly in an effort to assimilate it. This could not be good. "Wha' did ye hear?"

She moved closer to him, her arm brushing his, still staring out to sea as if she did no more than admire the view to the horizon.

"He is in love with someone else—the girl to whom he was speaking. She is carrying his child."

When Deathan did not speak, she shot him a glance. "You do not look surprised. You knew?"

"Aye." His mind struggled with it. "Wha' has that to do wi'

him wanting to—to *murder* ye?"

"I should say, it is the young woman in question who wishes me dead. She beseeched him to forsake our betrothal and marry her instead. When he said he must obey the king's orders, she—" Darlei stopped abruptly.

"Aye?"

"She told him to go ahead and wed wi' me, and then he could make sure I did no' survive long. As a widower, he could then wed wi' her, and their child would be the heir to—to all this."

"Caragh said that?" Deathan could not quite warrant it. Aye, he too had overheard Rohr and Caragh arguing. But the lass seemed far too sweet to make any such suggestion.

"So she did." When he did not speak, Darlei shot him another sharp glance. "Do you not believe me?"

"I do no' suppose ye would lie to me about such a thing."

"I would not. I would not lie to you at all, Deathan Mac-Murtray."

The significance of the statement did not escape him. "Is there a chance ye heard awrong? Or are mistaken—"

"Nay."

"My brother would no'—"

"Oh, he argued against it. Said there is no honor in murder. I have no doubt she will persuade him."

"Ye—ye did no' tak' this to yer father? Or mine?"

"Nay. Not yet. I am not sure they will believe me. He has only to deny it, and…it is such an unbelievable thing, withal."

"Aye."

"But someone has to know. In case he acts upon the deed. I thought on that all night. Knew I had to tell you."

He almost wished she had not. He would rather not know. And yet all his protective instincts rose. To be sure, he would defend her as he would his own life.

"My brother's situation is desperate," he said in a low tone. Down along the shore from them, a group of men—fishers—put out in a small boat, the sounds covering his words. "And will become more so. They cannot keep their secret forever."

"Indeed not. Should my father discover my bridegroom has fathered a child on another woman, well—I do not know if it would be enough to make him approach King Kenneth."

"Ask him to withdraw his insistence on the marriage, ye mean?"

"Yes. Then I could go home."

She withdrew her gaze at last from the sea and directed it at Deathan. He looked back at her steadily, ignoring the fishers and their activities, as his heart began to pound.

He might lose her. If the betrothal were dissolved, she might go from his life before whatever had taken root between them could flower.

Yet…if he had to choose between losing her and seeing her wed to his brother, which would be more unbearable?

The answer came to him swiftly. *Losing her.*

"If ye want my advice," he said, "ye should confide wha' ye ha' heard in your father. He will go to mine, who will question Rohr. Rohr will then no doubt confess. I admit, 'twould be better if Rohr was the one to step up and tell Da that he would rather ye dead than married to him."

If Rohr was man enough to lie with a maid and beget a child, he should be man enough to take responsibility—no matter how tangled and ugly the situation.

"I will speak wi' Rohr," Deathan decided. "Try to make him see his correct path."

"Will you tell him I overheard him?"

"Mayhap no'." The last thing Deathan wanted was to increase Rohr's anger against her. "Meanwhile, I want ye to ha' a care, princess. Do no' go out and about wi'out your woman for company. Spend time wi' my mother, or among your own folk."

"You think, then, she might yet persuade him to this act she desires?"

"Nay." And yet…Deathan's eyes moved over the scene. The water and the rocks. So many ways to prompt a fall or other dire "accident".

The very thought of any ill befalling this woman made the breath seize in his lungs.

"I am surely safe in your company."

Their eyes met. Deathan had a sudden vision of her *in his company*. The two of them alone together somewhere. Dim light and the soft rugs of a sleeping place. Neither of them clad, and all her glorious hair loosed to his touch. Time for the two of them to taste, to explore, to cherish.

"Aye."

"You could mayhap show me the sights o' the settlement. Between your other duties, I mean."

In the narrow gap between their bodies, where his arm hung beside hers, he reached for her fingers. No more than a passing grasp and release it was, yet it felt almost painfully intimate.

"I might do that." His voice sounded husky to his own ears. "Let me speak wi' Rohr first. See if I can persuade him wha' is right. Meanwhile, ye must no' put yoursel' out here like this, or go anywhere alone at night. Will ye promise me so?"

"I so promise."

"I will find a way to speak wi' Rohr."

"He is over in that field admiring the ponies." Darlei turned and pointed south.

"Is he? I shall go there, then, after seeing ye back safe to yer quarters."

Did she sigh under her breath as they turned away from the sea? Not easy for a woman such as she—one with a wild heart—to face confinement. To keep a halter on her behavior and her impulses.

"Trust me," he bade her as they started back up the slope.

And, gazing full into his eyes, she replied, "Oh, I do."

WHENCE CAME SUCH trust? he wondered after he left her in her woman's company and started off toward the broad field where the ponies were stabled and trained. Aye, he could see a group of men gathered there, standing in a dark knot. The animals had been led out, and not, as he saw when he drew near, their own, but those of the Caledonians being housed there.

An argument was in progress.

It may well have started as a friendly discussion of the differences between their animals and the Caledonians'. A rehash of the pony race. Now, though, Deathan could hear raised voices even before he reached the gathering.

Rohr was there, aye, along with their fellows who trained and cared for their stock. All the men of the Caledonian party save King Caerdoc. He and Father must be off somewhere else.

Deathan increased his pace to a lope and was in time to hear his brother declare, "There is no need to be boastful about it. I ha' nay patience, me, for arrogance."

That almost made Deathan snort. Rohr could at times be the personification of arrogance. Like now when he stood with his head back, color high, and eyes ablaze, facing…

Aye so, it would be Urfet, who held himself with such assurance and pride.

At the moment, Urfet looked slightly amused. Confident. Almost as if he needled Rohr on purpose just to get a reaction.

Did he want to provoke a fight? Aye, mayhap he did.

Eyeing the group of men, Deathan could not be sure. The Caledonian party had already been here longer than they had expected and likely grew bored. And Urfet appeared to be a man who would make his own sport, if none offered.

Swiftly, Deathan turned his gaze on his brother. Given his internal tensions, he could well explode.

Urfet turned his head and gave Deathan an assessing look when he jogged up. "All I said was, our animals are more agile than your own. You can tell by their build. A fact, that. How can you call it arrogance?"

"'Tis no' a fact—" Rohr began, and Deathan jostled him.

"Brother, a moment." If he could distract Rohr, perhaps he could keep this from going awry.

But Urfet kept goading Rohr. "Why do we not put it to the test"—he grinned—"as we did in the pony race? An informal contest here in your field." He took an exaggerated look around. "A pity the princess is not here to put you in your place—again."

"There is no' woman can put me in my place."

Urfet lifted scornful brows.

"That pony o' yours is half wild," Rohr declared. "It but ran awa' wi' her during that race."

"You think so? Let us put it to the test here and now."

Do not take the bait, Deathan beseeched his brother silently. It could not end well—he felt that in his bones.

Too late. Urfet had Rohr's measure and then some. "Aye so, we will do just that."

Desperate now, Deathan said, "Brother, Father needs ye. He is looking—"

Rohr turned on him. "Father bade me entertain our guests." His tone made of the word an epithet. "And that I will do."

CHAPTER TWENTY-FOUR

UNDER THE GREAT, wide sky with streamers of clouds sailing in from the sea, Deathan stood and sweated. A beautiful scene it should have been, with the young men and the healthy ponies all in motion. Lining up in a row, all the Caledonian ponies on one side and the Gaels' newly trotted out on the other.

Rohr and Urfet beside each other.

"Twice around the field?" Urfet proposed with that wicked gleam in his eye. As if, Deathan could not help but think, he still goaded Rohr for his own amusement. As if he knew he would win. And would further humiliate his host's prideful son.

"Just like the last race," he added. For an instant, his gaze met Deathan's.

"Aye!" Rohr called, and vaulted onto his pony. A good beast, but one that had lost to Urfet's half-wild animal before.

With Darlei on its back.

"Your brother can give the signal." Urfet waved an arm at Deathan, perhaps prodding him a bit also. "When we pass him twice, the leader will be the winner."

"I think—" Deathan began, but Rohr overrode him.

"Aye. Deathan, gi' the signal."

The ponies danced. Deathan raised his arm and brought it down again.

The animals, barely restrained, thundered by him, their hooves tearing the green turf. Misgiving rose to his head, and in that instant he knew what a bad idea this was.

No mild, orderly race this. More like the footrace that had pitted these very men against each other. This time the Caledonians did not play fair but jostled their ponies into one another. Barging, shoving, hoping to knock each other out of the running, they ran the length of the field in a mob that had Deathan's heart up in his throat.

At the turn, down the bottom of the field, he was sure they would crash in a knot and all go down. It sorted itself somehow and they headed back toward him, Rohr and Urfet neck and neck in the lead.

Only…

He narrowed his eyes. To him it looked like Urfet played with Rohr still, kept pace with him. As if he and his wild pony could outrun Rohr at any time the Caledonian chose.

He preferred this game instead. He would wait till the final moment, let Rohr think he could win.

A final humiliation of the Gael.

King Kenneth could give any order he liked—the animosity in the new Scotland would not die so easily.

They thundered past him, turned again. Did Urfet's tribe mates hold the other Gaels back? So fierce was the jostling, Deathan could not tell.

He caught a glimpse of his brother's face, stark white with determination. He did not mean to let Urfet win. Not at any cost.

Down to the bottom of the field once more with Urfet bumping Rohr's mount again and again. Rohr tried to follow suit but his pony was not used to such contact and balked, losing some ground.

Still, Urfet did not surge ahead.

It happened as they were heading back up the field for the final circuit, Rohr and Urfet still in the lead. Just as they were to pass Deathan for the final time, still nose to nose, Urfet crashed his mount sideways into Rohr's in a flurry of motion almost too swift to see. Rohr's pony shied and lost its footing, and Rohr flew off. Both pony and rider crashed to the ground.

Everything came to a halt then. To give Urfet credit, he pulled his pony up immediately. The other riders split and rode around the fallen pair, stopping beyond.

The scene burned itself into Deathan's mind. The light streaming in, the huge sky. The color of the fallen pony's pale coat and his brother lying on the green turf.

Hurt?

To be sure, he was. He must be. Deathan had known all the while that this would end badly.

He ran forward. To his immense relief, Rohr was sitting up when he reached him. Urfet, who had got there first, stood over him, an expression of either mock or real concern on his face.

Deathan shot him a glare. "Wha' were ye about? Did ye want him to break his neck? Or harm the pony?"

Urfet held up both hands in a calming gesture and backed off a step. "Now, Master Deathan, I would ne'er wish harm on that fine pony."

Deathan dismissed him and focused on his brother. "Are ye hurt?"

Others of their men, as he could see from the corner of his eye, had got Rohr's pony up and felt him over. Rohr, though, sat in the grass, face streaked with sweat and lips pressed tight. He did not make to rise.

"Rohr?"

"My arm." It was all Rohr said. He did not want to admit to pain, not here in front of this company, but aye, he felt it.

Deathan stooped and hauled him up, then asked in a low voice for Rohr's ears alone, "Is it broken?"

"Aye." Rohr stared into Deathan's face, his eyes wide, not with pain but rage. "He cheated. Ye saw."

"Aye." Deathan had seen. But how to prove it? Would Urfet not just argue—again—that the Caledonians played harder at their games?

Others of their men came running. The Caledonians stepped back, leading their ponies away.

"We need to get him to the healer's," Deathan told the near-est of his men, Dermot.

"Aye. The rest o' ye, tend our ponies."

"My mount," Rohr muttered.

"He is fine," Dermot assured him.

They led Rohr away between them. As they passed Urfet, Deathan could not help but see that the Caledonian was smiling.

HE CURSED TO himself as he waited outside the healer's hut, hearing far more vociferous language from inside. He'd wanted a chance to talk with Rohr about Caragh and the threat to Darlei—that opportunity now had flown. How would this affect relations with the Caledonians? Affect the wedding?

It did not take long for Da to come hurrying up with King Caerdoc at his side. Da focused on Deathan and asked in a tone that implied it was all his fault, "What's happened?"

"Rohr took a fall from his pony. They were playing—racing." Deathan looked at King Caerdoc. "Urfet took him out o' it."

King Caerdoc said nothing, though he looked thoughtful. Father added to the curses filling the air and ducked inside.

"An accident," King Caerdoc said mildly. "You saw, young Master Deathan?"

"I saw, and 'twas no accident."

King Caerdoc's dark eyes met his. Something hovered there, as wild and dangerous as the streak in Darlei's heart. "I am sure you are mistaken. Our young men play hard. Urfet especially. He is used to being at the head of our men. He would never endanger—"

"A pony?" Deathan interrupted, angry enough to lose his hold on courtesy. Angry and still with a ball of dread in his gut. "I think Rohr has broken his arm. Wha' if it had been his neck?"

King Caerdoc shrugged. He did not have to say. Then they

would all have gone home, any obligation to Kenneth MacAlpin flown.

"A strong young man like your brother will soon recover from a broken arm. In future, if he does not like to play rough, he should perhaps not accept dares from Caledonians."

How had King Caerdoc known it was a dare? Had he and Urfet somehow planned this between them? Or did he merely know his man?

"I must see to my brother," Deathan said, to avoid offending, and followed his father inside.

Two healers worked over Rohr, who sat, rather than lay, on a bench. He had gone white, his face still streaked with sweat. Da stood at a distance looking on critically.

He grunted when Deathan took the place at his side. "Tell me wha' happened."

"Urfet dared him to race. Rohr, the fool, accepted."

Another grunt. "Yer brother may be a fool at times, but he has a rightful pride. Did the bastard cheat?"

"They were jostling. Like the other races." Deathan did not add that Urfet had been playing with Rohr, though he believed it. How would that improve relations?

Da said nothing, though the expression in his eyes told that he bristled.

"He is no' hurt otherwise?" Deathan asked. "Just the arm?"

"'Tis enough. He will no' be able to draw a bow, to ride, to practice at arms."

"Still, it could ha' been much worse."

"That is wha' galls me. This has gone too far, and the Caledonians ha' been here too long. The wedding should ha' taken place already."

"Aye, but circumstance—"

"I no longer care for all that."

"Father, about the wedding. We ha' to talk."

His father turned and glared at him. "Wha' d'ye know o' it?"

Should Deathan say that Mistress Caragh had engaged in wild

and dangerous talk? It would be better coming from Rohr, but that did not now seem likely to happen.

Before he could part his lips to speak, the head healer stepped over to them.

"Chief MacMurtray—'tis a bad break, this. The bone did no' snap clean. 'Twill take time to heal."

"But he *will* heal?" Father asked. "He will regain use o' that arm?"

"If he is careful and keeps fro' using it for the time."

"I shall see that he does. Any other injuries?"

"Och, there will be bruises, and he bumped his head when he went down. 'Twill be sore for a while."

If anything, Father looked even more unhappy. He stepped forward to begin berating his older son.

Deathan left the hut.

CHAPTER TWENTY-FIVE

DARLEI STOOD HIGH on the wall that guarded the keep, where Deathan soon found her. She knew very well she should not be up here—two members of the guard had hurried to tell her so as soon as she and Orle ascended the steps.

But she felt so trapped and so beleaguered by the thoughts cramming her head that she'd wanted—no, needed—to escape. It was either try to make another break for freedom here in this country she did not know, or climb the walls where she could at least glimpse an elusive liberty.

"I just want to look out," she'd told the guards, two big, rough-looking, well-armed men. "I just wish to see."

That was before Orle began charming them, speaking prettily in her less-than-perfect Gaelic. The two men had eaten it up, softening considerably as they spoke to the diminutive maid. They still stood at a distance chatting, and Darlei took advantage, thinking, *It will not be long before Orle marries one of their sort, given we stay.*

Deathan came upon her leaning dangerously far over the breast-high wall, and gave a nod to his men before he joined her.

"Princess, wha' are ye doing up here?"

"Looking." *Dreaming.* She shot him a glance, one that became a long and luxuriously enjoyable examination. She could admire the view, yes. Or she could admire something far better.

The light up here was so clear, it showed her every detail. The myriad colors in his hair, all woven together—amber and honey brown and gold like the fine strands the jewelry makers drew out back home.

His skin wore a tan over those freckles she had detested on his brother, and on Deathan came to find, well, acceptable. More than acceptable. His eyes…

Yes, in the fine, strong light of midday she could see the deep blue of them, could almost count the separate flecks of green that made rings around each pupil. All shaded by those long brown lashes.

It made her hurt to look at him, to draw a breath. But she wanted to go on looking. She wanted to touch his hand that lay beside hers on the stone.

She wanted to kiss him.

That thought startled her, but the desire would not back down. She wanted to taste his lips. To kiss each separate freckle. Did they extend *everywhere*?

"There has been an accident," he told her, and then reconsidered. "It *may* have been an accident."

"My father?" The desire did take a half step back, but did not desert her.

"Nay." Deathan shook his head. "Rohr and the others were at the field with the ponies, as ye said. Rohr let your father's man, Urfet, talk him into a race. He fell."

"Urfet did?"

"Nay, Rohr. He's broken his arm. The healers say 'tis a bad break."

"Oh." Her mind raced even as she dragged her gaze from her companion. "What will that mean for the wedding?" *For us*, she added silently.

"I do not know. I went to the field to try to ask Rohr about what you heard, and the threat Caragh expressed. I had no chance."

Darlei frowned at the far distance. This section of the wall faced eastward—the direction of home.

Did she still want to leave here?

"I suppose the marriage could still take place," Deathan said in a low voice so the guards and Orle did not hear. He took a measured look at the three of them, the two big men clearly in thrall to Orle's sweetness. "But if there is a threat to ye, my father needs to know of it. Here at Murtray, ye be under his protection."

"I will go out of my mind if this goes on much longer." If she could not be with this man beside her. Could not touch and taste him. Explore all that could be between a man and a woman.

Why him, of all men? To look at, with an unprejudiced eye, there was not all that much to tell between him and his brother. Yet Rohr repelled her. And he…

He turned his head and looked her full in the eyes. "Would ye still be happy to leave here, princess? D'ye wish to say farewell to me?"

"Nay." She shook her head so emphatically, her hair flew. "Nay, and nay I do not." *Not ever.* "But—"

"Master Deathan?" The two guards stepped over to them. They had Orle tucked between them like treasure.

Deathan straightened. "I came up to tell ye that there has been an accident. Rohr has broken his arm and will be forced to rest awhile." Whether his brother would or would not was another matter, so his tone implied. "So for the time being, ye will tak' orders from me."

One of the men, the taller of the two, gave an easy grin. "Do we no' do that already?"

"Aye so," Deathan admitted ruefully. "I was also just telling Princess Darlei that ladies should no' venture up here on the wall." He offered Darlei his arm. "Let me escort ye back down."

A gift it was, an opportunity to touch him. Darlei wrapped her arm around his, skin to skin, his all warm and sunlit.

An image bloomed within her mind. The two of them together, naked, nothing between them but desire.

Oh, but somehow, she had to make that happen.

Orle, with soft words for her two swains, followed them down quietly. At the bottom of the steep stone stairs, Deathan said, "Princess, I suggest ye retire to yer room."

"I tell you, I will go mad pent up there."

"Just until we see how matters stand."

"Very well." She could do that. She could, for him. because her heart, always wild, now strained to belong somewhere.

With him.

DEATHAN WENT LOOKING for his brother and found him drowning his sorrows in the guards' warming room, which oft served as a meeting and drinking chamber for the men. Several beds had been set up there, and those who were off duty tended to gather, especially in bad weather.

The weather was not bad now, but gossip could also make them gather—and the subject of current gossip sat in one corner, drinking steadily.

The men, drifting in and out, rolled their eyes at Deathan and did not say much. The tale would have spread—like fire, it would—and it said something for Rohr's state of mind that he would rather sit here and brave the talk than languish alone in his chamber.

Or perhaps the ale merely helped dull the pain.

Deathan sat at the table opposite his brother. They had never been the sort to confide in one another, not even in their youth. They thought far too differently, and Rohr tended to look down on Deathan, or so he believed.

Rohr did not appear pleased to see him now. He would be less so before the conversation ended.

"How bad is it?" Deathan asked.

"Bad," Rohr answered, more frankly than Deathan would have expected. "Hurts like a bugger, but no' so much as letting that bastard best me."

"He did no', truly. The race ended when ye flew off yer

mount. The bastard did no' have a chance to finish and win."

"That will no' be the way he tells it. I wanted to wipe the smile off the arrogant serpent's face. Wha' reason have Caledonians to feel so superior?"

"Urfet is a confident fellow. Good at many things. Mayhap we ha' underestimated the Caledonians."

"See, brother, that is the trouble wi' ye. Ye are too soft and generous. Ye always tak' the line that others are as good as us. No one is as good as us."

"That, I suppose, is why ye sit here wi' a broken arm and Urfet is off bragging."

Anger flared in Rohr's eyes. "I can reach across this board and throttle ye wi' one hand, ye ken."

"I think not." If anyone proved arrogant, it was Rohr. And Deathan had taken his fill of it. "Ye consider me soft, do ye?"

"Aye so."

"Then I will tak' a hard line wi' ye. Settle this business wi' Caragh, once and for all."

"This, again?" Rohr squinted at him. "Ha' ye not done enough in that regard, failing to keep my secret?"

"Ye maun do the right thing."

"I am terrible weary," Rohr said bitterly, "o' people telling me what to do."

"Because Princess Darlei knows."

That made Rohr's eyes come up to meet Deathan's. They held surprise. "How? How could she know?" His lips parted in a snarl before he said, "Unless you told her."

"She saw the two o' ye together. Overheard ye talking."

"Och, shite."

"Aye so," Deathan said. "She feels threatened by the situation. Threatened by wha' she heard." Did he have to be more pointed?

Nay, for darkness flickered in Rohr's blue eyes. No doubt he recalled what he and Caragh had last said to one another. "How—"

"Does it matter? Ye maun confess what Caragh asked ye to do, tell Da before Darlei goes to the king."

"There is no need. Those were just words on Caragh's part. She did no' mean—"

"Is that wha' King Caerdoc will think?" Deathan leaned toward his brother. With deadly intent he said, "Go to Father and tell him what Darlei overheard. Or I will."

Before Rohr could protest farther, Deathan got up and left the chamber.

⸺ ❖ ⸺

CHAPTER TWENTY-SIX

ONCE AGAIN, THE argument could be heard all over the keep. No storm rumbled overheard to provide cover for the hard words, Da's shouting at Rohr to "stop wi' all the nonsense and put that lass in her place."

The servants heard, and the guards. The guests in their chambers may well have heard—that Princess Darlei not only knew the truth about Rohr's unfortunate position, but had overheard his pregnant lover demand he remove her from their way. *Take her life.*

Deathan heard as he crossed the hall toward his father's quarters, and a savage kind of satisfaction touched his heart. Did Rohr at last get what he deserved? Could he, Deathan, possibly be glad of it?

Nay, for it would not be a good day at Murtray.

Deathan went on to Ma's room, to find Darlei there before him. Both women, who sat close with Darlei beside the bed, looked up at him, startled, when he entered.

"Goodness, Deathan!" Ma said. "Wha' is all that about? Are we under attack?"

She knew very well what it must be. She would recognize the voices.

He tried to sound bland when he said, "Merely Father and Rohr speaking together."

"They do no' always shout when they speak. Wha' is amiss?"

"I canna imagine," Deathan lied. All night he had wondered

whether Rohr would go to Da with what Darlei had overheard. In truth, Rohr had little choice, if he believed Darlei would turn to her own father for protection. Would Da put his foot down once and for all, perhaps again bring forward the wedding to put Caragh and her threats behind them?

Darlei gave him an assessing look, and Mam, catching something in that look, patted Darlei's hand. "Do no' worry, my dear. Rohr is no' always so ill-tempered and should no' mak' ye an angry husband. He would ne'er shout so at his wife. Though"—she appeared to consider—"Deathan has always been the more even-tempered o' my twa sons."

To be sure, Deathan thought, at the moment it seemed Da did most of the shouting.

"No doubt," Mam went on, her cheeks flushed, "Rohr is out o' sorts at the moment because o' his broken arm. Deathan, how does he do wi' that?"

"I do no' ken, Mam. I ha' not seen him this morning."

"Aye, well, if he will go headlong into these competitions, there will be accidents. Deathan, do ye recall the time—"

Mam chatted on, bringing up old memories, and the argument they could all hear eventually died down. By the time Deathan and Darlei left Mam's chamber together, silence reigned, though there did seem to be a large number of people milling around.

The two of them stood in the corridor outside the great hall, watching for a moment.

"Something is afoot," Darlei said.

"Aye."

"Do you suppose Rohr confessed to your father that this woman—Caragh—threatened me? And if so, why?"

"I told him he should, before ye brought the matter to yer own father, and if he did no', I would tell Da the truth."

"Ah. Will Rohr ever forgive you?"

"Likely not. That does no' matter." Only she mattered to him.

Swiftly, so fleetingly he nearly missed it, her fingers brushed his. He felt the thrill of it all through him.

"What will happen now?"

Deathan frowned. "A question that occupied me all night."

"Will I still have to marry him? Oh," Darlei interrupted herself, "here comes Father."

Indeed, here King Caerdoc did come, sweeping down from his guest chamber with his holy man at his back. He entered the hall, and, peering in, Deathan saw Da there also, taking up a place at the head of the room. Not Rohr. Where was Rohr?

Da did not come and summon Deathan in. Certainly not. Nor, though his gaze swept over her, did King Caerdoc summon Darlei.

When the door of the hall closed, Darlei said, "So, it will be decided without me once again—my future and my life. Unbearable, it is."

"Come," Deathan told her softly, "we will walk the shore." Even though he was due up on the walls.

He did not know that he could make the waiting easier for her, but he was willing to try. A soft day, it was, the sea nearly calm, in contrast with what had just taken place inside. The white foam curled upon the stones of the shingle, and far out, light clouds sailed like white boats.

The people they passed gave curious glances, but no doubt supposed he was helping to entertain a guest. The woman who was to be his sister.

"How long do you think it will take," she asked, "for them to determine my future? Do you suppose this will be enough to make Father withdraw from the marriage? He must have heard enough to know my intended husband has a lover who carries his child."

Deathan did not suppose even that would be enough to put an end to the betrothal. He felt reluctant to admit it.

She looked angry and desperate and, aye, frightened. "It is not fair. I tell you, Deathan, I am tired of it. Why should I be denied a say in what is to befall me?"

No reason, save that she was a woman.

"I do not know what to hope for. I cannot live under Rohr's thumb. Told what to do, how to act. It will take the very heart out of me. On the other hand—"

She stopped speaking and ceased walking. They were not yet far up the shore. Deathan could still hear the bustle of the settlement behind him.

But when she turned and faced him, all he could see were the emotions in her eyes.

Beyond desperate.

"If they decide this is cause for the wedding to be forfeit, if my father takes me away home, I may never see you again."

Protest rose in Deathan's heart, so powerful it took him a moment to speak. "I will no' let that happen, Darlei. If ye leave here, I will follow ye. I will find ye."

Her eyes widened. "Give up your life here?"

"If that is wha' it takes."

"Live with strangers?"

"Anywhere, so long as I am wi' ye."

The expression in her eyes softened, going from hard agony to something else he could not name.

Because he could not help it, he touched her cheek. Soft as a flower petal, it was. Soft was his wild woman, her beauty covering the strength of iron.

She caught his wrist and turned her head to drop a kiss in the palm of his hand. Swift was the gesture, so swift, before she released him and resumed walking.

"As I say, I scarcely know what I should hope for. All night, I thought on it. I…I confess, I never thought ye would be willing to leave here. To be with me."

All women everywhere, Deathan supposed, asked for assurances. She did not yet know—or believe—that his heart was her own.

"I promise it to ye, Darlei—we shall be together. I do no' ken quite how. Or when such a thing may come about. I do know I will no' rest till ye be mine."

She stopped walking again. This time she gazed out to sea, fighting, perhaps, to master her emotions.

"Your father," he said softly, paused beside her, "will no' be easy to convince. I am naught but a second son and scarcely worthy o' a Caledonian princess, MacAlpin's order no'withstanding."

"I shall have to make Father understand."

"If ye can. He is a proud man and gey proud o' his daughter. I am…naught at all."

"You are everything, everything to me. If Father will not give his permission, we will run away together. Live wild on Caledonia's breast. Or—or we will sail away in one of those wee boats, begin a life in a new land." She cast a look at him. "So long as you come to me. Find me."

He repeated it, a vow: "I will always, always find ye. If I ha' to search a lifetime."

Her lips trembled in a smile. Amazing, Deathan thought—he had not yet kissed those lips. And yet he'd sworn his future to her.

"Then it is agreed," she said. "Ye will come to me."

But it was not to happen that way. By the time they walked back to the settlement, the meeting between chief and king had ended. Things had apparently been decided as they usually were, without Deathan's input.

Indeed, one of King Caerdoc's men was looking for Darlei and summoned her hastily.

"Princess, your father is looking for you. Come, please, to his chamber."

Darlei cast one look at Deathan, as tactile as a touch. She could not touch him here, nay, but as she moved off with her father's man, Deathan felt the ties that had formed between them pull and tighten.

Nay, though, those ties had not so recently formed. In some way Deathan could not explain, they had existed even before she and he met. Anchored in his heart. He'd felt them the first time he laid eyes on her. The first time she'd looked at him.

His life had always been hers. He merely had not known it.

He went in search of his brother, figuring Rohr, having been released from the meeting in the hall, would be his best source of information. He could not find him. Not in the guards' warming room, not up on the walls. Not even, when he peeked in, with Mam.

Had Rohr gone to Caragh? Indeed, if he truly loved the woman, he would, if only to share the trouble her wild words had caused.

It was exactly what Deathan would do, were their positions reversed.

To be sure, though, were their positions reversed, he could ask no more from life than to wed the Caledonian wild woman with the valiant heart.

✦

CHAPTER TWENTY-SEVEN

DARLEI'S LEGS TREMBLED beneath her as she followed Breh into Father's quarters. A grand chamber, it was, no doubt the best the keep could offer. Sunlight spilled in through the large window and lit Father's figure as he paced the floor. He and Moradoc, his holy man, were alone.

"Daughter," Father cried even as Moradoc slipped out, "terrible news has come to my ears. Woeful news."

Let him say the marriage is off, Darlei begged silently. *We will go home, and Deathan will follow me. We will be together.*

How did not matter. Where did not matter. Only that they would be.

Because her whole life up till now seemed to have been one great longing. For him. All the wildness, the dissatisfaction. The defiance. She had not known for what she longed till she saw him.

No explaining it. It just was.

She looked her father full in the face. "What is it?"

"Sit down." He indicated the bench near the window.

She sat, her stomach writhing. Father continued to pace as he spoke to her.

"It has all gone wrong, this marriage agreement we came to fulfill. There are things the king, when he ordered the union, did not know. I am sorry to say, it has now come apart."

Darlei licked her lips. Sorry? Nay. "What did the king fail to know?"

Rarely had she seen Father so angry. So indignant. "It has come to my ears that your bridegroom is…otherwise involved. He has a lover, and she is carrying his child." Father hurried to add, "Chief MacMurtray did not know of this when he welcomed us here. The truth has only just come out."

"Oh." It was all Darlei could say.

"Rohr insists he wants to marry this young woman, and also insists the child she carries may well be the legitimate heir to Murtray. Moreover, the young woman in question"—Father made a distressed face—"apparently wishes you harm. That is the only reason Murtray saw fit to inform me of this."

Darlei's heart leaped violently. A way out. "Ah," she said. "So—it is off, the marriage agreement? We are going home?"

"Nay, it is not so simple as that."

"What? Why? If he is already pledged to someone else, if the heir is assured, what else is to be done? He does not want me." Deathan did. *I will find ye.*

Father stopped pacing and fixed Darlei with a firm eye. "That does not matter. A threat put forward by a mere girl—how seriously can we take it? This marriage is by order of the king, a political matter for the benefit of a new Scotland. The king will have to be consulted."

"Nay." Darlei sprang to her feet, all the wildness she'd thought conquered leaping to the fore. "I want the agreement dissolved, done."

"Unfortunately, daughter, it no more matters what you want than what young Rohr wants. Have I not told you this, time after time?"

He had, over and over again.

"Well, but—"

"I will myself travel to Forteviot and consult with the king. Urfet will accompany me along with half our men. I leave tomorrow."

"Oh." Darlei puffed out a breath. "The rest of us will return home?" Deathan would find her there, certainly.

"Nay," Father said.

"I am sorry?" She must have heard him wrong.

"You shall remain here as a show of good faith and a sign that we are keeping to the king's order, until I return with his decision."

"I will not! I am in danger here."

"Daughter"—he turned on her—"you will obey me in this. If it all goes to pieces, the king will know we Caledonians did all we could to fulfill his decree. It was the Gaels who broke the agreement. Understand?"

"I understand. But you cannot leave me here alone."

"You will not be alone. You still have Orle. Some guards I will leave. You get on well with Rohr's mother."

"Yes, but Rohr does not want me here," she wailed. "I feel myself in danger. If he chooses to eliminate me—"

"The fool has a broken arm and can scarce attack you. I think you are safe enough. His father is furious with him. Rohr will not dare come near you."

Rohr would not come near her. But Deathan would.

She did not want to stay here, nay, especially without Father. But neither did she want to leave Deathan.

If she remained here—a sort of glorified hostage at best—she could see Deathan. Be with him sometimes. Watch the light come and go in his eyes. Mayhap touch his hand.

She dared ask for little more.

She drew a deep breath. "How long?"

"Eh?" Father had started pacing again.

"How long will you be gone?"

"It is impossible to tell. There is the travel to Forteviot. Hoping King Kenneth will be in residence. Waiting for audience with him. It could take a fortnight. Or longer."

Or *far* longer.

"Daughter, tell me I may trust you to behave decorously in my absence."

Decorously? Her?

Father hurried to add, "As befits the dignity of a Caledonian princess. In a very true way, you carry the weight of all our people upon your shoulders."

Well, that could not be good. On the other hand, she could show them of what a Caledonian woman was made.

"Tell me," Father insisted, "that I may trust you."

He too had a lot laid upon him. The need to resolve this morass fairly, yet without causing strife. To visit the king. He did not want to have to worry about her while he was gone.

Yet he knew full well what she was. No wonder he sought reassurance.

"You have my word. I will behave as befits."

He scowled.

"As befits a Caledonian princess," she added.

He did not look satisfied, but he let it go, perhaps figuring it the best he would receive from her.

She said, "I hardly know how to behave around Rohr."

"I doubt you will see much of him. After the dressing-down his father gave him, he will scarcely dare present himself."

"And the young woman? The one who wishes me dead?"

Father looked uncomfortable. "I doubt very much she will have the gall to put herself forward either."

Darlei hoped not. She could still hear the hate in Caragh's voice.

"Are you sure you must take Urfet with you? Can you not leave him for me?" She might at least turn to Urfet if she felt threatened.

"I am taking him with me. There seems to be a great deal of friction between him and Master Rohr. In fact, Rohr accused Urfet of causing the injury he now bears."

So, she would have no one to whom she might turn, save Deathan.

"Very well, Father. I ask you only, do not leave me here too long."

"Certainly, I will not."

Because despite Deathan's presence, there was ill will here for her. She could just feel it.

DEATHAN PACED THE wall, awaiting the outcome of that meeting. He knew it had ended when he saw King Caerdoc come out and cross the grass of the bailey to speak to a group of his men, including Urfet. No sign of Darlei and no hint as to how things had concluded.

He watched as the group of Caledonians crossed the grass back toward their quarters.

Preparing to leave?

He drew a long breath. He would have to resign himself to losing her, then. At least for a time. Could he bear it?

No.

He must.

He had barely touched her. Had not so much as kissed her lips, though he ached to. *Ached.* He could still feel the heat of her mouth in the palm of his hand where she'd bestowed that kiss.

He wanted to spend a year or so exploring that heat, the inside of her mouth, the rest of her body.

He grew hard just thinking about it. But what he felt for Darlei was not just physical. How could it be, when he'd not yet held her?

The need was for her company. Her voice. The light in her eyes and the thoughts in her head. If physical touch added to that, well, could a man be so fortunate?

The truth of King Caerdoc's actions was all over the keep by nightfall. Such things did travel, whisper by whisper, and this was far too rich to keep quiet.

King Caerdoc intended to ride, with many of his party, to seek out King Kenneth and consult him regarding his order for this marriage. For he'd learned—at last!—that another young woman carried Master Rohr's child.

Yet Master Rohr did not have the power to gainsay the king.

Princess Darlei, meanwhile, would remain here under Chief MacMurtray's strict protection to await the outcome and King Kenneth's wishes.

Deathan's heart leaped at that part of it. He was not to lose her.

Not yet.

Not ever, if he had aught to say in it.

There came a time when even a second son came into his own.

◆━━━◆◇◆━━━◆

CHAPTER TWENTY-EIGHT

T HEY WOULD HAVE to be careful. Darlei told herself as she watched her father and much of their party ride away from Murtray's stronghold the next morning.

Eyes were everywhere, particularly avid eyes given the gossip flying around the keep. Murtray's folk did not want to miss a look, a reaction.

They certainly would not miss her running to Deathan as she longed to do. But oh, she longed to!

She had to be clever about this. Even though she felt a bit like a hound let off the lead with Father gone. No one to chastise her. She doubted Chief MacMurtray would, in their present circumstances, even though she'd been committed to his protection.

But nay, she could not be obvious about her interest in her need for Rohr's brother. And she could not go out alone in the dark. A sharp knife might be waiting.

Her death would yet serve Rohr and Caragh well. And she would not put it past the young woman to shove the blade between her ribs, or employ a brother, if she had one, to do so.

She still felt uneasy about it and longed to tell Deathan so, to seek his reassurance. She hoped having seen her father's party off without catching sight of him, he might be with his mother when Darlei stopped in to see her.

He was not.

Mistress MacMurtray, though, was clearly troubled. The gossip had penetrated even into the peaceful space of her

158

chamber, Chief MacMurtray having told her just enough to keep her from worrying—so he thought. She worried all the same.

"My dear?" She caught Darlei's hand. "What is all this my husband tells me? Your wedding is put off again?" Her kindly, faded blue eyes met Darlei's, full of chagrin. "And for such a reason!"

"Yes. But naught that should trouble you, mistress."

She might have saved her breath for all the difference the words made. "I am so ashamed. That my son should do such a thing."

Compassion touched Darlei—not a particularly frequent visitor to her heart. Leaning toward the woman in the bed, she said, "I do not doubt Master Rohr loves this young woman. He has no such feelings for me and no more wishes to wed with me than I wish to wed with him. Love...love makes us do mad things."

Disconcerting tears filled Mistress MacMurtray's eyes. "But I so wanted ye for my daughter. My own girl, Kearana, is wed and moved far away. I ha' enjoyed spending time wi' ye."

"And I with you, mistress. We will have to trust my father to work this out."

The chamber door whispered open. Deathan stepped in.

Every part of Darlei's being came to life. As if she'd spent the morning half asleep, her senses awoke, stirred to his presence.

He must have been outside after all. He was clad for it, wearing his weapons and a leather tunic. His hair—that sandy golden mane—spilled down his back, and he brought with him the scents of the morning. He seemed overly large, overly male, in this quiet place.

His gaze moved to Darlei even before it found his mother.

"Och, forgive me interrupting."

"Nay," Darlei said. "Pray, come in."

Darlei wanted to fly to him. Lay her hands upon his bared forearms. Drink in his scent. She remained where she was, and he came to her instead, standing as near as the room allowed.

"Mam. Princess Darlei."

"Och, Deathan! Come sit wi' me. Explain to me wha' has happened. Your father came and spoke wi' me—but I confess, I canna believe wha' he said."

Deathan sat on the edge of the bed. "I canna speak for Da, Mam," he said. "Or for Rohr. He will ha' to come and tell ye all himself."

"I have been saying," Darlei put in carefully, "that Master Rohr no doubt has feelings for the young woman in question and likely always meant to wed wi' her. He had no idea King Kenneth would impose this marriage upon us."

"Aye. Aye so."

"Love"—Darlei captured Deathan's gaze—"can make us do many things."

"Is she no' a generous lass?" Mistress MacMurtray patted Darlei's hand. "To take such a view when my son has so damaged her."

"Mistress Darlei has no reason to feel damaged. She is beyond reproach."

"Aye, son. I agree wi' ye, and I did so want her for a daughter. I was looking forward to this wedding. And to attending it, even if I did ha' to be carried." Her eyes still brimmed with tears.

"Well but, Mam, this will afford ye more time to gather yer strength. And since Princess Darlei is staying here while her father is awa', 'twill give ye longer to spend wi' her."

"That is so. Tell me, Deathan, what people are saying. I wish to understand all."

With a rueful look at Darlei, Deathan spoke softly in a calm voice of what a scandal this had proven to be. He held his own opinions and said nothing of the conversation Darlei had overheard.

Troubled, Mistress MacMurtray said, "I know little o' this young lass, Caragh. MacDroit's daughter, is she?"

"Aye, Mam."

"A beauty?"

"Most would think so." Again Deathan's gaze touched Darlei. An assertion. A vow. *None so beautiful as ye.*

He thought her beautiful, this man she adored. She'd been many things in her life—headstrong, stubborn. Rarely had she felt wholly beautiful.

They talked on of other matters till Mistress MacMurtray seemed to calm. Darlei rose and made her excuses, pushing past Deathan just for the pleasure of touching him in passing.

He sprang to his feet. For the third time, their eyes met.

And it was alive with them in the room, this feeling—this intense desire and sense of belonging.

Could Mistress MacMurtray not feel it?

Darlei went out, nearly stumbling. Deathan followed her.

"Princess?"

She turned. The corridor appeared empty, but Mistress Mac-Murtray's woman would be hovering nearby. They must be careful.

"Come outside," she said.

The morning broke upon them, wild and beautiful, everything in motion. The trees upon the rise, the sailing clouds, the raking sea. Darlei drew in a breath.

"Are ye all right?" Deathan asked in a low voice.

"I do not know. Now that word of Rohr's lover is out, everyone expects me to be humiliated and cast down, but my heart rejoices because I might not have to marry him."

"Ye ha' no reason but to hold yer head high."

"Still, I wish I could escape all this. I have not seen your brother and do not wish to."

"Wi' your father and most o' his party gone, there will be no more grand dinners for the time. I do no' doubt Caragh's parents will keep her close to home. All the same, 'tis no' a good idea for ye to venture out alone."

Her gaze clung to his. "I do not suppose there is any way you might be assigned as my personal guard?"

She meant it lightly, but he did not take it that way. "Let me speak to my father about it. The post might be better taken by one o' the men yer father has left behind."

"But he, a Caledonian, could not show me around the settlement."

"Aye so." Deathan's gaze moved over her face, intimate as a touch. "And if ye could do aught ye wished, what would it be?"

I would kiss you. The answer flooded not only her mind but her body from fingertips to toes. *I would kiss you for a day and a night.*

She said, "Escape this place. The stares and the whispers. If only for a short time."

"Let me speak wi' my father. Wait here for me. I will no' be long."

He hurried away back into the keep, and Darlei lingered outside in the sun, becoming aware only then of—yes—the stares. The uncomfortable truth of being at the center of much gossip.

Being the woman she was—a princess—she gazed back defiantly and the clan's folk looked away. But there was a next stare, and a next.

It seemed an age before Deathan returned to her, though it could not have been long. He had lost his sword and his leather tunic, and gladness burned in his eyes.

"Father has bidden me entertain ye—at least for the morning. He insists yer woman must come along, though. For the sake o' propriety, ye understand. He has had enough o' scandal."

She had a chance to be with him. Who cared for propriety?

"Orle was not feeling well this morning," she lied barefacedly.

"I suppose, then, she would not enjoy a sail out on the sea."

"A sail?" Her heart rose impossibly.

"Aye. I thought to get ye awa' from all this, for a time."

"I should like nothing better, nothing in all the world."

CHAPTER TWENTY-NINE

DARLEI HAD NEVER so much as glimpsed the sea before journeying to Murtray. She had certainly never dreamed of riding out upon it in a tiny boat like a leaf on a stream.

The boat was, indeed, very small. Made of slatted wood and coated hide, it looked more like an oversized drinking vessel than a watercraft and tipped alarmingly when Deathan helped her in.

Terror might well have swamped her, had she not placed herself wholly in his hands.

In his hands, precisely where she wanted to be.

He had grown up here and, he told her, had sailed all his life. He handled the oars competently, and anyway, she gladly embraced the possibility of ending in a watery grave, if it meant she could be with him.

"Where will we go?" she asked once she was settled and he pulled powerfully on the oars. There was a sail on a slender spar, but he had not yet unfurled it.

"I thought we might hug the coast so ye could see how far our land reaches and"—he grinned at her—"ye might no' be too afraid."

"I am not afraid."

"Liar." He smiled again.

"Very well, I am lying. But people will be able to see us from shore. I long to get clear away." Alone with him. "Can we not sail out?"

"We can."

Away into the blue sea, which today held the exact color of his eyes. She longed for that almost as much as she longed for his company.

Because now here out on the breast of the water, once her heartbeat settled, this seemed strangely familiar.

Like everything else to do with him.

She sat where he'd put her and watched the beautiful way he moved, the serenity that came to his eyes, the color of his hair against the sea and sky. Never, never had she been so happy.

"How far can we sail?" she asked after a time, when the settlement had slipped out of sight.

The corners of his mouth crinkled and his eyes smiled. "All the way to Ireland, if ye like."

She liked. She did. They could make a life together there. Never come back.

"What are those lands, there?"

He named them, the islands that guarded Scotland's coast like sleeping dragons. He told her there were other lands far, far to the west.

"In the old days, our ancestors believed Tír na nÓg lay there. The place warriors went when they died. A land of revelry and ever-youth."

That caused her a pang, though she could not say why.

"Do you believe in such tales, Deathan MacMurtray?"

He shrugged. "There must be something better than the sorrows we face here in this place."

Sorrows. His mother was slowly dying, his family wrought asunder. Could she be his joy?

With certainty, she said, "I cannot imagine anything better than being here with you. And I would not embrace any prospect that would take you from me."

His gaze met hers, deadly serious this time. The oars froze in his hands. She leaned forward, rocking the little boat perilously, and pressed her mouth to his.

A kiss.

Ah, and she had been living for this. Living a lifetime, though she had not suspected it. His lips, warm and soft beneath hers, tasted of sweetness and desire. They tasted of eternity.

Surely she had done this before, somehow, somewhere, if only in dreams—kissed him and felt her very soul pull him in, lost a bit of herself as it did so, the one of them becoming part of the other.

"Darlei," he breathed, and suddenly she was in his arms, the oars in the bottom of the boat, for he had the presence of mind not to lose those.

The little boat rocked again and she did not care. *She did not care.*

For his arms were around her where they needed to be, as hers were around him where they needed to be, and their mouths were open, searching, taking, giving without measure.

She could feel his heartbeat thundering against her breast. She could smell the sunshine on his skin, and she could ask for no more of life.

There was no more to be had than this.

How long that kiss went on, she could not say. It lit her, calmed her, excited and yet reassured her. There was a place she belonged. *Here.*

After a time, he began to murmur. "Beautiful lass, glorious lass." He lifted each of her hands and dropped kisses into the palms. Kissed each corner of her mouth, her cheeks. Blessed her with a kiss upon her forehead. "My lass."

"Yours. I am yours. For all time."

The little boat drifted, its sail still furled and the oars at angles in the bottom. The motion of the sea matched what filled Darlei, fluid and dreamlike, half wonder and half memory.

She reached out and touched his face. The freckles beneath the tan. The golden hairs growing along his jaw.

"I want you, Deathan MacMurtray. I do not just mean—" Though she did want him that way, shockingly, as she'd never desired any other man. Between her legs. Covering her body with his. The most natural of things. "I want you. At the center of my life."

"I believe," he told her most certainly, "ye are already there—at the center o' my life, I mean. Beautiful lass."

She gave a broken laugh. "You keep saying that. Fool! I am not beautiful. I have this nose and this wild hair that will not—"

"Ye be the most beautiful thing I have ever seen."

His eyes said so, and his hands as they cradled her, cherishing her. His lips when they returned to hers. Their tongues met and twined, the bonds between them strengthening impossibly.

The little boat bobbed, aimless as Darlei's life. Love for this man. Only this man.

Eventually she glanced back, searching for the shore. She could not see it.

"Where are we?"

How long had they been out here? Impossible to say. There existed only the sun on the water and the light in his eyes. The warmth of him. Those kisses.

"Deathan, Deathan, I do not want to go back. Not ever."

Amusement filled his eyes. She loved it when he smiled at her that way, with his eyes.

"Darling, I doubt there is any going back fro' this."

He drew her down to lie against him, her cheek against his shoulder and her head tucked beneath his chin as the sea rocked and rocked them. The sun arced high overhead, and for the first time in more days than Darlei could number, she let go of her worries.

But even if they both desired it, they could not go on so forever. At length he sighed in her ear and said, "We maun go back. Let me tak' up the oars."

"Nay."

"Darlei, my heart, we are a long way out. 'Twill be a hard pull. And people will start looking."

"Not yet." To silence any further protests, she kissed him, and the little boat bobbed on while they remained so, one attached to the other. The taste of him was now hers, as was the feel of him. But that had always been so.

"How is it," she asked, still cuddled to his chest and gazing into his eyes, "I can love you this way?"

"Ye love me?" His eyes grew intent and once more serious.

"Fool," she said again, with affection. "I have never dreamed of loving anyone the way I love you."

"And I ye." Another kiss that stole her breath and nearly her sanity.

"Yet it does feel," she persisted, "as if we have done all this before. Kissed one another. Lain together. Sailed in a wee boat. As if my heart…my heart knew all along without knowing that you existed, and it needed you, would not stop needing you till it found you."

He said nothing for several moments. The boat rode a swell and tipped its way down again. There might only be the two of them, the water and the sky, in all the world.

In all time.

"I do no' ken what yer people believe," he said then. "Some o' our holy men teach that we live life after life. Time after time." He stroked her hair tenderly. "They say the gods send us back through the cauldron o' creation to learn lessons. To perfect our spirits and become heroes. Heroines."

"I am far from perfect."

"I ha' yet to meet anyone who is. If 'tis so—well, to learn the lessons we must, they say we are thrown into similar situations. We even meet the same people in differing guises, in order to understand the meaning they hold for us."

"Do you believe all that, Deathan?"

"I never gave it much thought, not till now."

"It would explain much. But if it is true, if I knew and loved you before, how may we now seize hold of the fabric of life, and shape it so we can be together once more?"

He shook his head with regret. "That, I do not know."

"And how"—her emotions came up in a storm—"having

tasted you, been with you this way, am I to go back and behave as if you are naught to me?"

"Faith," he told her. "Ye must believe that if we were born into this world to be together, all will come right—so long as we believe."

"Hard. So hard," she whispered, "when all is in strife and confusion."

"Save for this," he reminded her, "ye, and me."

"Yes. Being with you feels like—well, like I can breathe freely for the first time ever."

"Aye so. Promise me, Darlei. Promise ye will keep faith wi' me when we return."

"I will. I will. But—must we return?"

"Aye." He sat up, making the little boat rock like a leaf upon a river and setting her from him gently. "'Twill no' be easy. Yet aye, return we must."

━━━◆◇◆━━━

CHAPTER THIRTY

A TIME AWAY from time. Deathan did not know how often he termed those moments in the boat so, in his mind. How frequently he returned there in spirit to relive them over again. The sense of eternity that enveloped him when he held Darlei in his arms. The ease and warmth of her.

The familiarity.

He had wanted, aye, to keep on sailing. To journey on—to Ireland, say, just the two of them together. Could they not be happy there? Build a life?

But his roots were here in Scotland, deep in the granite beneath the soil. As were hers, to speak true. His Caledonian wild woman.

Anyway, was he not the levelheaded son? The practical one who saw to his duties and never kicked up a fuss? Not for him arguments or defiance.

Not for him, either, tumbling head over heels into love so deep he could no longer see the surface. Yet here he was. Making promises and talking of past lives and of eternity.

Destiny had him in its grip, aye, as did desire. He'd never known it possible to desire a woman the way he did Darlei. More than her kisses, the feel of her soft body beneath his hands, he longed to be inside her so that their bodies might be joined as were their spirits.

He must be mad, but he could not stop thinking of it even after they arrived back at the settlement to her woman's frantic search, which had once more brought in others, including his father.

And after he had a fierce dressing-down for keeping their guest out so long, one he endured in silence with the taste of her still on his lips, after they'd parted, his heart protested the separation so loudly that he could scarce believe no one else heard.

Darlei heard. He knew by the look she cast over her shoulder as she walked away from him.

The trick was to keep anyone else from guessing that he'd done aught more than seek to entertain a guest at an awkward time.

Father did indeed holler and rail, saying, "Did I no' tell ye to tak' her maid wi' ye, where'er ye might go?" Fortunately, he was too distracted by the question of what to do about Rohr and Caragh to spare much more than annoyance for Deathan. For once, being an afterthought did not bother Deathan much. Da soon retired to consult further with his holy man and contemplate what should happen when King Caerdoc returned.

No sight of Rohr anywhere, still. Deathan had no inkling as to where his brother might be hiding himself. Not a glimpse to be had of Caragh, either. Her parents must be keeping her close.

Deathan paced the walls and thought. And thought.

Christian monks had long since brought their teachings to these shores, mostly from Ireland but also from the south. Stories of eternal fire and redemption. But as he had told Darlei, the old beliefs died hard here, as did the old gods. Just as his roots were down in this stony soil, his spirit clung to what had been. The old beliefs of life after life. The circular nature of it, all that brought a man around again and again upon the wheel of the gods, just like the wheel of the year, to face the same challenges.

And overcome them.

He'd never thought about what he believed, not consciously. But aye, he believed that like hard masters, the gods sent them back again and again to face and perhaps overcome their failings.

It would explain so much. How he felt about Darlei. The way he'd seemed to know her instantly when they met. The intensity of the longing.

But he came to realize, as he pondered, that it did not mean they would be together in this life. It did not, for the obstacles were many. And even if he believed, and believed fiercely, it did not mean they could overcome whatever they must.

Nearly impossible, when he did not even know what it was they must overcome. Circumstances, most certainly. But also something within.

Within each of them.

What was the greatest enemy? He pondered that also as he paced the walkways high up on the stone walls, as he assigned the men. As the sun began to go down upon this day of days unlike any other.

Fear.

Aye so. The greatest enemy must be fear. His. Hers.

He feared, and always had, that he would not be enough. Strong enough, dutiful enough, skilled enough with a sword. It pushed him during times like training sessions to be first among the men, even though he knew he could not be.

Rohr must be first. Best. Their father had always insisted upon it.

Just as Rohr was to have the prize—Darlei—for whom Deathan would be willing to give his life.

The knowledge did not cheer him, for his fear was a deep one. It stemmed from being a second son. Knowing no matter how hard he worked or what talents he possessed, he could never be first.

Save, perhaps, in Darlei's heart.

Was that why he loved her so? Nay, there were a thousand reasons.

Had it been so for him in past lives? Had he striven for acknowledgement that had not come? Or had he achieved it?

Whatever the case, he feared not being good enough. What

did Darlei fear?

He knew her now, on a deep level—he did. Still, he could not answer that question.

"You are in love with him, are you not?"

Orle's question spun Darlei around where she stood, at the window of her chamber. She'd been thinking of Deathan—to be sure, she had—so when Orle spoke, she had no doubt as to whom she referred.

She stared dismayed into her companion's eyes.

Orle came and stood close, lowering her voice even though there was no one to hear. "You can tell me. I am your friend. I should hope you would tell me anything."

"I—" It was not that Darlei did not wish to tell. She longed to shout out what she felt for Deathan, the miracle of what had taken place out upon the water. She did not have proper words, however. Only feelings.

Orle's dark eyes filled with compassion. "Your betrothed's brother. How did it come to be?"

Darlei sagged where she stood. "I scarce know. With all that has happened—"

"Yes, it is a terrible tangle."

"How did you guess at my feelings for him?" She had to be more careful, lest others also guess the truth she and Deathan shared.

"I saw the way you looked at him when the two of you came ashore today. The way he looked at you."

"Do you think anyone else noticed?"

"I could not say. I know you very well, Darlei. You keep going off with him—up the shore, out to sea. Were you not frightened out in that little boat?"

Yes, she'd been frightened. Not so much of the water but of

the enormity of what she felt for the man.

"I trust him. He knows how to sail. And..." She could not possibly tell even Orle that it felt as if they'd done all of it before. Sailed off together into the unknown, clinging soul to soul. "I trust him," she repeated lamely.

Orle shook her head. "It is not like you to fasten your attentions to any man. Well, there were a few, like Urfet, who caught your eye, but this is not the same, is it?"

"Nay." Not the same.

"What is it about Master Deathan? That is to say, he is handsome enough. So are many of the men here. But he looks very...Celtic."

Darlei laughed unsteadily. "Orle, it would not matter if he had a head like a turnip and two noses. I would want him anyway. Though, I have to admit, I have come to appreciate everything about him."

The warmth of his skin beneath her fingers in the little boat. The crisp hair above the opening of his tunic. The strength of his arms cradling her, and the response of his body beneath her own.

The depth of those blue-green eyes, like gazing into eternity.

"Darlei, I do not need to warn you that you must be cautious. We do not know what may happen between your father and the high king. You may still have to marry Master Deathan's brother."

"Yes." He who was in love with someone else even as she was in love with someone else. "I know."

Orle's eyes met Darlei's again. "You would not do anything foolish, would you?"

"Foolish?"

"Like lying with him. You are unbreeched, just like me. And if this wedding goes forth, there will be expectations."

Ah, did she care what Rohr MacMurtray expected? What his father did, or the high king? She wanted to lie with Deathan the way she wanted to keep breathing.

It would happen. She could not guess how or when. But it

would.

"Yes, I must be careful. Orle, you will not tell anyone what I have confided?"

"I will not. But others may guess as I did, by the way you look at him."

She must try to control her feelings while in company. She had never been what might be called disciplined in her emotions. A wild woman, those here called her, and so she was.

A wild woman in the grip of destiny.

✥

CHAPTER THIRTY-ONE

E AGER TO SEE Deathan in his mother's room the next morning, Darlei once more arrived ahead of time and so sat long chatting to Mistress MacMurtray before he arrived.

He entered the chamber with a soft sigh from the door and a slight rattle of his light weapons. He moved so quietly, this man she adored.

How could he change the very complexion of the air when he stepped in?

He looked tall and very composed, wearing his sword and that leather tunic. A warrior's garb—a Celtic warrior's. Her people had spent generations battling his for this land.

This land they both loved as desperately as she loved him.

He must have been out about his duties already, for he brought the scent of the morning into the stale room, as well as the other scent particularly his own. The one that made Darlei go dizzy with longing.

"Master Deathan." Her voice quivered, but surely Mistress MacMurtray would not notice.

"Princess." He gave her a slight bow. "Mother, I trust you feel well this morn."

"Och, Deathan, ha' ye spoken wi' yer brother? Will ye no' ask him to come and see me?"

Deathan stepped forward, bringing him close to Darlei. Not close enough.

"I ha' not seen Rohr, nay. He must be hiding himself awa'. I ha' no idea where."

"He will be feeling the disapproval, aye, and the condemnation. But I must speak wi' him concerning this lass, Caragh, and the child." Mistress MacMurtray blinked rapidly. "My first grandchild. 'Tis my duty as Rohr's mother to speak wi' him. He must do what is right by the girl."

Darlei's heart rose in a bound. If Mistress MacMurtray urged Rohr to wed with Caragh, would that not open a path for her and Deathan?

She cast a look at him and he returned it, a cautionary flash between long brown lashes.

Yes, as Orle had said, she needed to be careful.

"Mam, all must wait upon what the king decides."

"Aye so, and King Caerdoc has gone to consult wi' him. I understand all that. But wha' will become o' my grandchild? I so want to see it born before—" Mistress MacMurtray paused abruptly.

"Mam." Deathan brushed by Darlei's skirts to take a place on the side of the bed and capture his mother's hands. "Ye ha' been growing stronger. Are ye no' working at getting out o' this bed? Ye will soon be well."

Doubt clouded Mistress MacMurtray's pale eyes. "I ha' been working at it, aye. I do no' ken if I will ever leave this bed."

Deathan touched his mother's hair with the gentleness that characterized him. As much a part of him, Darlei decided, as his strength. "So ye will."

"Perhaps, if ye carry me."

"Nay, Mam, ye must believe."

"Deathan, ye be a fine son. Will ye tell Rohr that I need to see him?"

"I will." Deathan leaned in and kissed her cheek. "I go now to lead the men at practice, since Rohr is no' there to do it. I wanted to see ye first."

He rose from the edge of the bed, brushing past Darlei again. Unable to help herself, she followed him to the door.

"I need to see you," she whispered under the guise of opening it for him.

A check in his step betrayed his reaction. "How?"

"I do not know. Or care—"

For the briefest instant, his gaze touched hers. It said, *I will find a way.*

Too brief a time together, she thought as she regained her seat beside Mistress MacMurtray. Too few moments with him. She looked up and encountered Mistress MacMurtray's gaze.

"Darlei, ye ha' become gey friendly wi' my son. Wi' Deathan."

I cannot live without him. Suddenly, Darlei wanted to confess it all to this kind woman, even as she had to Orle. But how could she? Mistress MacMurtray was sorely ill and as bound by the restraints of their society as she.

Gazing into Mistress MacMurtray's pale-blue eyes, she wondered if she needed to confess, and what this woman suspected.

Orle was right. She needed to be far more careful. If not for her own sake, then for Deathan's.

But how to balance her desire for him—what had become more than desire—with caution?

She was not the woman to answer that.

A MORNING SPENT sweating on the training field did not help relieve Deathan's feelings as much as he'd hoped. Anger kept assailing him, and frustration. His brother should be here in his place. What was Rohr about? Where was he? Though Deathan had asked around as discreetly as possible, no one seemed to know.

The men just rolled their eyes. Everyone, to be sure, had heard the tale of Rohr and Caragh by now. Deathan supposed he could not blame Rohr for wishing to avoid the gossip and Da's condemnation. But he'd expected his brother to have more backbone.

So he worked beneath the autumn sun, and he tried without success to discipline the emotions that swamped him. Anger at Rohr, aye. Frustration at the wishes of kings who knew nothing of the lives they affected.

Desire.

What was he to do about the desire?

He never should have kissed Darlei in the first place—or more precisely, let her kiss him. He never should have touched her, for it had opened up a need inside him, gaping as a mortal wound. Not just for the taste of her, sharp and sweet. Or the feel of her in his arms. But for her company, her presence, the way his very world shimmered to rightness when she was near.

Naught but the promise of passion had ridden him hard all night. He'd had very little sleep, his thoughts running like a maddened creature in a cage. Seeking ways and means for them to be together.

As he saw it, the best thing that could happen would be for King Kenneth, hearing of the situation, to withdraw his insistence upon the marriage. Caerdoc would take his daughter home. As soon as decently possible, Deathan would follow and make his suit, plead his case to the Caledonian king.

The thing was…

What had he to offer for a princess? Him, a second son. What, besides his heart?

Would what Darlei wanted matter to Caerdoc? Perhaps if they both pleaded with him, he would relent and allow them to wed.

And if nothing could persuade Caerdoc that Deathan was good enough for his daughter?

Do not think about it, he bade himself sternly. *If it is true ye knew her before, loved her before, then ye have come together now for good reason. There must be a way.*

His father came down at the end of the training session and

watched as Deathan finished up and dismissed the men. He stood watching until Deathan put aside his weapons and joined him.

"Deathan," he said heavily and with rare approval, "'tis good in ye to tak' over your brother's duties. D'ye know where he may be found?"

"Nay, Da. D'ye no'?"

Da shook his head. "I am troubled," he admitted, "sorely troubled. No' so much by wha' he has done—after all, young men ha' needs, and he had no way o' knowing what the king would decree. I believe he intended to wed this lass, Caragh. But the way he is behaving now… A man, a chief's son, should hold his head high even when things become difficult."

Especially then, Deathan thought, but did not say so.

"Instead, he hides. It fair makes me ashamed."

Father had never said such a thing before, not of Rohr.

"Mam has been asking for him, but I could no' find him to give the message."

Da looked rueful. "All yer mother hears is that she has a grandchild on the way. Something she did not hope to see before. I do no' ken whether she grasps the bigger ramifications o' all this. 'Tis good to have King Kenneth's favor, to be singled out as leaders in this new, united Scotland. I would do naught to spoil that."

Deathan looked at his father with new attention. "Ye think he will still insist upon the marriage despite the changed circumstances."

"I do not know."

"How soon can we expect King Caerdoc to return?"

"I do no' ken that either. Only that we maun take the best care o' the princess until the answer comes down. She may be my daughter yet."

━━━◆❖◆━━━

CHAPTER THIRTY-TWO

"PRINCESS DARLEI," DEATHAN said very formally, and gave her a bow. "If ye would be so kind as to come wi' me, there is somewhat I should like for ye to see."

Darlei's entire spirit leaped when Deathan spoke her name. It did not matter how formal he was, or pretended to be. The connection between them flared strong.

Two days had passed—two long days—and apart from their visits to his mother, she had found no fit excuse to be with him.

Had he found one now?

She glanced into his face, which revealed little, before gazing at Orle with a wordless demand. She was supposed to venture nowhere, save in Orle's company. Yet Orle had watched her suffer these past two days—suffer like she had an illness—and understood what was now required of her.

"I—uh—Princess, if you will excuse me…"

She hurried off, not pausing to give a reason. Likely because she had none, save kindness.

"Master Deathan, what is it you have to show me?"

"Somewhat to give you pleasure, so I hope."

He would give her pleasure. Being alone with him would. She'd dreamed of him these past two nights—at least, she'd dreamed of being with a man who felt like him. Kissing and doing more than kissing. So detailed were the dreams that though she'd never been with a man, she felt as if she'd had this one.

Felt him inside her. The two of them made one.

Either what he'd said about past lives was true, or she was going mad entirely.

And now, now because there were so many eyes watching them as they passed, his clan's folk far too curious, she had to act polite and proper.

"A cool day today," she remarked, matching her steps to his as they headed toward a group of stone outbuildings.

"Aye, it feels more of autumn than aught else. Are ye warm enough?" He eyed the shawl she wore, and she wished he would tuck it up higher around her ears. As she could tell he wanted to do.

I would be warmer in your arms. But she could not say that aloud.

"Where are you leading me?" Somewhere—*please, all the powers of earth and sky*—where they could be alone. Where he could kiss her. She could not live much longer without his kisses.

He smiled. "You shall see. I ha' been hoping ye are no' too lonely here wi' us. I ken fine ye ha' yer woman for company, but I hoped another sort o' companion might brighten yer days."

"Oh?" He'd been thinking of her. Even as she thought of him.

He led her into a small stone structure, passing a young lad just leaving, who flashed him a smile.

"One o' our bitches had a litter some time ago. The hound pups are just ready to leave her. I thought ye might like to choose one."

"Oh. Oh!"

The interior of the stone shed smelled of clean straw and dog. The dame hound lounged at her ease, a great, shaggy gray beast, with her pups tumbling over her and each other.

"Oh!" Darlei cried again, and fell to her knees in the straw beside them.

"A few o' them are spoken for. That one there wi' the white blaze, and the tan female. This one, I think. But ye can see 'twas a grand, big litter."

The dam looked at them with calm amber eyes. Fully half the

litter came tumbling into Darlei's lap, and she laughed for the first time in days, with delight. Ah, she had not laughed so since before Father told her of the king's decree.

The pups climbed over her knees. They nipped her fingers and tugged at her clothes. Tumbled over one another like furry acrobats. With their chubby legs and stubby tails, she could scarcely believe they would ever be as sleek and magnificent as their mother.

She raised eyes full of mirth to Deathan's. Saw his spirit take light from hers.

"I used to have a hound of my own," she said. "When I was young. He grew old and—well, did what old hounds do."

"Would ye like to have another?"

"I would." Oh, she would. "But"—she shook her head—"will it be wise? With all the uncertainty."

"If ye go back home, ye can take the pup wi' ye."

Could she? But what of after?

Gazing at him steadily, she said in a soft voice that would not carry beyond the pups' yips and mews, "What if King Kenneth dissolves the marriage agreement and yes, we do go home? You have said you will find me."

"And so I will," he promised. "If I ha' to travel half of Scotland."

"I take that promise, Deathan MacMurtray, to my heart."

"As ye should."

"I think," Darlei told him, putting the pups away from her with regret and getting to her feet, "I should wait till we learn the high king's decision. For though I should love one of these pups for company, there is one thing my heart desires more."

Emotions chased one another through Deathan's eyes. "Ye think—"

"I think if it comes to it and you have to follow after me in truth, my father may not approve of the match."

He took it like a blow, which was not her intention, to hurt him. With far less enthusiasm he said, "Aye, I see. As naught but a second son, I ha' little to recommend me to a king o' the Caledonians."

She stepped closer and touched the front of his tunic with both hands. "It would be my greatest honor to wed wi' ye, Deathan MacMurtray. I cannot imagine anything finer in all the world."

"But your father will no' see it that way."

"Perhaps not. And"—she tossed her head—"if he does not give his permission, then we will have to flee together. Because as you have promised that you will always find me, I so promise to always follow when you do."

"Darlei." He barely breathed her name, yet the emotions leaped in his eyes. The future was the future, unknowable. The past, with its secrets unfolding inside her, was the past. He was here, warm and strong beneath her fingers, love brimming in his eyes.

Love.

She leaned up, not even pausing to wonder if there was anyone save the dam and her pups to see. Their lips met, warm on warm, and the world snapped into such perfect focus, it made her ache. For a few precious moments she drank of him before remembering where they were and what they should not do. She stepped away.

Not far.

"I think," she mused again, "I should wait to find out how things lie before claiming a pup. If I am to stay here"—if the marriage to his brother must take place—"then yes. I will choose one, and gladly." For consolation in a life most unbearable.

But would parting from him, subject to her father's will, be still more unbearable than living in his proximity while married to his brother? In truth, she did not know. She did not know for what to hope.

"Come," he said with rueful regret. "This was a poor idea."

"It was a wonderful idea."

"'Tis only that"—his beautiful, broad-palmed hands came up

but did not touch her—"when I think o' ye, I see ye wi' a great hound at your side."

"Do you think of me?"

"Constantly. Darlei—"

The lad came in and they stepped apart, Darlei's pulse leaping.

In a voice not quite steady, Deathan asked the boy, "How many o' the pups are spoken for, Kai?"

"Only about four o' them, Master Deathan."

"Well, hold one back. Princess Darlei may wish for one. She is no' yet decided."

The lad gave an easy smile. "Which one, mistress?"

"It does not matter." Darlei had a sudden and near-overwhelming prescience of doom. Something dire and terrible came to them. She found it difficult to smile at the lad when she said, "They are all splendid."

"'Tis a fine litter," Kai agreed. "Very well so."

"Wha' is it?" Deathan asked Darlei when they stepped outside. "I felt yer mood change back there. Is it because ye canna choose a pup? I am that sorry. I would no' ha' brought ye here if—"

"It is not that. Walk with me."

They went away up the shore, their steps matching without thought or intention, Darlei wrapping herself tight in her shawl against the cool breeze.

So close did they walk that several times Deathan's elbow bumped hers. Not till they were well out of sight from the settlement did he stop walking and turn to her. "Tell, Darlei."

"I am not sure I can." Helpless now against the feelings that assailed her, she shook her head. "I feel, here—" She pressed both hands to her chest.

He captured them in his. "Wha' did I tell ye about faith? About believing? Darlei, if 'tis true we ride on the wheel of destiny, then wha' has been must be again. D'ye no' see?"

She wished she did. "I believe in *you*." Her faith in him had become absolute. "In any promises given by destiny, not so much. I fear—I fear—"

"Do no' fear, darling. Do no' fear, love."

Suddenly she wanted to weep. Because she could not make him understand what she felt coming, how dire and terrible it might be.

He was a warrior, this man she loved. His instinct was to fight. Fight for her, if need be.

She knew to her heart that all such battles did not end well. And she could never bear to see him fall.

"Och, now," he told her, "do no' weep." Only then did she realize her eyes brimmed with tears.

Gravely and deliberately, he raised each of her captured hands to his lips, dropping kisses in the palms. Bestowed soft, sweet kisses at each side of her lips, her cheeks, her brow.

"Trust me," he bade her.

And she whispered, "So I do."

But the future frightened her still.

CHAPTER THIRTY-THREE

THE CALEDONIAN PARTY returned a fortnight later with King Caerdoc riding at their head and Urfet close behind. Deathan was himself among the first to sight them, as he was on the walls at the time, and he called out the order to open the gates even as his heart began to pound.

Their answer, his and Darlei's, was upon them. From the moment they heard what news King Caerdoc had to tell, the fates would lie cast. Everything would change.

He knew very well that Darlei feared so. As the days had stretched out, her apprehension had only grown. Naught he said seemed able to shift it from her, no reassurance, and no promise.

Though she refused to come out and say so, she expected some dark and terrible outcome upon her father's return. One that would serve to separate them. It was why she would not choose a pup. It was why even when they were alone together, he glimpsed apprehension in her eyes.

"Do no' borrow trouble," he'd told her. And yet it came to him that mayhap she borrowed it from the past.

If they had known each other before, on some previous turn of the wheel, and if it had ended badly, would not the fear carry over just like the love? It did not mean their lives would end the same way this time. He would make it right. He would, for her, no matter what he had to do. Had he not proven that?

But aye, he understood her fears. He'd been naught but a second son all his life. Second to a brother he no longer respected as once he had. For, aye, he had discovered where Rohr had been hiding out all the while—in a private place up the shore, most often with a jug of heather ale and sometimes, he suspected, with Caragh, though Deathan could not prove that last.

He'd expected better of Rohr. Ah, well, he would now have to surrender his hiding place, so Deathan thought as he watched the Caledonian party ride in.

He, like Deathan himself, would have to *dree his weird*, as the old ones put it. Accept his fate.

But his stomach turned sour as he ran down the narrow steps from the wall and went to meet King Caerdoc. Did the man look grim? Or merely weary?

"Run and get the chief," he told one of the men standing by. "And Master Rohr." If they could find him.

And the princess? *Och…*

Hurrying forward, he caught King Caerdoc's bridle. The man's dark gaze swept over him as if he did not exist.

"Send word to the chief we are returned from Forteviot."

"Word is already sent, King Caerdoc."

"I will need to meet wi' him at once. And my daughter."

The king swung down. Urfet followed and took the pony's lead from Deathan with a disdainful look. The bailey bustled with activity.

Deathan stepped back. He had to be in that meeting.

His father came hurrying, alarm hovering in his eyes. He shot one look at Deathan and said, "Find your brother." Swiftly, he stepped to Caerdoc and extended his hand. "Greetings, King Caerdoc. Ye ha' brought an answer?"

"I have," Caerdoc replied, very grimly indeed.

"Come, we will meet in the hall."

Da shot another look at Deathan as they passed, one that made Deathan turn and pelt down toward the shore.

Even though that was not what he wanted to do. Every instinct bade him go to Darlei, seek to reassure her. For, aye, having seen King Caerdoc, he feared she'd been all too right.

Something dire came rushing toward them.

He found Rohr lying in his hidey-hole above the shore, half slumped on a stack of cloth used to make sails, the inevitable jug beside him. Not till Deathan tried to revive his brother did he realize Rohr was more than half drunk.

"Wha' is the matter wi' ye?" he bellowed, the emotions that roiled in his gut making him impatient. "Lyin' here wi' the sun up. Where is yer shirt?" For Rohr lay there in no more than his leggings.

Rohr opened a bleary eye and looked at Deathan. "Leave me be."

"I will no'. I canna." Rohr's hair was uncombed, the front of his leggings untied. It came to Deathan then—while he had been performing his brother's duties, organizing the guard and drilling the men, Rohr had been here with his woman.

"Where is she?" Sharply, he pushed his brother upright. "Caragh?"

"To be sure, long gone. But she comes here to me." A besotted smile curved Rohr's lips. "She is carrying my child, ye ken."

"I ken it, aye." It was unfair for Rohr to have a lover and possibly Darlei also. Did he mean to keep Caragh on the side after the marriage?

"She comes," Rohr reiterated, "so we can decide wha' to do about our s-situation."

"Well, ye ha' run clean out o' time. Da wants ye."

"Da?"

"Aye. The Caledonians ha' returned, no doubt wi' an answer from the king. Ye canna go looking like that. Where are the rest o' your clothes?"

"Somewhere about." Rohr climbed to his feet, looking like a man who'd been struck a hard blow, one that had at least partly cleared his head. "I do no' wish to wed wi' that wild woman."

And I do no' wish for ye to wed wi' her. She is mine.

"I do no' like her." Rohr wrinkled his nose. "Conceited bitch."

A little more of Deathan's patience slipped from his grasp.

"Where is yer self-respect, man? Pull yoursel' together."

"I wish to wed wi' Caragh. Even though she often carps at me and leads me on a merry chase. She is the woman I—"

"Aye, well, it scarce matters wha' ye want, does it? 'Tis all down to the king."

Deathan was to recall speaking those words a few moments later, after he dragged Rohr up the slope most hastily clad and the object of stares.

Under the guise of bringing his brother into the hall, he lingered. Because he just had to hear.

Darlei was there ahead of them, standing not far from her father, and his. King Caerdoc's face bore a heavy frown. Several of Da's advisors stood by.

No one else.

Darlei turned to look at them, and Deathan's heart fair seized in his chest. Silvery eyes bright, she held hard to her composure, fighting for it with every sinew, but he could feel her apprehension.

"There ye be!" Da cried as Deathan pulled Rohr forward. "Step up, step up. We ha' an answer from the king."

Rohr went forward to stand beside Darlei, who cast one more look at Deathan before turning her attention to her father.

"King Kenneth kept us waiting several days before granting us an audience," Caerdoc said somberly. "And when he heard me out, he was not best pleased with what I had to tell." He turned his dark gaze on Rohr, sharply critical. "I fear, Chief MacMurtray, you and yours have fallen some in the king's estimation."

Da gave a heavy sigh and likewise raked Rohr with a disparaging look.

This is it, Deathan thought. *There will be no escaping the decree now. The marriage will follow swiftly. Darlei will be my sister.*

"The king pondered well and long over what should be done, and left us waiting several more days before making his decision."

"And what," Da asked, "is that decision?"

Deathan could see Darlei trembling now. Her head was still

high, but her hands quivered where she clasped them together.

King Caerdoc said, "This marriage will not take place."

Darlei sagged. Rohr made an inarticulate sound in his throat that smacked of relief, and Deathan's heart bounded. A good outcome.

But swiftly, King Caerdoc turned to his daughter. "The king has chosen another husband for you, instead. We leave as soon as ever we may and will journey to Killin for the wedding. King Kenneth sends word ahead of us."

"What?" Darlei gasped.

What? Deathan echoed in his head.

King Caerdoc spoke rapidly to Darlei in their own tongue, as if he feared she had not understood his words.

A dull flush rose from her bosom upward. She did not look at Deathan, though he felt her emotions flying to him.

Nay.

Nay.

"Who?" Darlei asked in Gaelic, like a woman stunned. "Who is this man to whom I am being given?"

"His name is Dunstoch MacNabh, and he lives a goodly distance east of here. Closer to home, it will be for you."

"I know of Dunstoch MacNabh," Da spoke up. "He is a widower and a strong chief."

Darlei began, "I will not—"

Swiftly her father told her, "You will do as the king commands. There has been enough delay, and we can see what comes of it. Chief MacMurtray, we will be ready to leave here in two days, as soon as my men and ponies are rested."

Two days. They had but two days together.

This was not what Deathan had expected. He'd thought, if the wedding were canceled, Caerdoc would take his daughter home. Deathan would follow and somehow, *somehow* persuade him they should be together. As, in truth, they already were.

But she was to be swept away. Into the arms of another stranger. How could he stand and let that happen?

"Father—" Darlei began again.

"Hush. I wish to see this settled and done. For once in your life, daughter, you will do as you are told. Now go to your woman. Begin to pack up your things."

Darlei, too, looked like she'd been struck a hard blow. But she turned to leave the hall. As she walked past Deathan, she sent him one burning look.

I will find ye, he promised silently. *I will always find ye.*

❖

CHAPTER THIRTY-FOUR

ANOTHER STRANGER. QUITE likely, if he was a widower, an old man. Nay, that was not the way it was meant to be.

Clamor filled Darlei's head as she walked from the hall, silent. Angry thoughts, protests, desperate longings. She could not feel her feet hitting the ground. The pain inside was far too bright.

Deathan.

As she passed him by there at the rear of the hall, she cried out to him. Her heart did and her spirit. *Save me. Please save me.*

The look on his face showed him as shocked as she. He had not seen this coming. Neither of them had.

Curse King Kenneth MacAlpin and all that belonged to him down through eternity.

What was she to do? Oh, what?

She'd believed all this while that the worst that could happen would be an order to carry through with the marriage to Rohr. Unbearable, yes. But at least she'd live here, where she could see Deathan every day. Mayhap talk with him. Survive on whatever crumbs they might share.

Or she would journey home, and he would follow. Yes, she'd believed in that promise.

This… *This!* To be snatched away from him. Given like a prize heifer to a stranger, a widower. As if her heart did not matter in the least.

She was not a woman to weep and moan. She might scream, yes, but only in anger.

She managed to keep a grasp on her dignity till she reached her chamber. Orle was there waiting and swung round to gaze at her in alarm when she entered.

Darlei cast herself onto the bed and sobbed. Sobbed and sobbed.

Two days. In two days, she must leave her heart behind.

NO ONE SEEMED to notice that Deathan remained in the back of the hall after King Caerdoc left, gone to take his rest. Da, mightily displeased, lit into Rohr as Deathan had rarely seen him do.

Rohr, the lucky bastard. Once more, things had worked out for him as they always seemed to do. Off the hook he was, and at liberty to wed the woman he loved. What was a tongue lashing in the face of that?

Though, aye, Da did tear into Rohr without reserve.

"Look wha' ye ha' done, ye fool o' a lad! Cast us into disgrace. Disgrace wi' the king! Did ye no' understand that choosing ye to wed wi' a Caledonian princess and help unite the country meant we were held in the highest favor? No more."

"I did not know," Rohr said. "When I started seeing Caragh, I did not know I would be held in high favor by the king. Or chosen to marry some savage lass from the dark lands—some woman I do no' want."

I want her, Deathan thought, and could have hollered it with his anger and frustration.

"And for ye to get yer bairn in yon lass's belly beforehand—I did no' need the king to know that is how I run my house."

"Does it matter? I always meant to wed wi' Caragh. I did before all this happened. At least the succession will be seen to."

"If ye got her a son," Da said scathingly. "I doubt ye can do e'en that right. Look at ye. Coming here before our guests half dressed and reeking o' ale! I am fair ashamed o' ye."

That seemed to penetrate Rohr's indignation. He sobered abruptly.

"I do no' doubt King Caerdoc believes his daughter has had a narrow escape."

"I am sorry, Da. But I did no' ken—"

"Neither did ye conduct yersel' as I would expect from my son. We shall ha' to do our best to mak' it up to the Caledonians before they leave."

"Aye, Da."

"And wha' am I to tell yer mother? Sore eager has she been for this wedding. Now I maun tell her ye are in disgrace."

Rohr bent his head, but Deathan, watching, did not quite believe in his remorse. He'd got what he wanted after all.

Yet again.

Deathan left the hall, and his father did not see him go. Outside, he stood and took great breaths of air, trying to calm his tripping heart. Unbearable, this was. He had to see Darlei, speak to her. Make this right. But how?

If he tried to get word to her, her woman would know. Could she trust her woman? The last thing he wanted to do was place Darlei in greater difficulty.

As if there could be aught worse than going away from him.

He went out and walked the walls, just for space to think. The men on guard there shot him sharp looks, which made him think his distress must show. He stared out over the land he loved and beseeched, "Gi' me an answer."

And received one.

He ran down from the walls and into the keep, stopping the first servant he saw. A young girl, she was, who usually served in the kitchens.

"Go to the princess's chamber," he bade her swiftly, "and tell her Mistress MacMurtray wishes to see her at once."

"But Master Deathan, I—"

"At once," he reiterated. "Your mistress is distressed."

"Aye."

The girl ran off up the stairs toward Darlei's chamber. Would she do as asked? Trying to act as if his stomach did not roil and his heart did not pound, Deathan walked to the corridor outside his mother's chamber and waited.

Waited.

Would she come? If anything could bring her, it would be his mam's request.

He could hear faint sounds from inside his mam's chamber, the door shut. The voice of Mam's woman and Mam's murmurs from time to time in reply. He hated to use his mother this way, but...

Soft footsteps skittered on stone. Darlei came, head bent and long brown hair streaming over her shoulders. When she saw him, she froze for an instant.

He caught her hands and drew her into his arms. Light flared to silver in her eyes.

He held her for one precious moment. "This was the only way I could see ye," he whispered.

"Yes."

"I had to see ye. Go up the shore alone, if ye can manage it. The place we walked before. Can ye?"

"Yes." She did not question the request or argue the difficulties of getting away alone. Only gazed into his eyes, her spirit finding and clinging to his.

He wanted to tell her it would be all right. But how could he? He wanted desperately to tell her he could solve this dilemma in which they found themselves, but he did not know how.

"I will go ahead," he told her, and left. One of the hardest things he'd ever had to do.

The cold air followed him up the shore, a hint of the winter to come. Winter of his spirit, perhaps. If he lost Darlei, if she went away from him where he could not follow, there would be naught ahead for him but winter.

Far up the shore, out of sight of the settlement, he paced the stones. He wondered about the past and about fate. About facing destiny.

If all this had in some fashion happened before—in a previous life—if he had known Darlei and loved her with a love that would not die, what was the meaning in what befell them now? What was he intended to learn? What must he do to be with her?

It could not all be about hurting and pain. The turn of the wheel, life into life, could not be meant only to torture him.

She came walking up the shore path with her cloak wrapped around her. When she saw him waiting, she ran.

Ran to him.

Their hands met first, grasping. She'd been crying—his wild and valiant maiden—as he could clearly see here in the strong light.

He did not want her ever to weep.

Their bodies met next as he drew her in. Then their lips, as irresistibly as breathing.

An effort at comfort it was, on his part. But she needed more than comfort from him now.

CHAPTER THIRTY-FIVE

"L IST TO ME," Deathan said, and Darlei drew away just far
enough to look into his eyes. The taste of him, of their
kiss, remained on her lips. His hands still cradled her.

The one place in all the world she needed to be, in his arms.
Yet there was no hope in it, for she could see the fear in his eyes.
The man she loved wanted desperately to comfort her.

What comfort was there to give?

Fresh tears spilled over from her eyes—she who so seldom
wept. She was undone, all her courage lost for love of him.

"I am being sent away," she cried out. "To this—this Dunstoch MacNabh. Do you know of him?"

"I ha' heard the name. A powerful chief. No doubt in favor
wi' the king."

"And I am to be his reward," she said bitterly. "Me."

"'Tis too cruel. I—"

"Nay." Lightly she laid her fingers across his lips. "Do not
make more promises. There are none ye can keep."

Agony flooded his eyes. "Darlei—"

"I have been thinking about it ever since...ever since.
Deathan, I know you have promised to follow me, to find me.
And I know you would save me if you could. But I do not see a
way."

"We will leave here now, before your father can take ye east.
I will go and fetch a boat."

For an instant, Darlei did hope. It would be like that glorious afternoon they had shared out on the water, a time apart from time. Only it could not last.

"Where would we go?"

"To Wales. Or Ireland. I can hire out my sword."

A dangerous life, that. If he fell while trying to win their bread? If she lost him? An old fear, that. One rooted in her very soul.

She swiped tears from her face. "And would no one come looking?"

"Let them. We would ha' time together."

Some time.

"Or," he offered, seeing the doubt in her eyes, "I will follow after yer party when ye leave. Fight ye free."

"You would take on all my father's men? Urfet?" Oh, that was worse even than the prospect of him hiring out his sword. For she had seen Urfet's skill with a blade.

"Darlei, list to me," he said again. "Would fate—would life— ha' brought us together if 'twere no' meant? If there should no' be a way, however difficult?"

Lovingly, she touched his face. "I do not know. But I have this great and terrible fear inside me."

"Fear may be overcome."

"It may. And I always believed I might spit in the eye of my fears. That was before I met you. Before I loved you."

"I ha' loved ye always."

"Yes."

"Darlei, I will no' surrender the belief that we are meant to be together."

And she could not quite surrender the idea that he might die for her sake—this strong and humble man she adored.

To leave him would half kill her. To live knowing she was responsible for his death…

Nay, not that. Better to *dree her weird*, accept her fate, if only for his sake.

Turning her back on the very idea of him risking himself for her, she turned for the settlement.

"Darlei." She thought she heard him whisper her name as she started off back up the shore. But she ran on.

THE MOOD IN the great hall that evening was strained and grim. Few of the clan's folk were in attendance, and those of them that were—MacMurtray's own advisors and senior members of the guard—clearly saw no cause for revelry.

Deathan's father made a speech about how his wife had hoped to attend a gathering before the Caledonian party had to leave, but her illness still forbade it.

Mam. Deathan would have to make a few moments to see her before he followed Darlei's party.

For he *would* follow. He could not simply stand and watch her ride out of his life.

It would mean breaking ties with those here. If he interfered with the king's wishes, his father might never forgive him. It could mean being loose in Scotland's wilds.

He did not care. This land he loved would provide for him, and for the woman he loved.

But he had not much time to prepare. Just tonight and to-morrow, when the farewell feast would occur. The Caledonians would leave the following morning, and he must have all he needed to take with him packed and ready.

Rohr, in forced attendance here and looking far happier than he had, sat looking at no one and did not notice when Deathan rose from beside him early to leave the gathering. But Urfet did and gave him a long, thoughtful stare as he slipped out.

Urfet. Would he be a problem? Darlei seemed to think so. She did not believe Deathan could best her father's champion, if it came to a fight.

She did not yet realize he could do anything, *anything* for her sake.

He was packing up a leather bag when he heard a sound at his door, no more than a scratch upon the wooden frame. Darlei came slipping in.

So stirred were Deathan's emotions, he scarce knew how he felt to see her. She had no doubt come to continue the discussion they'd had on the shore, to try to dissuade him from following after and risking himself for her sake.

She'd clearly come straight from the hall, with her hair all dressed, wearing an amber-yellow gown. She looked so beautiful, it fair stole his breath.

"Darlei," he said, "I do no' wish to spend more words in—"

"Nor do I." She came to him, having closed the door carefully behind her. "No words. No more."

She moved into his arms and pressed up against him. Her eyes made two bright silver shields, holding hard to her emotions, but he could see…he could see her desire, and it made him weak, as his own longing rose to meet hers.

"Darlei."

"Hush. Please, Deathan. *Please*. Love me. Because, well, I may be able to bring myself to leave you, but not without"—light and darkness flickered in her steady gaze—"not without lying with you first."

The emotions that poured through him then near took him to his knees. "We canna."

"Are ye not listening? I cannot leave you unless we do."

"Then do no' leave me." If she could beseech, he could also. He buried his hands in her hair. "Come awa' wi' me now. Tonight. I am more than half packed—"

"And if I do, and they come after us? If they catch us, and it costs your life? Deathan, I fear this has happened before between the two of us. I know not where or when. But the fear inside me is so bright, I would do near anything to escape it. Though," she added softly, "I will have you first."

"Darlei, I believe, aye, we are stuck on the wheel o' time. That does no' mean each turn o' it will bring us to the same events. We maun be meant to learn something."

"I have learned I love you above all others, above all else. Do not ask me to live knowing I have brought you harm. Or without having shared with you all a man and woman can share."

He wanted her. By all the powers of the earth and sky, he did. Yet his heart insisted it could only make things worse for her.

"Please," she whispered, and kissed him.

Ah, and he was lost, his intentions crumbling so fast it made him tremble. Could they be joined in spirit and not be joined at the root, as well?

But what would it do to him, having her once while knowing they must part?

Her fingers moved on the laces of his tunic. And aye, it felt familiar having her undress him, though they'd not done this before. They shed their clothes without modesty, one for the other, and she took a half step back on her small, naked feet.

"Let me look at you, Deathan MacMurtray."

He stood and let her look, his lust near overwhelming but his will like iron, for her sake. It gave him a chance to look also.

Perfection, she was, her skin smooth, her waist slim, her breasts high and round. She might have been made to please him in all ways.

She had.

She touched him softly, the movements of her fingers following her eyes—his shoulders, down his chest through the crisp hair she found there and lower still. When she sank to her knees and embraced him, pressing her cheek against his belly with her fingers wrapped around him, he very nearly succumbed.

"Please, Deathan. Love me now."

"Aye. Come to the bed."

He lifted her and carried her there, pushing his pack and scattered possessions to the floor. His urgency, nearly overmastering, answered to the rein of love.

This must be fine and memorable for her, as much as he could make it. He would worship her, show to her just what it meant when a man adored his woman.

And that meant kisses. Over every part of her, possibly.

He started with her lips. She met him hungrily, open mouth to open mouth, all heat and welcome. And he knew—he knew they would burn up together this night.

A curse upon the morrow.

He kissed his way down to her breasts, latched on with his tongue because he knew how that pleased her. How could he know it, when they'd never before been together this way?

By all that was holy, he just did.

A single light—the one by which he'd been working—burned in the room. Enough to allow him glimpses. Of the passion in her silvery eyes. The way she spread herself in offering. The abandon with which she invited him in.

A holy act was this mating, a thing as destined as her breath and his. But nonetheless passionate, for that.

When he pushed inside her, her body drew him in, wild as her spirit, and primitive as time. He tried to pull out before he came—the last sort of complication she needed was to arrive at her next destination carrying another man's child—but she locked her heels behind his back and held him, held him to her.

"Deathan." She breathed his name. Kissed his face over and over again, desperate little kisses. Held him tight.

He remained inside her and lay marveling at the sensation. Two made one. Never had he known such peace.

Despite what must come.

"My lass. Beautiful lass." He breathed in the scent of her hair. Of her skin.

"Do not move," she implored him. "Do not speak. Just be with me."

CHAPTER THIRTY-SIX

T IME, SO DARLEI decided during that night and the day that followed, was a strange commodity. It dragged when she waited to be with Deathan. Flew when she knew she had not much more of it with him. Went away entirely when she was in his arms.

She left him three-quarters of the way through the night when she thought no one would see her slipping away. Orle, to be sure, would know. Orle, she could trust.

She felt like a different woman when she slipped away. Not just a new sort of Darlei, who had lost her maidenhead and flown into womanhood, but someone else entirely. One who already knew how it felt to lie with a man—this man. One who had already done so, perhaps at other times. In other lives.

He had tried to talk to her about that before she left him, standing there naked and oh-so earnest, he had. How sure he was that they'd come round on this turn of the wheel for a reason. That there was something they must learn. Something they must do differently to avoid living through this kind of pain ever again.

That there was pain—pain amid the great love and joy— neither of them could deny. It had broken her heart to walk away out of his chamber. What it would do to her to leave him…

It made it hard to breathe just thinking on it. Yet she had but one more day. And time being what it was, that would slip through her fingers like water.

That, even more than the learning of lessons or the embracing of their destinies, remained on her mind as she slipped back into her own chamber. The man she loved had perhaps more faith than she.

Fear made it so hard to believe.

Orle was sleeping when Darlei arrived, but sat up in her little cot to stare.

"Are you all right?" Darlei had, of course, told Orle where she was going before she slipped off to Deathan's chamber. Now the girl eyed her searchingly. "How—how—"

Darlei doubted she had words for what had taken place between herself and Deathan. She doubted there *were* words, though she did surely owe some to this girl whose reticence had allowed for it. She could not say she felt wonderful, for leaving Deathan had torn the heart from her.

Softly, she whispered, "I had what I wanted. What I sought."

"Oh!" Orle blushed. She got up and came to Darlei, keeping her voice soft. "I hope it is what you wanted, for it was a terrible chance to take. One of the first things my mother told me was that if I lie down with a man, I may come away with his babe. And you are to go to another man."

"Yes, it was a terrible chance to take. But worth it."

She half expected Orle to go on chastising her, or fretting. Instead, her friend drew her into a tight embrace.

Darlei wept. Wept and wept.

"I do not want to go to another man, Orle. I want Deathan. No one but him."

"I know it is hard to bear." Orle smoothed back Darlei's hair. "But the king's orders must be obeyed."

"Orle, I am so afraid. Not just because I do not know how I am to live without him. I fear he will follow after me, make some attempt to win me away. Die for it."

"Oh, Darlei, why should you think such a thing?"

Because it had all happened before. He had risked himself, as a warrior he had, time after time.

"Better," she whispered, "I should pass into lifelong misery than he should die for my sake."

"Neither of those things need happen. You may well grow fond of this Dunstoch MacNabh whom you are to wed. And though I am sure you do not believe so now, your longing for Master Deathan may fade."

It never had, in the past. It never would.

"Now come. Get some rest. Tomorrow is likely to be a difficult day."

Darlei went to her bed, but she took no rest.

ALL THE FOLLOWING day, Darlei's mind remained like a mouse trapped in a ewer, running endlessly, trying to find a way out. She went early to see Mistress MacMurtray, intending to say her goodbyes.

Deathan was not there, and the grief of it hit Darlie all out of proportion.

"Och, lass," Mistress MacMurtray said, her pale-blue eyes full of regret, "I am that sorry to see ye go from us. I was looking forward to yer wedding, and to you becoming my daughter. Do no' greet."

"Nay." Darlei swiped at her cheeks. She had done enough of that in Orle's arms. What had come over her? Was she not a strong woman? A Caledonian princess.

"But I understand why the marriage agreement is broken and why ye maun leave—to be sure, I do. My husband has explained to me what my son has done."

Her son. Deathan. But nay, Mistress MacMurtray did not speak of him.

"For Rohr to have got another lass wi' his child—"

"He loves her. And it happens." Darlei understood that now in full.

"Aye, so it does. But I doubt his father will ever forgive him.

For our clan to fall out o' favor wi' the king"—Mistress Mac-Murtray's gaze softened further—"and for us to lose ye, 'tis a blow."

Yet life here would go on after Darlei left. Rohr would marry his lover and raise his child. Mistress MacMurtray, sweet woman that she was, would likely linger in her illness. Deathan…

What would become of him without her? What would become of her, without him? Sitting there with Mistress MacMurtray, she could feel the wheel of life turn, with herself helpless upon it.

Slow. Inexorable. Immeasurably cruel.

Despite all her best intentions, tears pricked Darlei's eyes when she said, "I wish to thank you for your great kindness while I was here. You welcomed me at once, and it made such a difference."

"I only wish ye could stay."

"As do I."

Mistress MacMurtray squeezed Darlei's hand. "May the gods go wi' ye, lass, on your journey. And may ye find much happiness in yer life."

A blessing. Yet Darlei felt as if her happiness had flown. She expected no more.

"Ye leave us in the morning, aye?"

"Yes, mistress."

"Pop back in and see me before ye go."

"If I can."

Darlei hurried out so the woman would not see her tears. Orle was waiting.

"Your father wishes to see you, Darlei."

Her father's quarters were in disarray, his man packing. Caer-doc gave Darlei a sharp look when she came in. "Daughter, are ye packed and ready to leave?"

"Most of my things have been gathered, yes."

"Make certain they are. Chief MacMurtray wishes us to feast tonight, an effort to assuage his guilt, I do not doubt. I will not deny him, even though 'tis a terrible inconvenience for us to travel on." He sighed. "This marriage should have been over and done long since."

An inconvenience. Was that all her future meant to him?

"We will give him his feast, as I say, but I wish to be ready to leave by first light tomorrow."

"So early?"

"Our journey is a considerable one. And I want the dust of this place off my feet. It has not been a rewarding experience."

Not rewarding? Her fingers trailing over the warmth of Deathan's naked skin, across his taut belly and lower still. His mouth at her breasts, calling up a passion she'd never imagined. The heat of him inside her, the deep and thrilling sense of belonging.

There could be no greater reward in all of life.

And standing there amid the chaos of her father's chamber, she knew whatever it took, before she left Murtray she must have Deathan again.

CHAPTER THIRTY-SEVEN

DARLEI COULD LOCATE Deathan nowhere. Though she walked the settlement while Orle finished packing, searching high and low while trying to pretend she did not, she caught no glimpse of him. Not on the walls where he so often shared the duty of keeping watch. Not over in the training field. Not on the shore.

She even walked a way up along the rocky trail beside the water, thinking he might have gone there ahead of her, and they might snatch a few moments alone.

The water was restless, dark blue flecked with green, like Deathan's eyes. The seethe and pull of it matched the emotions that filled her.

He was nowhere, and walking back her heart broke all over again. They had so little time. She wanted only to see him before it ran out.

But ah, she lied to herself, for she wanted far more. She wanted to touch him. To lie with him once again.

As, if she could manage it, she would.

She did see Rohr in passing. He jerked his head away when he encountered her gaze and pretended she was not there. She might despise Deathan's brother, yes, and had never wanted to wed with him. But better to accept even marriage without love than to be snatched away from this place where Deathan remained.

Why must life be so cruel? If she was indeed pinned to the

wheel of fate, she wanted off.

Not until after she and Orle had shared a few bites to eat at noontime, sitting among their gathered possessions in Darlei's chamber, did she go back out and catch a glimpse of the man she sought.

He was in the field where the Caledonians so often gathered and saw to their ponies. Indeed, when she caught sight of him, he stood speaking with Urfet in what looked like stilted conversation.

The emotions that filled her as she hurried thence made her breathless. Gladness—yes, gladness first. Great relief and joy at merely seeing him. Regret. Grief.

He looked round as she joined him and Urfet, and as swiftly away again. But she had seen, yes, seen the flare of joy in his eyes, the hope, the desire.

"Princess." Urfet bowed to her.

As did Deathan. "Princess Darlei."

And just the sound of his voice affected her right down to her bones. That soft voice in her ear as he'd caressed her. When he was inside her.

"I came to make sure there will be a pony available to me so I will not have to ride in the wagon all the journey." It seemed like forever ago that she had injured Bradh in her futile attempt at escape. She added for Deathan's benefit, "Father says we are to leave at dawn."

"Yes," Urfet said, "I have spoken with the king. It is why we are here. The ponies are in good condition and will be eager to leave." As would he, his tone implied.

"Good, for we have very little time." Darlei's gaze stole to Deathan's face, which looked like a mask. Gazing away at nothing.

"Leave it to me, princess."

Darlei nodded, reached out to pat the nearest pony, and walked away praying Deathan would follow.

After several moments, he did.

She dawdled, abandoning her usual swift stride till he caught up with her.

"Darlei—"

"Where have you been? I looked everywhere."

"There is much that must be done for your father's party before morning."

"I have to see you. Talk with you." But that was not all she needed. She needed to touch him, taste him. Needed it with a raw kind of desperation.

He shot her one look that betrayed only a small measure of what he felt. "Aye. But 'tis impossible."

"It cannot be." She would not allow for it. She felt sick with wanting him.

"Darlei—"

"Take me for a sail. One last sail."

"There is no chance for that. The feast is set to begin—"

"Curse the feast. Walk with me up the shore."

"There are eyes everywhere."

"List to me. During the feast, everyone will be occupied." She ached to touch his hand but refrained. "If I get up during the feast and leave—when I get up, follow me out."

"But—"

"Folk absent themselves from the hall all the time. No one will think aught of it. I have to be with you."

"Madness," he breathed.

It might well be just the wildness in a woman's heart.

"You will follow me?"

He nodded and veered away, saying no more.

After that, it was all waiting. Waiting while Father engaged her in conversation, seeking to determine whether she was going to make a fuss here at the end of their prolonged stay at Murtray. If she would continue to battle against her fate. While Orle prepared her for the farewell feast, all their possessions piled ready for leaving.

While they took their places in the hall, the clan's folk filing in, the tables loaded with food, Rohr was there looking sullen—though what reason did he have?—and refusing to so much as look at her.

Deathan was there sitting at the other end of the head table where she could barely see him.

She tried to choke down some of the food presented to her and found she could not. The honey wine went down better and managed to calm her a mite by the time Chief MacMurtray's harper came in. A final show of entertainment for the guests.

The man began with a long and winding tale, telling of Murtray's ancestors, in particular a warrior called Ardahl, of Ireland. Beyond compare, this warrior was said to be. With scattered notes upon the harp, the shanachie related his attributes.

Darlei could wait no longer.

With a murmured word for her father beside her, she rose and, moving discreetly around the perimeter of the place, left the hall. She did not look back to see if Deathan noticed. If he followed.

He could not follow too soon.

She lingered just outside the hall. Dark had fallen—the season moved into autumn, and it came earlier now. She waited like a shadow, her back against the wall of the building, still listening to the old Coll's voice rising and falling within, a beautiful cadence marked with notes that sparkled through the dark air.

A shadow moved beside her and her whole being breathed for the first time all day.

"Deathan—"

"We canna stay here. Come."

He led her not away but around the side of the hall and through a small doorway in the rear. The music immediately grew louder.

"What is this place?"

"Hush. 'Tis my father's meeting chamber, and the hall is just there." He nodded to a curtained doorway, through which the exquisite music flowed. Deathan drew Darlei into his arms, hard up against him, proving his need matched her own. He buried his face in her neck and breathed in, trembling.

For several moments there was no more than this. Only their heartbeats falling into time and the music beyond—for the bard had concluded his tale and now played an intricate tune, glorious music that sparkled and danced and filled the hall. An occasional rustle and cough from the assembly reminded Darlei that the entire clan—and her own people—sat just beyond. For yes, this tiny, dark chamber separated them by no more than the width of the wall.

"Darlei." Her name was but a breath on his tongue. When his mouth claimed hers, she melted so swiftly that she had to clutch at him to remain upright.

That kiss told her everything she needed to know. That he ached even as she did. That he wanted her the way she wanted him. That he loved her.

"Darlei, I canna see ye go from me," he gasped when it ended.

"Then please. Deathan, please. Make love to me."

CHAPTER THIRTY-EIGHT

T HEY HAD NOT much time. Only so long as it might reasonably take either of them to visit the nearest privy and return, before someone would come looking for Darlei.

True, the bard had successfully woven a spell, and the hall full of his listeners, only steps away, had fallen into a kind of enchanted stupor. Silent.

"Please. Please." Darlei did not mind begging the man she loved. "The last time."

She could feel Deathan's hesitation. She could feel the moment his will broke and he capitulated. He kissed her again and his need came flooding upon her, a match in full for her own.

The wondrous music played on, a backdrop to what they would share.

For the last time.

Gently, he laid her down on a rug by the wall. She could barely see him for the gloom, but oh, she could feel. His hands shook as he drew up her skirts and loosened the ties beneath. As he pushed up his kilt and untied his leggings.

Time for little more. She would not have his mouth at her breast. His fingers all over her skin.

At that moment, she did not care. She opened herself to him, drew him in, and, mouths fused, they rocked to the flowing music while everyone they knew sat but a hand's reach away, unaware of the great need met and answered.

After, when Darlei still had him hot and spent inside her, she wept. Lying with his weight atop her, she listened to the ancient song played upon the magical harp, each separate note passing through her like an echo of longing. The tears ran down into her ears.

I must remember this. How he feels, how he smells, each separate heartbeat, at this moment when he is mine. I must live upon this for a long time.

But they could not remain so, and he withdrew from her, leaving a wound so deep it made her gasp. He kissed her cheeks and found the tears.

"Weeping? Nay."

What else could she do? What else was left in the wake of these beautiful moments?

"I must go back."

Beyond the wall, the bard was speaking, saying he would play one last song tonight.

Yes, she must return.

He lifted her up. Smoothed her skirt. Fastened his own clothing.

"Deathan—promise me something."

"Aye?"

"You will not follow me." It could only end badly. This, she felt to her heart.

"Ye expect me let ye go?"

"Yes." This she did ask, rather than expect.

Before he could answer, she ducked outside. The night air struck cool. No colder than the chill that beset her heart.

When she returned to the hall and took her place beside her father, he gave her a questioning look, but she focused all her attention on the harper, who, indeed, played a final song to end the night.

As for Deathan, he did not return.

AND WHAT LESSON, so Deathan wondered amid pain so bright it nearly made him numb, was he to learn from this? Being forced to stand in the morning so young it had not yet earned its light and watch the woman he loved ride away from him. In aid of what seeming enlightenment could he attribute this flaying of his soul?

The morning, crisp and cool, argued good travel, and he was glad of that, glad for Darlei's sake. Yet old Coll's song—the one he had given his audience last night while Deathan held Darlei in his arms—continued to play through his head as it had all night, and the pain...

Impossible to bear.

What were life lessons in the face of this?

Da and his advisors stood by to bid farewell to honored guests. Deathan could see the relief in his father's eyes.

No one questioned Deathan's presence, since Rohr had failed to turn up, and it might be argued he represented the house.

In truth, he merely wanted to drink in the sight of Darlei while he could. Brown hair all braided for travel, her grand cloak upon her shoulders. He had run his fingers through that hair. He still carried its fragrance on his skin.

Her pony stood ready, and she had not looked at him even once.

Ah, but he could still feel the softness of her cheek beneath his lips. Wet with her tears.

"Go safely," Da told King Caerdoc. "And I wish ye all prosperity ahead."

The king nodded. Urfet stepped forward to help Darlei mount. Deathan reached her first.

"Princess, allow me."

His hands closed on her waist, beneath the cloak. The last time he would touch her?

She did look at him then, a searing look as bright as the glint of a war shield. A warning. *Do not follow me.*

She feared for him. Had she so little faith in his abilities? Did she not know that Ardahl MacCormac—the man of whom Coll had sung last night and one of the greatest warriors ever in Ireland—was his ancestor? That he carried the man's blood?

If ever he would fight for anything, it would be for her.

Yet she rode away from him, already she did, her borrowed pony falling into place behind Urfet and her father, her woman in the wagon behind. She did not look at him again.

Did she weep? He could not tell. But the pain inside him was beyond bearing, and if she felt anything akin to that…

At the last, when the jingling of bridles had near died away, she did look back, one telling glance, swift as pain.

My love.

My love.

Da gave a gusty sigh. "Good riddance to all that. What a trial! I suppose now I shall ha' to set a swift marriage for yer brother, if only to see things right."

So Rohr was to get everything he wanted, was he? The blessed firstborn. While Deathan watched his life disappear into the distance.

Hard not to grow bitter. But was that what he was meant to learn through this ordeal?

Nay. He believed he was meant to follow his heart, no matter the cost.

He watched the train out of sight, some part of him hoping for a miracle, that they might turn back at the last moment, that Darlei might persuade her father to let her stay. A mere child's hope. The air grew bright, folk bustled around pursuing their business, and he could stand there no longer.

He did not truly have to think about what to do. He'd done so for long enough. The heart did not care for objections, nor what the head might argue.

He had only to figure out the way of it. He could not just disappear. People would worry. His ma would.

By all that was holy, it would be hard to leave her. Not as hard as watching Darlei ride away mayhap, but still difficult.

She had forbidden him, had Darlei, from following after her. But he had promised always to find her. No matter where.

Perhaps that was the lesson in all this. That naught, however terrible, could keep them apart. And perhaps it was her lesson, not his, to learn.

His headstrong lass, his wild woman who sought to protect him. Was he not a man? Was he not her man?

If she thought he would stay here meekly to pick up the pieces and go on without her, she did not know him.

Or she did not remember everything about him. Not yet.

CHAPTER THIRTY-NINE

S O GREAT WAS Darlei's sorrow when she rode away from the keep at Murtray, she felt sick from it. He had lifted her onto her pony, touching her once more, for the last time. She had looked into his blue-green eyes and beheld the weight of his grief, backed by another emotion that terrified her.

Determination.

Please, my love, please do not risk yourself for me. I am lost.

The morning was crisp, and all around her Caledonian voices filled the air. She had grown accustomed to the sound of Gaelic in her ears. His voice, like music.

Like the music that had played for them last night.

She had no doubt old Coll had played for them, woven his magic for them as they joined flesh to flesh and spirit to spirit for the last time.

She was doomed, and Deathan MacMurtray was better forgetting her, if he could.

He would not.

He'd best try, because she rode to a fate from which no one could rescue her. Headstrong and willful all her life, a princess most often granted her way, she'd run up against the stone wall of the high king's decree. She saw no escape, and the knowledge made her want to lose her hastily consumed breakfast in the heather.

The rest of their party seemed so happy, giddy with escaping the keep beside the sea. She alone contemplated disaster. She closed her eyes and recalled the day they'd had out upon the sea in the wee boat. The first time they had kissed.

If only she could have sailed away with him forever.

Now she rode in silence, and no one noticed. Or if they did, they left her alone. Spoke around her, leaving her wrapped in misery. Father knew how she felt about all this. But Father had taken his fill of it. He wanted only to go home and resume his life. A Caledonian king in a new Scotland.

Darlei choked down the sickness inside. Better, better she be sacrificed to an old man, a stranger, than endanger Deathan. She would live for that now.

She would live for him.

DEATHAN WENT TO Rohr, since he could not approach Da and he had not the heart to tell Mam. And anyway, Rohr had a part in this, whether or not he acknowledged it.

After a search, he found his brother on the shore. Not in the stone hut where he'd spent so much time hiding after his lover threatened Darlei, but bareheaded beneath the morning sun, working at repairing one of the boats there.

Excepting himself from clan life, Deathan could not help but think. From the gossip and the staring eyes, as was his way. Fool. Did his brother not know he would be chief here someday?

"Wha' d'ye want?" Rohr asked with scant respect and no welcome. He straightened from his task of scraping at the hull of the craft overturned at his feet. "Are they gone? The accursed Caledonians?"

Deathan had to bite back his ire. Ignoring the query, he said, "I want ye to do something for me."

"What?"

"Gi' Da a message."

Rohr snorted. "I am going nowhere near Da for the time

being. He—"

"I am leaving."

"Wha'?" If Deathan had drawn a *sgian-dubh* and attacked his brother, Rohr could not look more surprised. His gaze moved over Deathan with more attention. "Going? Where?"

"Where does no' matter."

"If ye are goin' off hunting, I will go wi' ye. I could use some time awa'."

"I am going alone. And I may no' come back. You ha' responsibilities here. A child on the way. A clan to someday lead—"

"What are ye talkin' about?" He had all Rohr's attention now.

"Tak' up yer place, brother, for I will do it no longer." Deathan had done that far too long. Organized the watch. Drilled the men. Looked to the safety of the holding.

Being the dutiful son.

"I know my place fine," Rohr said.

"Then step into it. Tell Da I ha' gone off to clear my head."

"Yer head!"

"And no' to follow me. I will come back when I am ready. If at all." Deathan had no idea how this would work out.

"Have ye lost yer mind?"

"Do no' let Mam worry. That above all else, Rohr."

"Listen to me, Deathan. This is madness. Ye canna—"

"I take naught but my pony. My weapons. Naught but what belongs to me."

"'Tis no' that." Rohr's eyes widened. "Wha' will we do wi'out ye?"

Rohr had never before said such a thing. Deathan would have sworn he'd never thought it. "Ye will manage, I do no' doubt."

Rohr snagged Deathan's arm in a hard grip. "How long—"

"I do no' ken. Just do no' let them worry, eh? And do no' let them come after me."

He turned away, and Rohr stood open-mouthed and watched him, only calling at the last moment, "Go, then. Get whatever it is out o' yer system. Ye'll come back. Ye've nowhere else."

He might come back. Or he might end up dead and buried in the breast of this land he loved. Impossible to tell.

At least the Caledonian party was easy to follow. Such a large group left a clear trail, and he was not all that far behind. They had a wagon and baggage. He could catch up.

First he had to decide what to do. How to handle matters when he did.

He thought he should speak with King Caerdoc, explain the situation and how things were with him and Darlei. The man loved his daughter. Mayhap the two of them together could persuade him.

To act against the high king?

Another choice was to steal Darlei away, perhaps under cover of darkness. The two of them could approach King Kenneth at Forteviot. Petition him and explain their feelings for one another. Seek permission to wed.

If he sought a union between Caledonian and Scot, well, they were that, were they not? Just because Deathan was second-born and had no claim upon his own lands…

A third option: Deathan could seek to win Darlei's hand. Challenge her father for her, just like in the old stories. Fight for and win her.

This was what Darlei feared, so he knew—a fear buried so deep within her, it did not answer to reason. She did not believe he could win such a challenge.

And if he could not?

He refused to countenance that. Fighting for her, he could not lose. This he believed down to the root of his soul.

Yet if fate proved unkind, if the turn upon the tortuous wheel allowed Darlei to watch him die for her sake?

She would never recover. *Never.*

If he loved her, he had to consider her physical safety, her heart, her spirit.

He rode on and the morning strengthened around him. A beautiful day did Scotland offer her son.

And he could feel her, Darlei. As if an invisible cord ran from him through the very blessed ground, to her. And he had to be careful of that, mindful of his thoughts. He did not want her to know he followed, lest she worry and fret for him.

Best, mayhap, if she did not know he was there until she saw him. And so as he rode, he prayed to the very soil of Scotland: *Protect her. Do no' let her worry. Bring her comfort. And let her forgive me what I do.*

CHAPTER FORTY

"**D**ARLEI, YOU MUST eat something. Please, before we resume travel. You will fall ill," Orle beseeched Darlei, a portion of barley cake in her hand. After one swift glance, Darlei refused to so much as consider accepting the food.

They had just passed their first night upon the trail, Darlei and Orle together in their narrow tent. Darlei, unable to sleep, had considered flight even as she lay in her blankets, though she knew her father's men stood on guard and she could not possibly get far.

Now, as inevitably as every other aspect of her life, morning had come. They mounted up for another day's travel.

She must face her fate and, as Deathan put it, keep faith. For his sake.

But oh, she did not feel well, had not since they left Murtray, and she swayed on her feet. Father, who had more or less ignored her all day yesterday, walked up and looked at the proffered cake in Orle's hand.

"Daughter, will you eat?"

"Nay, Father."

His dark, impatient gaze swept over her. "You had best ride with Orle this morning. I do not trust you on the back of a pony."

He did not trust her? Because he believed her too ill to ride, or because he thought she might break away?

She scarce cared. She crawled into the bed of the wagon and curled up tight, seeking to shut the world away. They soon jerked into motion.

Yesterday had been a glorious day of bright sunshine with a cool, rattling wind. Today, clouds closed in and promised rain. A reflection of her mood, perhaps. She squeezed her eyes shut and—

She could feel him. By all the gods, she could. As if he hovered with her in spirit. A warmth at the place where he had been. And his face danced in her mind, the way he looked when he smiled. The light that came and flickered in his eyes when he spoke to her. Kisses dropped into the palms of her hands.

She wept.

Orle let her be, or perhaps she did not hear, for it began to rain, the drops pelting against the wooden awning of the wagon.

Darlei slept. She dreamed.

She dreamed of a man riding a chariot. Tall and slender he was, and taut with strength, a red-brown mane of hair tumbling down his back. Eyes of bright hazel, eyes that anchored her world.

He rode away from her into battle. A terrible, fierce battle it would be. If he did not return—

She awoke to the jolting of the wagon and a crashing cacophony that she realized meant it rained still harder. She sat up to find the interior of the wagon full of gloom.

"Where are we?"

"I am not sure." Orle tried to peer out. "Do you feel better for the sleep?"

Darlei did not. Had her heart been pulled out by the roots, it might be better. At least then it would eventually stop hurting.

"Have we traveled far?"

"It is difficult to tell. We go slowly for the rain."

A terrible thought burst upon Darlei's mind. He could catch them if he tried. Deathan could.

He will not, she assured herself. *Did he not promise?*

Nay, he had not. He had stopped short of that. And she could feel him.

"We are stopping."

To be sure, the wagon drew over to the edge of the track and one of the men—Mordoc, his name was—came to the opening.

"We have found a good stopping place. It is raining too hard to go on. Stay in the wagon. We are under the trees and will make camp."

"Yes," Orle said when Darlei did not speak.

The wagon shuddered. Orle came to Darlei's side.

"We will spend the night here, I do not doubt. Now will you take something to eat? Darlei, I am worried for you."

The very prospect of food turned Darlei's stomach. Might that be caused by hunger, under the sickness?

They sat side by side on the cot in the wagon and Darlei sought to choke down a bit of barley cake. They listened to the men trying to care for the ponies and set up camp in the driving rain.

Darlei wondered what had happened to her life. Once, she had been strong. Confident. Sure of her place as a princess. Her choices had been taken from her. Sent to wed with Rohr MacMurtray, she had for the first time been subject to command.

She'd fallen in love.

But nay, that did not describe it. She'd *remembered* love. Reached out with both hands and reclaimed it.

To no avail. For now, she was being sent like a prize cow to someone else. An old man.

That did not mean she could allow herself to become weak. Was she not still the girl who had possessed such strength, beneath all the misery? Just as, all along, she had been Deathan's love.

Some things, she was beginning to learn, did not change, not even as the wheel of fate turned. Beside her, Orle dozed, exhausted by the hard travel. Outside, the rain crashed down. No campfires tonight, and the men would be miserable. They—

What was that?

Voices, barely audible above the rain. Raised voices. A challenge. A query. Then a voice she would know even when she was dead.

She flew to the opening at the end of the wagon.

A curtain of silvery water fell, obscuring everything to mere blurs. To one side beneath the trees, the ponies had been picketed. Someone had bent a number of tree boughs and thrown a skin over for shelter.

The men, including Father, emerged from that cover now.

A man stood facing them, rain sluicing him down. Tall, lean, and facing away from her, he had a pony behind him and a sword in his hand.

Nay. Oh, nay, nay, nay—

Her heart leaped at seeing him—leaped impossibly—and then slammed so hard in her chest that she could feel it in her teeth.

He had come. By all the powers of the earth and sky.

He spoke to Father, who posed facing him. Though she heard the rhythm of his voice, she could not catch the words.

A challenge.

Nay, oh nay.

Everything she had feared on a level so deep she failed to comprehend it arose inside her. She launched herself from the wagon out into the crashing rain.

Deathan's head jerked around and he looked at her. Soaking wet, his hair darkened by the rain and his clothes dripping, she might not have known him, except she would know him anywhere. In the dark. If she were blind.

He had followed her. Just what she'd begged him not to do.

Their eyes met. *Oh, my love.*

She stumbled toward her father, who reached out and snagged her arm. Drew her to him.

"You are mad, boy. Go home. Turn about and go back home."

"I will not." Deathan could not be more implacable had his back been set to an oak. "I am taking Princess Darlei wi' me."

Darlei's heart bounded. Poor, abused heart. For it came crashing down so hard again, it nearly shattered.

"Deathan," she said.

No one heard. Except he did. His gaze moved to her and back again to focus on Father. He said, "I will no' let ye take her away to a marriage she does no' want."

Father, clearly shocked, sneered, "Oh, and I suppose she wants you?"

"She does."

"I do," Darlei echoed, but no one heard. No one heard. Her life—her being—at stake, and no one heard.

"You fool," Father barked, "she goes by order o' the king."

"The king will ha' to be disappointed, as will the chosen bridegroom. She comes wi' me."

"He is mad!" Father declared, and the men around him echoed it.

Deathan raised his chin and his sword. "I issue a challenge. I will fight any o' yer men for Princess Darlei's freedom. To the death, if it be your demand."

Nay. Nay!

Darlei tried to step forward. Father's grip on her arm prevented it.

"Any of us?" It was Urfet who stepped forward. Even through the rain Darlei could see the confident smile on his face. In an aside to Father, he said, "King Caerdoc, allow me. I can end this. It may prove amusing."

Nay.

Not Urfet. Not this.

"Father," Darlei began. She could not look at Deathan now. She turned instead and stared at her father beseechingly. "Do not agree to this."

For an instant, Father's gaze met hers. She beheld speculation there. Did he wonder or suspect what lay between her and Murtray's second son?

"Nonsense," he said from between clenched teeth, and then called to Deathan, "We accept your challenge." To Urfet, he said, "Go ahead and end it."

CHAPTER FORTY-ONE

THEY STEPPED OUT into the cleared space beside the wagon where there was room to fight, Deathan facing Urfet, who wore a broad smile. Indeed, the Caledonian champion wore that accursed, confident look on his face, the same as when they'd contested at games together back home.

This, though, could not be more serious.

As if to emphasize it, Urfet called to Deathan in his heavily accented Gaelic, "To the death, you said, MacMurtray? Then say goodbye to the world."

Deathan did not waste breath in answering, too busy seeking his bearings. The world looked blurry with rain. It might well affect his aim and timing. At the same time, he felt something rising within him, a kind of fire that stilled his quivering knees and lent sure strength.

If he won this battle, Darlei would ride away with him. *They* would win.

But he could not look into her face and behold the protest there—even through the rain he could see that. More than protest. Terror.

She still did not believe he could win.

He wanted to tell her not to fear so, but no time for that either. Urfet was circling, circling. His blade in his hand. That smile on his face.

The Caledonian blade was a beautiful thing, not as long as Deathan's own—he should have the advantage in reach. But the weapon, touched with bronze, looked magical, and it moved in a blur. No shields. No protection. Only metal and flesh.

As Deathan might have expected, Urfet became the aggressor. Almost before Deathan could draw breath, the warrior came swooping in, the strike so swift that Deathan barely caught the blade on his own.

He shook his head and tossed the wet hair back out of his eyes. Urfet struck again. Again.

Let him tire, said something or someone in the back of Deathan's mind.

Would the man tire? He was like a young horse, swift and full of power.

Deathan circled, back and back. Urfet struck once more and Deathan turned the blade, stepped in to give the man a taste of what he had.

Urfet's smile widened.

He struck for Deathan's legs. Deathan leaped aside, barely in time. So it was to be that way, was it? As he should have expected.

He waved his sword around his head and came in crashing upon his opponent. Somehow, Urfet caught the blade before it took his head. His smile slipped.

A few more like that and the man would lie dead, or as good as. Deathan and Darlei would ride off together.

A flurry, a desperate struggle, the slip of a blade. Reengagement, and a line of red appeared on Deathan's sword arm. He did not feel the pain.

But Darlei cried out. He heard her even above the crash of the rain. He heard her inside his head.

Nay, my love. I will not allow you to die for me.

Deathan set himself to fight on. But, tearing free from her father, Darlei ran forward. With a wordless cry, she planted her body between Deathan and Urfet, her back to the Caledonian champion.

Urfet stilled his sword just in time. Darlei did not seem to notice how close she had come to death. Eyes huge, staring into Deathan's face, she hollered, "Stop. Stop! I will not allow this!"

No one made a sound. The pounding of the rain became twice as loud. The pounding of Deathan's heart fair possessed him.

"Father!" Darlei spoke with her gaze still fastened to Deathan's. "This man is mistaken. *Mistaken.* I do not wish to go with him. *I do not want him.*"

Deathan took a step toward her. "Ye do no' mean that."

"I do. Believe that I do. Turn right around. Get on your pony and—"

She still did not believe he could win this fight. Even though the hard part—convincing King Caerdoc to countenance the challenge—was already done.

That hurt far more than any wound. Yet he could see in her wide silver eyes that her fear was greater still than any belief.

Ignoring the men behind her, ignoring the rain, she stepped forward and gazed at him earnestly. There were just the two of them, naught else existing, when she said, "You should not die for me. No man will ever again die for me."

"Darlei, come!" King Caerdoc, with a livid glare for Deathan, leaped forward and seized her arm. "You heard her," he spat at Deathan. "She does not want you. It is done."

A greater lie had never been spoken. But the lie stood behind the silver war shields of Darlei's eyes. She let herself be pulled away back toward the wagon. Urfet stepped back also, not without a glance of speculation.

Deathan stood there in the rain, his world crashing down around him and blood running from his arm.

As he saw it, he had two choices left to him. He could ride away back home. He could battle against that lie in her eyes and follow her.

For now he must take his answer, the one that was a lie.

He mounted his pony, which stood as miserable as he, and rode away. Rode away with nothing more than his life.

DARLEI SOBBED. SHE had never wept so, not in all her life. As she had discovered, especially lately, a woman wept tears from time to time, no matter how strong she thought she was. Most of hers had been angry tears, or those born of pride.

This, this was grief. Grief such as she had not known existed.

He had come for her. She had sent him away again.

She had sent him away in order to save his life. At least he had that, still.

She had seen Urfet fight before, as Deathan had not. She knew the ins and outs of the man's tricky mind. He never played fair. And when the blood had flowed, she had reacted without thought.

The fear that had fountained up through her was deep and fierce as fire. It had roots in her soul.

It had overwhelmed her. Spoken for her. But…

Had she done the right thing?

Yes. Yes, never doubt it. For nothing—not even marriage to a stranger—could be worse than seeing Deathan lying dead on the ground.

Nothing.

Yet had he won, she might have ridden away with him. Free.

She had condemned herself for his sake. Was it so different from what he had tried to do for hers?

She wept so long that Orle begged her to stop and then despaired of her. She must at last have gone out to fetch Father, for suddenly he was there beside her.

"Darlei, daughter." His hand on her hair was not unkind. "You must get hold of yourself. This will not do."

Darlei said nothing. She could not speak.

"Do you love him, that young man?"

Love. Could the meaning of the word even approach what she felt for Deathan?

"Life is not easy, daughter, and often not as we would choose." His hand still rested on her hair. "The path ahead of you is cast. You have done right to obey the king."

Was that what he thought she had done? Was it, truly?

"It will go well for our people to be in King Kenneth's favor. So if you have made a sacrifice, it is a worthy one."

She had not sacrificed for her people. For him, only for *him*.

"But you are a princess and must behave like one. Now call upon your pride and make up your mind to accept your fate gracefully."

Pride, yes, she'd always had that. Could it see her forward?

She had chosen this. Could she be woman enough to live with it?

She pictured Deathan riding away through the rain. Returning to the settlement he loved so well, the place beside the wide sea. She'd once rued the necessity of spending her life there.

Now she could imagine nothing better, so long as it was with him.

His trail lay in one direction and hers another. Blessed she had been that their trails had ever crossed, that she'd known him for a time. Gazed into his eyes. Held him inside her.

She held him inside her still.

She sat up and mopped her eyes. That, if anything, would be her strength.

✦

CHAPTER FORTY-TWO

A WOMAN COULD live with a broken heart. Darlei discovered that the next day when they moved out and continued their journey through a sodden world. The rain had stopped by then, but a gray mist clung to the trees and crawled down the hillsides. Everything dripped, and the party traveled mostly in silence.

They made their way south and east. Darlei had no idea where MacNabh's lands were located, where she would spend the rest of her life.

At Orle's persuasion, she tried to eat a few bits of breakfast as they jounced along in the wagon and then gave it up as impossible, too sick of stomach, too sick of heart. A dull numbness came over her as the day progressed. It was better not to feel, not to think at all, than to think of what was gone.

But her heart, her broken heart ached. How did a woman silence her heart?

She supposed a sharp blade would do it, and she considered that, she truly did. Better perhaps than the marriage ahead.

And anyway, if Deathan were right, if they'd known each other before, loved each other before, then she need only wait—alive or dead—for the wheel to turn once more.

Alive or dead.

Orle worried for her, tried fussing over her, and at last left her alone. Weary to the bones, but unwilling to succumb to tears again, Darlei endured the day's travel.

Far they went. Far over the stony shoulders of the mountains.

Over broad streams when she and Orle had to get out and ford on foot while the men got the wagon across. The streams were swollen from the rain. All the trees dripped water and the mist refused to rise.

The world wept.

But she could not. One more night on the trail, so Father said, and they would arrive at MacNabh's holding.

By the time that second morning arrived, Darlei had come to a conclusion. A woman strong enough to send away the man she loved, rather than see him die, must be strong enough to keep her chin high. To face what would come.

That morning, Orle fussed over Darlei's appearance as best she might in the confines of the wagon. They were both cramped and sore with jolting by then. Everything was damp. But they would arrive by noontime and Orle had determined that Darlei, a Caledonian princess, should look her best.

Indeed, at the last, when Urfet called to them that they approached MacNabh's lands, when guards met and halted them, then sent them on, Orle hung from the front of the wagon alongside the driver, trying to catch a glimpse.

Darlei took the opportunity to secrete a long knife beneath her overdress. It was stealing, for the men had left some of their extra weapons in the back of the wagon, but a woman, however strong, should not go unarmed to face her fate.

The sun struggled out as they rumbled along the stony track, and voices sounded ahead. Calling out to announce their arrival no doubt, and alert the chief. Darlei would see him soon. The man she was to wed.

"Darlei, come look," Orle called.

"What is it like?"

"A…a rough sort of place."

They had not been particularly welcome at Murtray. Even less so here, at Scotland's interior, where more recent battles had been fought. All one country now, as Kenneth MacAlpin commanded by decree.

She supposed a king could not be a king without imposing his will.

The wagon stopped moving. Father appeared at the front beside the driver.

"Daughter, come."

Her knees wobbled beneath her as she descended, but she managed to keep her chin high. A stone building stood before her, not as large or as well built as Murtray's keep. It lacked the walkways high behind the parapets where she'd so often seen—

Nay, do not think of that. Do not think of him.

A man was descending the stairs that led down from the main gate. A big man, he was, made to look even larger by the thick cloak he wore. Of middle years with black hair heavily streaked with gray, he carried an impatient, disagreeable expression.

Was this to be her husband? *Please, by all the powers, nay.*

Father led her forward, his grip tight on her arm. They met the large man at the bottom of the steps.

"Chief MacNabh?" Father asked. "I am King Caerdoc, and this is my daughter, Princess Darlei."

MacNabh's gaze swept over Darlei. Pale-blue eyes, he had, set disconcertingly under heavy black brows.

He snorted. "King, is it? And princess? There is but one king to my understanding, and he is busy interfering wi' our lives."

Father, seeming taken aback, said nothing.

MacNabh made a rough gesture. "I suppose ye had better come in. A hard journey, was it?"

"A wet one," Father replied, and gave a look to his men that said, *Some of you with me, and look lively.*

Three Caledonians came, including Urfet, their hands at their weapons.

MacNabh led them across an elevated entry to a second gate that opened to the keep proper. Curious faces stared from every hand. Only steps within, the hall opened up. A tall, chilly room full of wood smoke and containing still more people, who stared.

Darlei shivered with foreboding. She would not be happy

here. How could she be happy here?

All happiness lay behind her.

But she'd experienced it once, she reminded herself. She'd had him more than once. At least she'd not be sent here first to…

Suffer and perish. If her body did not, her spirit would.

"Come," MacNabh said. "This is my mother. And my mistress."

That put a check in Father's step. He parted his lips but did not speak.

The old woman, MacNabh's mother, was a crone. Clad in layers of rusty, dark clothing, she had a mouth devoid of teeth and scarcely any hair. Hardly the woman's fault, Darlei reminded herself. She could not help the changes brought by age.

But what of the disdain in her eyes? Might she help that? She was a far cry from gentle Mistress MacMurtray.

And the mistress—did that mean what Darlei thought?

As if to answer the question, MacNabh squeezed the woman's thigh as he passed her. "Roisin warms my bed."

The woman, surely two score years of age, directed at Darlei a look of sheer hate.

"These are Caledonians?" the old woman screeched. "Let us see. Are they blue?"

MacNabh waved a hand at her. "That died out long since, Mother."

To be sure, Caledonian men still carried tattoos. Designs that denoted their tribe, acquired when they pledged their fealty.

Darlei felt the men at her back stiffen, at least those who understood the Gaelic tongue.

"Ye are to marry that…lass?" Roisin sounded as if she'd wanted to select a different word for Darlei but had not quite dared.

"Aye, so I ha' told ye and told ye again. The king's orders."

"I did no' expect her to be so young."

"I can hear you, and understand your words," Darlei said in Gaelic.

MacNabh stepped up to her. His heavy features did not lighten and his pale eyes glared into hers. "Ye will speak when spoken to, miss."

Father's arm stiffened beneath Darlei's. She experienced her own surge of anger. Good. Mayhap anger would come to her rescue, make it possible to go on breathing.

Anger was easier to bear than grief.

Father said, "Chief MacNabh, I apprehend you are not in favor of this union."

"I am no'. I tell ye fairly, King Caerdoc, I had matters here arranged to my satisfaction already. My scold of a wife died last year—"

"Scold o' a wife!" the old woman echoed.

"—and I was set to handfast wi' Roisin when we had notice fro' the king." He scowled from beneath his brows. "His letter was quite specific and left little room for argument."

"Yes," Father said. "Still and all, if you are otherwise pledged, perhaps we should apply to the king." He sighed. "Though I have just come away from Forteviot."

"Nay, it will no' do a bit o' good. Naught to be done, but I'll tak' the lass off your hands."

Darlei nearly fell down where she stood, her despair worse for the glint of hope that had preceded it.

Father, bless him, seemed to ponder it and said, "I am not so certain."

Darlei turned to him and spoke low in their own tongue. "Father, please. Do not leave me here. I do not want—"

"Daughter, I can no longer tell what you want. You did not want to travel to Murtray. You did not want to wed with Rohr. You did not want to wed with that young man, his brother, who came after us seeking you. Now you do not want to be here either. Can I take such a complaint back to King Kenneth?"

"Yes," she beseeched him. "Please."

Slowly, even as her gaze clung to his, he shook his head. "Nay, daughter, let it be done. You chose your path back there along the trail."

Darlei nearly fell down. She had chosen her path, yes, merely to spare Deathan.

She was lost.

Father turned back to MacNabh. "Forgive us," he said, again in Gaelic. "I wanted to be certain of our intentions. When is the wedding to take place?"

MacNabh eyed Darlei unhappily before turning back to Father. "Will ye stay for it, King Caerdoc?"

"I will. But I must get home and back to my own affairs. This has all stretched out hideously long."

"I shall fetch the priest and the weddin' can take place in the morning. Ye can leave directly after, if it suits ye."

For one more moment, Father hesitated before he nodded briskly. "Yes. Let it be done."

He would leave her here in this dark and terrible place. Alone, save for Orle.

Less a wife than a captive, by order of the king.

$$\cdot\!\!\!-\!\!\!\Longleftrightarrow\!\!\!-\!\!\!\cdot$$

CHAPTER FORTY-THREE

MacNabh's keep, more a fortified house than aught else, proved a poor sort of place. Darlei was given a room to share with Orle that was small, cold, and, quite frankly, filthy. As they settled their belongings and tried to prepare for dinner—all their clothing being damp—even Orle fell silent, as if shocked out of her usual attempts at comforting optimism.

Darlei spoke to herself steadily. This was worse, far worse even than she'd imagined. MacNabh was worse, as was his terrible old mother—and the other, Roisin, that he kept at his side. How could she survive in this grim and comfortless place?

She would surely die by bits, body and spirit.

Yet Father was right. She had chosen this. Oh, not being sent away to wed by order of the king. But she had chosen to continue the journey here, to stop the combat between Deathan and Urfet that might have freed her.

She had chosen her fate. She must now be strong enough, woman enough to endure it—for his sake. But oh, she did not know how.

Dinner proved a poor meal served in a hall that was malodorous, barren, and cold. Dusty webs hung in the rafters. The food was meager, the meat stringy and, so Darlei feared, turned bad.

She could not eat and pushed her portion away. No one seemed to notice, or if they did, they ignored it. Conversation languished. The Caledonians sat on one side of the chamber and the clan members on the other, staring as if, indeed, they expected the blue men to draw swords and attack them.

If only they would.

Father's attempts to talk with their host fell flat. MacNabh ate like a ravenous boar, which Darlei concluded he fairly resembled. Mercifully, the ordeal did not last long, the courses being few, and ended when MacNabh said, "I ha' sent for the priest. He will be here by morning."

"I have my own holy man," Father put in. "If you want it done tonight."

Even as Darlei stared at Father in horror, MacNabh, with a glance at Roisin, said, "Nay, mornin' will be soon enough." He belched. "So long as the king's demands be met."

Darlei had never laid eyes on King Kenneth, she thought as she returned to her barren room, yet his demands ordered her life.

She and Orle lay in the same bed that night, for comfort. Darlei did not expect to sleep, though she must have dropped off before dawn, for she dreamed.

She dreamed of Deathan, only he was not Deathan. That was, he felt like Deathan, and her heart knew him as such, but he appeared different.

They were in a wee boat out upon a silver sea, naught but water to be seen in any direction. And, wonder of wonders, there was a hound with them in the bottom of the boat, a great, shaggy gray beast. It looked very much like a large version of the pups Deathan had showed her, back at Murtray.

A name flittered into her mind. *Wen.*

The man who was and was not Deathan pulled at the oars, taking her away—away from a place she loved.

He spoke to her, though in the way of dreams, his lips did not move. *Ye ha' done this before, alanna. Chosen as ye thought ye knew best. Made your choice out o' fear. When will ye believe? Believe in me.*

I will be my own woman. No one shall die for my sake.

He had beautiful gray-green eyes brimming with grief. *I will find ye. I will always find ye.*

She awoke with a start so violent it turned her stomach. Who was he, that man in the boat? Was he the Deathan who had been before?

Orle lay beside her, breathing deeply. The fire had run out of fuel and died.

Darlei faced a future so bleak that she did not know how she would survive it. She had the refuge, still, of dreams.

Morning came inevitably on the turn of the wheel. Gray light stole through the single, narrow window of Darlei's chamber as if it were offered as stingily as everything else here. Father came early to her door to make certain she would be ready for her wedding, though he did not linger long, as if he feared she would beg him for release.

She would not. She was her own woman now, and expected no one else to save her.

That strength, though, came accompanied by a numbing sense of unreality. She could not warrant that she had landed in this position, ended in this place. She could not be about to wed with that horrid, aged man who, if possible, wanted her even less than had Rohr MacMurtray.

A maid brought breakfast to the chamber, and Orle—who appeared nearly as upset by all that had happened as her mistress—once more begged Darlei to eat.

"You must take something. Scarcely any food passed your lips yesterday. You cannot go on so."

The breakfast, clearly leavings from last night's dinner, did not look appealing. Darlei shook her head.

"Darlei, please. It will be a long and difficult day. You will need your strength."

"I dare not, Orle. I will never keep it down."

Father returned to fetch her, when it was time. Dressed in his grandest clothing, he had Urfet at his back. The warrior eyed Darlei curiously, appearing detached from all sympathy, and she wondered, *How could I ever have thought him attractive?*

On the way to the hall, her knees trembled so violently that she had to clutch Father's arm. He said to her, in their own tongue, "Courage, daughter."

Easy for him to say. He would ride away from here, his obligation fulfilled.

As soon as they entered the hall, the merciful numbness took over. She could no longer feel the flagstones beneath her feet. She barely took in the tableau—MacNabh and another man who could only be the priest standing with Father's holy man, waiting for her with MacNabh's crone of a mother and, oddly, Mistress Roisin at his back. The dim air of the room danced before Darlei's eyes as if she were about to faint.

She barely heard and never after remembered the vows. Did she speak them in truth? She must have, for everyone looked satisfied and it was all swiftly done.

Was she wed? Wed to this dark and burly man whom she could smell even from two paces away?

It must be so.

Orle stepped up on her side and clutched her arm, or she would have fallen. MacNabh and Father stood talking, and Father told MacNabh, "Yes, we are near ready to leave." He turned away.

He never once looked at Darlei.

Yes, she had been willful in the past. A difficult daughter at times. A trial to him. Now he had washed his hands of her and showed no real regret in it.

She clutched Orle's hand. "Do not leave me."

"I will not."

"Ye"—MacNabh cast a look at her—"gae to yer chamber. I will be there anon."

He would be there?

"To complete the business," he told her as if he had heard the question.

Oh, nay. Oh, nay, not so soon. She had hoped, given the presence of Roisin, that he had no interest in *that.*

She must stop hoping.

They went, she and Orle, with Darlei's feet tripping on the stones. An argument broke out behind them.

"Ye will no' move that slag into yer chamber, will ye?" cried Roisin.

"Nay, nay, no' now."

"It is *our* chamber. I did no' wait so long for your scold o' a wife to die, only to be pushed out o' it."

"Calm yoursel', lass. But ye ken I maun finish the joining. Once I get her wi' child, it will be done."

Get her with child.

Orle's fingers tightened on Darlei's arm and clutched hard all the way to their chamber.

"Is there a way to bar the door?" Darlei asked then. Yes, she had chosen this. Opened herself to it. But now the wheel turned and she could not bear where it stopped.

"There is no bar." Orle sounded breathless. "And the furniture…"

The furniture was sparse and far too heavy for them to move, even working together. A chest. A tall cabinet. The bed.

Oh, by the gods, the bed.

"Can we get away?" Orle asked. "Before he comes."

"The window is too narrow." A mere slit in the stones. "He will not come till after Father leaves."

"Yes, but our party was ready to go."

"Mayhap he will not come till night."

Women survived this. She knew they did. But she belonged to Deathan. Deathan. *Deathan!*

His name became a cry in her mind. Oh, why had she sent him away?

She must be strong. Surely she possessed the required courage? She was a princess. A Caledonian. A woman with a wild heart. But oh, the numbness that sustained her failed. It failed her fast.

CHAPTER FORTY-FOUR

DEATHAN, HIDDEN BY the trees and well back from the heavily trodden trail that led to MacNabh's holding, studied the place through narrowed eyes. A fortified dwelling it was, built of stone on two levels, the ground floor no doubt being used for storage and for billeting animals and perhaps the guard, with an attached wall. The residents would live above, behind the sheer expanse of stone.

A grim sort of place, it made Da's holding look like a palace, which for certain it was not. He could scarce stand to think of Darlei here. He could scarce *stand*.

Yet he'd watched her enter yesterday afternoon. He'd watched her. Riding in the wagon with her woman through the rain.

He, himself, had been soaked to the skin. Hidden, invisible.

Now the rain had ceased—thank all the powers—and a chill struck him as he thought of her inside that place. Trapped. Frightened. He could feel her heart beating, sense her agitation.

"Please." He spoke to the air and the trees and the land itself. He did not know to whom else, save God. "Please."

He knew not what to do. How to make this terrible thing come right. He could not go riding in. They would not admit him. He could not challenge this MacNabh for her hand.

She had sent him away.

The morning light grew stronger around him. A gray sort of day it was, yesterday's clouds lingering. He could feel autumn in the air, the year beginning to die.

As must his heart, if Darlei was lost to him. He had followed her as always he must. He did not know how to win her free.

All the same, he did not, *could* not accept she had passed beyond his reach. If all he'd been imagining were true, if he had known her, loved her before in other lives, did that not mean they were meant to be together again in this one?

Mayhap not. They had met. Loved. He had possessed her for those fleeting, magical moments in his room and later, while his father's harper played.

Mayhap that was all. A kind of solace, as she'd claimed, meant to last the rest of his life.

For, eyeing the grim edifice of the house, he did not know— he did not know how to win her free.

His pony stirred behind him and snorted, as miserable as he. The poor beast wanted to go home. Deathan did not know if he could.

Yet he could not remain here forever, watching a stranger's dwelling while Darlei sought to take up a new life.

The trees around him dripped moisture. It sounded like a heartbeat. Hers, perhaps.

A spear of alarm went through him as the gates of the house opened and men began to spill through. Darlei's father, it was, emerging first, and was that MacNabh also, come after him? All King Caerdoc's men. Was Darlei with them? Had the plan changed? His own heart began to hammer double time.

With hope.

But nay. He did not see Darlei. Or her woman.

The Caledonians were leaving. The ponies were led out, and the wagon. King Caerdoc spoke with the dark-haired man who could only be MacNabh, and who after a few words stepped back.

The Caledonians rode out in fine order, moving in that fluid, almost magical way they did, heading east.

Without Darlei.

She had stayed. Stayed with the man Deathan could now see

reentering the house.

Her new husband.

Aye. Aye, it must be over and done, that wedding.

Grief swamped him. Grief and loss and despair so black that for several moments he could not see beyond it. Could not think, could not breathe.

How cruel, that the turning of the wheel had brought her to him, only to take her from his reach once more.

"GET OUT," MACNABH said to Orle as he came through the chamber door. He had not knocked or otherwise requested leave before he entered. He owned the place. Darlei supposed he believed he owned her.

Orle clung to Darlei, bless her, until MacNabh fixed those pale eyes on her and again snarled, "Get out."

Orle went with a terrified, regretful look for Darlei. Where, Darlei could not begin to guess.

MacNabh turned his gaze on her. Eyed her up and down slowly.

"I suppose ye will do. Yer father says ye be un-breached. In fact, he was quite indignant about me askin'. As if a princess could no' be other than a virgin. I told him, and I'll tell ye, I will be certain ye do no' come to me wi' another man's brat in yer belly."

Another man's child. Deathan's. Could it be?

Not waiting to hear her answer, MacNabh began unfastening his cloak. His belt.

"There will ha' to be a child. Among other reasons, I need an heir and Roisin is past it, even if I am no'. My bitch o' a wife never gave me sons. There were daughters—long married and gone now. Though ye would no' warrant it likely, I am nearly sixty years old."

He laid aside the belt that held his knife and other weapons

Darlei did not pause to identify.

"Mayhap ye'll do better, eh?" He flipped up the folds of his kilt. He wore nothing beneath.

"Oh—" Darlei began on a gasp of air.

"On the bed. Let us get this o'er with. No' that way." She scuttled on her bum atop the counterpane, away from him. "On yer face, so that I do no' ha' to look at ye."

He tossed Darlei face down on the bed. Hauled her so her legs hung halfway off. When he tossed her skirts over her head, he found the long knife she'd stolen from the wagon, seized it with a grunt, and flung it away, toward the door.

Leaving her defenseless.

"Brace yersel', lass." Her undergarments tore.

Darlei did not have to feign the discomfort of a maidenhead breached. What he did to her hurt. Pain, outrage, terror, and violation all chased the numbness away. She kept silent only because her face, buried in the counterpane, did not afford her the breath to scream.

Once he finished grunting, he fell silent. Darlei lay where she was with tears trickling down her cheeks.

When he spoke again, it was in another tone—angry.

"So, yer father lied to me."

She drew herself up and away, limbs under her, onto the bed, and stole a look at him. He examined the counterpane.

"Ye are no' un-breached."

"My father did not know." From somewhere she summoned the dignity to speak. "I—"

"Filthy savage." To her complete astonishment, he struck her across the face, knocking her sideways across the bed. The sting of it broke through the last of her numbness and set her senses screaming. "No' bad enough I am forced to wed wi' an accursed blue wench, to keep the king's favor. Now I'll ha' to wait till ye bleed, to be sure whatever babe I get upon ye be mine."

He put his belt back on around his portly waist and snatched up his cloak, fixing Darlei with a stern eye.

"Ye will let me know."

Let him know? As if she might be eager ever to have him touch her again. The breath left her body in a hiss.

"Meanwhile," he tossed at her, "stay here in yer room unless I send for ye. We do no' wish to lay eyes on ye." He caught up the long knife from the stone floor and slammed out of the chamber.

Orle ran in, eyed Darlei crouched on the bed, and opened her arms. "Oh, Darlei, are you all right?"

Was she? Physically, no. A welt rose on her cheek where MacNabh had struck her, and she felt battered inside, as she never had at Deathan's hands.

Deathan.

Spiritually, she was near shattered. Broken. She wanted naught so much as to hide—here in this terrible little chamber, if possible.

No one was coming to save her. If she survived this, she would have to save herself. Become the wild woman the Gaels thought her.

How? How might she drag herself up from this abject misery?

"Darlei." Orle smoothed the tangled hair back from Darlei's face and asked again, "Are you all right?"

"I will be." As soon as she stopped shaking. She was a princess, was she not? A Caledonian. The woman Deathan loved.

Out of the fear and dread, another emotion came stealing.

MacNabh might be her husband. But he would never do that to her again.

CHAPTER FORTY-FIVE

DEATHAN RODE THROUGH the gates of MacNabh's fortified dwelling at an easy pace, doing his best to appear nothing more than a humble supplicant. Not too difficult a role to play. After days of rain, he was damp and filthy, and no doubt appeared as desperate as he felt.

But nay, *desperate* did not fully describe the emotions that filled him. He was indignant, apprehensive, and fearful on Darlei's behalf. So angry he could barely see straight.

Her father, who claimed to value her, had ridden off and left her at this grim place.

Deathan, who loved her, would not do the same.

He had been watching for two days and had caught not so much as a glimpse of her. Now the sun had come out, and the place had awakened, armed men hanging about and women emerging to do laundry.

The gates stood open when he rode in beneath the morning sun, but guards stepped forward immediately to bar his way.

"Who are ye and wha' d'ye want here?"

"A traveler looking for work," he stated with a casualness he did not feel.

They eyed him, the one man older and the other still green.

"We ha' all the help we need," said the elder. "On yer way."

"I am good wi' horses and no' bad at all wi' a sword," Deathan said as if he had not heard. "I was wi' MacLeod of Lewis before he disbanded us. I will work for my keep, just need a dry place to sleep if I might."

The two men exchanged a look.

"Our chief is Dunstoch MacNabh. He does no' hire swords. I am called Ardroch, head o' the guard and overseer o' pretty much all else." He eyed Deathan once more, thoughtfully. "That is a fine pony."

"Aye. Trained him up mysel'. But he could use a good feed."

"I suppose I could use help in the stables. If ye will work for yer food and yer pony's feed, I can tak' ye on for a few days."

"Master Ardroch—" the youth began to object.

"Whisht, Seumas. The chief does no' have to know."

"I'm grateful." Deathan swung down from his pony to find Ardroch continuing to eye him.

"That is a good sword, as well."

"I earned it. And then I hired it out."

"Ye will no' get the pay ye likely deserve here." Ardroch's expression turned sour. "Nobody does. But if ye work well, I can offer ye room in the stable."

"I ask nay more."

He was in. Ardroch gestured the lad back to guard the gate and led Deathan off toward a group of tumbled outbuildings.

Not a very prepossessing place, this, and Deathan wondered how MacNabh had found favor enough with the king to win a Caledonian princess.

"Wha' sort o' family is it here?" he asked as they went, the folk in the yard slanting him curious glances.

"Och, MacNabh is a careful sort o' man."

"Careful?"

"Wi' his coin and wi' his affairs. I will no' say overmuch, as he is my cousin."

"Och, aye. I do no' mean to offend."

"Ye ha' not. This is an old holding he got from his brother, who dropped down dead one day, unexpected."

"A sudden illness, was it?"

Expressionless, Ardroch said, "A dirk in the back. I tell ye this only to warn ye, this can be a fractious sort o' place. MacNabh has a temper and is no' afraid to unleash it."

A chill chased its way up Deathan's spine. He did not want Darlei at the hands of such a man.

"I would," Ardroch continued, "keep out o' his way, if I were ye. In fact, I will no' tell him ye are here. A few days work only, aye?"

"Aye. Is it a large family, in the house?"

"Nay. Just our laird's old mother, the *cailleach*. The chief's wife died last year and his daughters are grown and gone. But he has taken a new wife now, so who knows?"

"Ah. Ha' ye seen her?"

Ardroch gave him a sharper look, as if that were a strange thing to ask. "Just a glimpse before the wedding. But I will tell ye—she is a Caledonian. One o' them wild savages, ye ken. Supposed to be some kind o' princess."

"Och, I would like a glimpse o' a wild woman."

"Ye will no' have it. Like I said, keep out o' MacNabh's way. Come on."

The quarters were not good, and the work—a mountain of manure to be raked out and moved away past the retaining wall—hard and lowly. But Ardroch did feed Deathan first and allow his pony feed and a rubdown.

Deathan did not mind the hard work. He'd often done as much at home. But it took him behind the wall and out of sight of the stone house, where he had a hope of seeing Darlei.

Not much of a hope at all.

But she was here, and he could almost feel her behind the sheer stone walls. She rode the wheel of fortune.

He wanted to seize that wheel in both hands and drag it to a halt. Pluck her off.

How did MacNabh treat her? Had she been forced to lie with him? Frustration combined with the sheer torment of not knowing. If he could only see her with his own eyes.

Only he did not. Two days blurred into three. Ardroch must

have liked the way he worked, for he kept him on and set him working with the ponies, bidding him only, "Keep out o' sight. The chief still does no' ken ye be here."

"Understood," Deathan agreed. But he wanted to storm that stone wall. He wanted inside. To see her, to save her.

For now, he was near her. He told himself it must be enough.

DARLEI DREAMED OF Deathan. Again and again, she did.

There was not much to do here at MacNabh's stronghold but sleep. She and Orle were shut into her chamber all day and all night, and boredom fought with the sickening fear that MacNabh would come back looking for his rights.

If he did, Darlei just might have to kill him.

The anger had not deserted her, but it simmered like a covered pot on the fire. She had no weapon. She'd lost her small knife somewhere, possibly at Murtray, and MacNabh had taken the one she'd stolen from the cart. She and Orle both had searched the chamber for another, to no avail. Unless she wanted to bash MacNabh over the head with a filled chamber pot—a fitting end for him, in her opinion—she stood helpless. Armed only with this anger and the remnants of her pride.

So she slept away as much time as she could, and she dreamed of Deathan.

At least, she thought she dreamed only of him, though he came to her in more than one guise. The tall man she had seen before with the bright-hazel eyes and the auburn mane, a silver sword in his hand, riding aboard a chariot. The man from the wee boat with the rich brown hair and gray eyes, speckled with green. *Her husband.* The man she knew with the quick, rare smile, the gentle hands, and eyes that reflected the sea.

He was near to her, so near she could feel him. Only, how could he be?

She had sent him away. Back home.

Yet she dreamed he spoke to her. Made love to her in all his guises. She woke longing to weep and would not give in to the tears.

The dreams made her begin to understand, to comprehend what Deathan had tried so hard to tell her. Their love was not new. They had loved each other before on previous turns of the wheel.

That meant she had lost him before, this man she adored. She must have parted from him, if only at the impetus of old age.

More merciful, perhaps, not to remember. And if this dream of living life after life proved true, was that not so? People did fail mostly to remember.

She knew why. Remembering hurt too terribly.

Almost better never to have known Deathan MacMurtray.

Nay, not that. She would trade her very life for what she'd had of him.

She began to believe she would die here, shut away in this dim, airless room. Prey to her fear and her dread.

Only her anger, and her love, kept her alive.

CHAPTER FORTY-SIX

T HE KNOCK AT the chamber door caused both Darlei and Orle to jump violently. For days uncounted they had been left alone. That was, a maid brought their food and drink. A lad brought fuel for their meager fire and took away the soiled chamber pot. A furtive-looking woman did some minimal cleaning.

When the knock sounded, it was the wrong time of day for any of them.

She and Orle looked at each other. Dread clenched Darlei's belly, enough to turn her sick.

"I must answer it," Orle said.

Oh, and what would she have done all this while without the brave Orle? Loyal and steadfast she was, even while sharing this dreadful imprisonment.

"If it is him," Darlei said, "pray, do not leave me." They spoke in their native tongue so they did not fear being overheard.

Orle nodded and hauled open the door.

It was not MacNabh but his aged mother.

The old woman came pushing into the chamber wrapped in her ragged shawl, already squawking. Of all the Gaels Darlei had met so far, she found this woman most difficult to understand.

The old woman tottered past Orle and half mumbled, half screeched something at Darlei.

Darlei shook her head. "I am sorry?"

"Are ye deaf, wench?"

Even a deaf person would be able to catch that penetrating whine.

"I said my son sent me."

Apprehension tightened Darlei's stomach still farther.

"He wants to ken, are ye bleedin'?"

"What?"

"Ha' ye had yer monthly! Daft bitch," Mistress MacNabh added, not quite under her breath. "He needs tae ken."

Darlei exchanged a desperate look with Orle. She had indeed been visited by her round and had herself washed the cloths, hoping to keep it secret.

She dared not let MacNabh know.

"Not yet," she said with what dignity she could muster.

"Ye're lyin'! The woman what cleans in here says she saw the blood."

"That was me." Orle stepped forward bravely. "Mine."

Mistress MacNabh turned a fierce gaze on Orle. She had the same pale-blue eyes as her son, stark in her impossibly wrinkled face.

"Liar," she said again. "There was blood in yon bed."

"We share the bed, my servant and me." Orle was so much more than a servant. But Darlei had to speak what this old woman would understand.

Mistress MacNabh snorted. "Is that wha' ye Caledonians do? Women sleep together?"

"When we need comfort." The words went over the crone's head.

"I will tell my son. I will tell him I think ye be lyin'. He will come to see for himsel'."

See for himself? How, by stripping her down? Darlei shuddered.

"Meanwhile, ye are to come out to supper."

"Me?" Darlei laid a hand upon her breast. "Why?"

"How should I know? Ye be his wife. Ye will do as he commands."

The crone went out. Orle hurried to shut the door behind her, giving them a glimpse of the guard who stood beyond.

Darlei and Orle stared at one another in horror.

"She did not believe us," Darlei said.

"Nay."

"Oh, what am I to do?"

DARLEI HAD FORGOTTEN how badly the hall stank. Her chamber did not smell fresh either, having two women shut in with a chamber pot and precious little water for washing.

She had never in her life lived so, and these people called *hers* savages. But MacNabh's hall smelled of spoiled meat, and the rotted straw on the floor, and the urine of dogs—of sheer filth.

It smelled of MacNabh himself, and when the wave of it hit Darlei, it took her immediately back to her first day of marriage. MacNabh pushing her face down on the bed.

She'd been wrapped in a cloud of his stink while he did what he did.

It made her falter as she entered the chamber, caused her hard-held dignity to waver. She did not know what she'd expected when summoned to dinner. That there would be company, mayhap. That Father and his party might have returned to take her away again.

The room, though, contained but a single board. The few attendees were MacNabh himself, his mother, Roisin, and assorted servants.

"Come, sit," MacNabh called to her.

The day had seemed more like late than early autumn, the air coming through Darlei's slit window cool. The hall felt cold, and the fire struggled to burn, filling the space once more with smoke. A meager meal already lay spread out.

The three sat ranged on one side. A single bench faced them.

Darlei seated herself there.

MacNabh eyed her with a conspicuous lack of welcome, Roisin with open hatred. The old woman—well, she quite frankly appeared mad.

A servant came and began passing the platters.

"How are ye finding your stay?" MacNabh asked.

Darlei stared. She said nothing.

"How d'ye find your room now ye've had time to settle?"

"Small. We find it small." *And cold. And barren.*

"'Tis no' a grand house," the old woman whined. "No' big at all. My own husband raised it, ye ken."

"You may send your woman to the servants' hall, if ye will," MacNabh suggested.

"Nay, I want her with me," Darlei replied.

"There is no larger chamber. Save mine." His pale-blue eyes met Darlei's for an instant. Her stomach turned over.

"Nay. We are well enough."

"I will no' have it," Roisin wailed. "I will no' ha' *that* in your chamber. She should be housed out in the stables." She bared her teeth at Darlei. "Animal."

"Are you afraid of me? Like a wild beast?" Darlei fixed the woman with an unwavering stare.

"Afraid? Nay, bitch, why should I be?"

"Enough o' this. I had *hoped*"—MacNabh accompanied the words with a stare of disapproval—"we could get along. Ye be my wife and canna be shut awa' forever."

"Should the king come," the old woman said, wagging her finger at Darlei, "he will need to see ye."

"*Is* the king coming?" Darlei asked, startled.

"He may be, he may be. 'Tis rumored he will do a tour this autumn wi' his new wife. He will want to see ye." MacNabh fixed her with a stare. "He will want to see ye with child."

"Oh." So that was it. No kindness, this, no concern. Only the fear of accountability to a higher power.

"I ha' sent word to him by messenger," MacNabh said dutifully, "that his decree has been carried out, and we are wed. Should he decide to come and see…"

MacNabh did not finish the thought. He did not need to. Should the king include this place in his tour, all must appear well. And he would want to assure his liege that she carried his child.

She pushed her platter away. "If the king comes, I shall tell him how you have mistreated me."

"Wha'?" MacNabh roared, and his old mother squealed.

"I will tell him I am naught more than a prisoner here. That you shut me away from the daylight and half starve me."

"Wicked wench!" Roisin breathed. "Dunstoch, ye should do awa' wi' her."

MacNabh swiveled to look at his mistress. "Do awa' wi' her? With the king on his way?"

Roisin's eyes gleamed with malice. "Ye can say she suffered some mishap. Fell down the well, mayhap, and that ye be a widower—again. Ye will ha' obeyed him all the same, aye?"

Darlei pushed to her feet. The same end for her that Caragh had suggested. The very same. "You will keep away from us, from my servant and me. Else I will tell the king how you mistreat a Caledonian princess. How you forced me and starve me."

MacNabh rose to his feet also, though he made no move to come around the table. "Ye mad bitch."

"Aye, she is mad!" Roisin agreed. "Ye do no' want a child out o' that."

Nay, he did not. So Darlei hoped.

Her legs trembled beneath her as she left the chamber. And she had to remind herself again that she was strong. She was angry. She was a wild woman.

And even though her heart had been torn from her chest, she would fight to survive.

CHAPTER FORTY-SEVEN

THE DAYS CREPT by, all back-breaking labor and short rations, deeper into autumn. Deathan lived in the stables with the animals for which he cared, and ached for a glimpse of Darlei.

Ardroch kept him on because he worked hard and was indeed a good hand with the ponies. Deathan doubted MacNabh knew he was here. He had not seen the man but in passing.

He saw Darlei not at all. No one in the household so much as spoke of her. Deathan began to think she was not still here after all.

How could it be that the master of the place had a new wife and yet no one spoke of it?

He did not see her, nay, nor hear of her, but sometimes he could swear he felt her. There behind the face of the sheer stone wall. Shut away from him.

It might be fancy, and more than once when his heart flagged, he contemplated leaving. The wheel of time upon which they both rode may have turned, taking them away from each other, to meet no more.

The very idea made him ache, and he rejected it. Leaving here without knowing, without seeing her, felt like abandonment. He must be available and close at hand, if she needed him.

A rumor circulated that the high king might be going to visit as part of an autumn tour, though why the man should want to view such a squalid place as this, Deathan could not imagine. But MacNabh must be held in some favor, or King Kenneth never would have chosen him to wed the Caledonian king's daughter, in Rohr's wake.

Those with whom Deathan lived and worked were quite excited by the prospect of a royal visit, despite the fact that there was much to be done in preparation. A large measure of the routine work fell to Deathan, as the others were called upon to repair walls and even perform work inside.

"Though I hate to say it," stated Ardroch, "the hall smells like a killing field. I canna imagine welcoming in a king."

Ardroch had taken to speaking to Deathan as he might to himself in unguarded moments. Since Deathan rarely answered and merely absorbed what information came his way, the man no doubt did not consider such talk indiscreet.

"I could maybe help in the hall," Deathan did say from time to time. He had to find a way to get inside. To lay eyes on Darlei, if she were still there.

"Nay, nay, ye are best keepin' to yer own patch."

The members of MacNabh's guard were a taciturn lot who did not speak much either. Despite the excitement over a proposed royal visit, they did not appear happy to be taken from their regular duties to tote stone or, worse, be compelled to help with women's work inside.

Deathan labored. He watched. He ached. Sometimes late at night, when he lay alongside his charges, he willed Darlei to know that he was here. Close at hand. Defiant of her orders to leave. How could he leave when it had taken him a lifetime to find her? Until the turn of life's wheel proved they had been truly parted, he would not stir. No matter how grim his life became.

DARLEI HAD SLIPPED into a state of despondency so deep, she did not know how to climb out again. A pestilence, she discovered, having nothing to do. She and Orle devised a few games to pass the time in their imprisonment—for she could term it naught else—but soon tired of even these.

Her heart longed endlessly for Deathan. For his touch. For the scent of him and the smile in his eyes. For his kisses dropped into the palms of her hands.

She had sent him away.

Yes, and it was for the best. He could not save her from this—and, were he here, he would try. Risk himself yet again. Her greatest fear.

She imagined him back at Murtray. Picking up the pieces of his life. Moving through his days. Would Rohr marry? He must, for Caragh's pregnancy would have progressed by now. Clan life would go on, and people would forget to talk. Eventually they would forget their future chief's first child had arrived early.

But none of that concerned her now. She lived in a constant state of boredom mixed with dread, always listening for Mac-Nabh's heavy step.

Only her anger sustained her, and she fanned it as she could. Was she not a Caledonian princess? Proud enough and strong enough—so she hoped—to save herself.

But not too proud to cry. For some nights while Orle slept, tears trickled down into the bolster like rain.

So close had they come, she and Deathan, to spending this lifetime together. Only to be parted. And she was to endure this life without him.

One afternoon, a step did indeed sound outside the door. An order was given to the guard stationed there and the bar lifted. Darlei's heart leaped with apprehension.

It was not MacNabh come calling, but Roisin.

The woman wore a sour look on her face and had a bundle of garments in her arms. Their bright colors seemed to make her look older by contrast, her complexion turned sallow.

Her dark eyes snapped at Darlei as she pushed her way in.

"MacNabh has sent me. I would no' be here otherwise, so ye may be certain." She paused, the clothing clutched to her chest, and drew a breath. "We ha' had a message. Fro' the king's herald."

"Oh?" Darlei exchanged a swift look with Orle.

"We are on his planned route, though the messenger was no' able to tell us when His Majesty will arrive. No matter. We maun be ready when he does. Ye"—Roisin raked Darlei with a glance of pure hatred—"maun be presented to him then, and ye canna be wearing any savage Caledonian clothing. Ye being a proper MacNabh woman and all, now."

Darlei was nothing of the sort, but surprise kept her from saying so.

"I will fit ye for proper dress. These garments are mine that no longer fit me. We shall see wha' may be done."

"You?" Darlei managed.

"I was a seamstress once before I caught MacNabh's eye, and am still a good hand wi' a needle."

Incredulity nearly kept Darlei silent. She gazed at Roisin and said, "I do not want you touching me."

"List to me, mistress. I would as like see ye dead and cold as look at ye, but I am doin' this for Dunstoch's sake, none other. Now, strip down."

Darlei did, down to her chemise and not without embarrassment.

Roisin eyed her disparagingly. "No' much to ye under that garb, is there? No doubt ye are no' increasing—yet. I doubt ye'll be able to gi' him the son he craves, scrawny as ye be."

Darlei said nothing.

"Here, come to the window that I may see about this color for ye. Face the light."

Darlei did so, gazing past the woman in an effort to combat her humiliation, reaching for what little freedom she could see. The afternoon sunlight slanted from the west. She had but a glimpse of green lawn, here at the side of the house away from the yard. And there...

Nay, it could not be.

A man pushed a barrow, one heavily loaded with manure, on an angle that just caught her line of sight. The afternoon sun shone down on him, pricking out copper lights in a mane of dark-blond hair.

She knew him. Knew the way he moved. The bunch of muscles in his arms and back. Her heart knew and her soul did and—

Nay, she must be mad. She must indeed have lost the last of her senses. He could not be here. She had told him she did not want him.

But she had lied, and he knew it. If he knew anything, it was that.

She threw herself at the window, brushing Roisin aside from where she stood trying to use the light. The woman swore and stared in affront.

"Wha' are ye doing? Ye be a madwoman."

The man was gone, moved out of the narrow view on offer. Darlei's heart pounded so hard that she thought for an instant she would pass out.

"Are ye ill?" It was Orle moving forward to Darlei's side, speaking in their own tongue.

"Yes," Darlei said. "I do not feel well."

Orle turned on Roisin, speaking now in her heavily accented Gaelic. "She is ill. You will leave her alone."

Roisin's features drooped with offended dislike. "Do no' speak to me so. Ye upstart! I will no' be ordered about in my own home."

"It is her home, is it not? Darlei is the chief's wife."

"I maun get her fitted for a gown. When the king comes—"

Orle plucked a gown at random from the lot. "This one. Alter this one to fit her."

Roisin harumphed and glared at Darlei, who now leaned against the narrow stone windowsill like a woman who had been struck to the heart.

"Just go."

Roisin flounced out, and the door clanged shut behind her.

Orle swiftly put her arms around Darlei. "Princess, what is it?"

"I think—I think I am going mad."

"Small wonder, with all you have had to bear. Come sit down. There is some water yet."

They were strictly limited on daily water being provided—but one ewer a day for the both of them. A prison.

Darlei allowed herself to be led away from the window where she had seen—

Nay. It could not be so.

Yet everything within her leaped with belief, and she felt the wheel of her life turn.

CHAPTER FORTY-EIGHT

"COME," DEATHAN CRIED as cheerfully as he could, though he felt anything but. "A man canna work all the time. Will no' one o' ye give me some sport?"

He sat in a group of MacNabh's men gathered in the yard, taking what passed for a breather in the pale sunshine.

They had come to accept him, these men. Especially since news had arrived that King Kenneth's tour of the country would indeed swing by this place. MacNabh had decided the holding must present a respectable face. There was work to do from morning to night, and an extra pair of hands, willing to labor hard, was welcome.

Deathan had wormed his way in. He just did not know how to make it serve him.

He doubted MacNabh's dwelling could achieve respectability even if they labored for years. But much of the litter had been cleared away, and he could attest that the stables at least were tidy, their inhabitants, which included his own pony, benefiting much from his attentions.

What might be said about the house, he did not know. Female servants emerged on occasion to shake out clothes and tapestries.

He had never set foot inside and still did not know if MacNabh realized he had taken on a new man.

He had made it his sole intention to get inside. To lay eyes upon Darlei if he could. Because he'd begun to doubt she was there, even though…

Aye, there were still times he could almost feel her, feel her beating heart. A wild woman, pent up. Hurt. *Angry.*

She had spirit, did his Darlei. Spirit enough to tell him to go away and leave her, for his sake. That had happened before, so he suspected, on other turns of fate's wheel, in other lives. She feared for him enough to sacrifice herself.

He loved her enough to stay.

But he did not know what had happened behind those sheer stone walls. Had MacNabh abused her? Beaten her? Raped her repeatedly? If she was his wife, none would gainsay him.

And how much could even a woman with such a valiant heart as Darlei's endure?

He maun get inside.

Ardroch rolled his eyes. "Wha' d'ye ha' in mind?"

Deathan liked Ardroch. In fact, he liked many of this motley crew, having got to know them. They suffered as he did and served MacNabh mainly because there were ties of blood and loyalty.

He hoped Ardroch would not get into trouble, having hired him on, after he killed MacNabh.

For he did intend to kill MacNabh.

Playing at the careless rogue—a role he'd adapted here— Deathan said, "A contest at arms, perhaps. To prove we are still men and no' mere maids. I will tak' on any o' ye."

He had told them he was a western mercenary fallen on hard times, which explained his good pony and his even better sword.

There was a collective groan. "Och," said Ardroch, "who has the strength left to fight? If ye do, ye must be born o' the gods."

"Ye have turned into scrub women." Deathan put scorn in his voice. "Is there no one who will face me as a man?"

Ardroch eyed him with some interest. As the head of Mac-Nabh's guard, he was reputed to be among the best of his fighters. "Wha' do I get if I win?"

"The right to boast o' it."

"Och, well, that is naught."

"If ye best me—that is, either disarm me or draw first blood—I will do some o' your work as well as my own."

Another of the guards, Nielan, sat up straighter. "Does that go for any o' us?"

"Indeed it does. I will face all o' ye, if ye like."

"And do all our work after?" someone said, laughing. "That I would like to see."

"I will perform some o' your tasks, aye. No' all."

"If ye'd haul stone fro' the quarry, I'd be grateful," Nielan said.

"Face me, then." Deathan got to his feet. "I will fetch my sword."

"Ah, now," Ardroch objected, "wha' if MacNabh should find us all bleeding?"

"The chief need no' ken. And the westerner canna best all o' us." Nielan likewise got to his feet. "Go on, then, mercenary. Fetch yer sword."

Deathan did, his heart beating high up in his chest. He might have one chance to make this work—but one.

His sword felt good, if a bit foreign, in his hand. It had been a while since he'd trained with the members of Da's guard back home. He'd spent far too much time with the handle of a shovel gripped between his fingers.

He grinned as he jogged back out. In his absence, MacNabh's men had formed a rough circle, eager for a show.

He meant to give them one.

Nielan, too, had fetched his sword. A man of a score and some, maybe a few years Deathan's senior, he wore shabby MacNabh tartan and had tied his long brown hair back out of his eyes.

Not a complete stranger to combat, then.

Deathan measured him carefully, his thoughts racing. Could he best the man? Aye. For Darlei, he could do anything. But he would have to try to make it look convincing.

From the first the two swords met, Deathan knew he would have to be careful. Nielan possessed a wicked arm, and his lazy demeanor disappeared into a cool and calculating mien. He wanted to show off before his clansmen, against the boastful interloper.

He just might.

They circled and struck and circled, and the observers backed off a respectful distance, their bone-deep weariness quickly evaporating in enthusiasm. Like Gaels everywhere, they loved a show. Especially one that interrupted tedium.

Most of them called out encouragement for Nielan, but there were a few quips and cheers when Deathan got in a good blow. He felt better, stronger, as his muscles warmed. A measure of skill awoke inside, coming from so deep a place he barely recognized it. He grinned at his opponent.

The combat became a dance. Strike, step, turn, strike again from a different angle. Whirl. He was careful to measure his blows and make sure Nielan could block them.

Nielan began to sweat. Eyes narrowed in a face gone tense, he increased the pace, determined not to be bested by a hired sword. Him, one of MacNabh's best.

Step, block, absorb the impact of Nielan's strength, turn. Deathan let the inner knowledge arise and possess him.

A flurry, a bunching of muscle, a burst of speed, and Nielan's sword went flying out of his hand to land embedded, point down, in the turf of the yard.

The onlookers cheered. They did, regardless of whom they had backed, because they were Gaels after all, and because it was such a beautiful thing to watch.

Deathan lowered his sword, breathing hard. What would Nielan do? Meet him with aggression? Had he made an enemy he did not need?

To his surprise, Nielan grinned ruefully and shrugged at the onlookers. He retrieved his sword and looked at Deathan with a new expression in his eyes.

"How did ye do that?"

Deathan shrugged also. "Practice." *Ancient practice, mayhap.* "I thought ye had me there, once or twice."

"Aye." The onlookers, Nielan's friends, after all, took it up and showed him admiration. But there were those who congratulated Deathan also, and eyed him with speculation not unlike Nielan's.

Would he be able to convince another to take him on? Would a string of victories win his way inside the house?

"Come," Ardroch said. "Enjoyable as that was—and I canna say I've had a better time in a fortnight—we maun get back to work."

Aye so. Deathan followed him meekly back to the stable where he both lived and labored. He put his sword away carefully. He would do whatever he must to get near the woman he loved.

⬦

CHAPTER FORTY-NINE

Mistress Roisin returned the next day with a garment for Darlei to try on. She eyed Darlei warily and seemed unwilling to get close to her, bidding Orle instead to help her mistress try on the garment.

"Och," she said in disgust when the garment hung on Darlei's frame. "'Tis still too large. There is naught to ye."

"Can you wonder?" Orle faced off against the woman again. "It is not healthy shut in here all the while. She needs leave to go outside."

Darlei's heart leaped. Was it possible? If she were permitted to go outside, she might glimpse the man she'd seen yesterday. Discover whether she'd deceived herself, and sheer longing had made her think she saw what she had not.

She might even be able to spy a means of escape.

But Roisin's eyes narrowed. "So she can run like a hare? Nay, no' with the king coming."

But the mistress must have spoken to MacNabh about it, for later that day MacNabh's old mother turned up at the door, a stout guardsman behind her.

"Ye're to come out to supper," she croaked.

Darlei's heart fell. *Not that, again.* "Why?"

"Ne'er mind that. Ye will do as yer husband directs."

Darlei exchanged a look with Orle and snatched up her shawl, though she could think of few things less appealing than another meal with that crew. She hated leaving Orle imprisoned

270

here alone.

As before, MacNabh and Roisin were already ranged at the table when the old woman ushered Darlei in. The room, though, had been cleaned, much of the random debris gathered and disposed, the rushes swept up and fresh ones put down over the stones. The great wafts of dusty webs that had stretched aloft were gone. As was a goodly portion of the reek.

Indeed, much of the remaining bad smell came from the current occupants.

"Sit," MacNabh ordered Darlei without wasting breath on any other greeting. But he examined her closely. "Ye're to eat."

Servants began passing the platters. The food—pottage and a portion of greasy boiled meat—did not look appetizing.

"Are ye sickening for somewhat?" MacNabh demanded as he tore into his food. "Roisin says ye be naught but skin over bones."

Darlei said nothing. She stared at her platter with dismay.

The old mother said something to MacNabh that Darlei did not understand.

MacNabh barked at Darlei, "Be ye sure ye are no' wi' child?"

"She is no'," Roisin answered for her. "I would ha' seen."

"There has no' been time to show," MacNabh told his mistress. "I bedded her but the once."

"'Twould be a fine thing," the crone whined, "could ye tell the king she is bearing, when he comes."

Darlei began to shake. She could not endure that again, could not allow this beast of a man to violate her when she loved—

Deathan.

Her heart cried out for him even as her lips remained silent. Had she not chosen this path for his sake? Could she not then endure the price of his safety?

But nay. *Not that.*

"It would," MacNabh said, speculation in his eyes.

"She will ne'er carry to term if she is skin and bones," Roisin declared. "Ye maun get some flesh on her first. Eat, lass."

Darlei poked at her food, unable to choke down more than a

morsel.

Roisin gestured at her and said to MacNabh, "Ye canna show *that* to the king. Pale o' cheek and scrawny as a dyin' hen."

Darlei spoke for the first time. "I need to go outside. I need the air. I cannot survive shut away in that chamber day and night."

They all stared at her as if they'd forgotten she could speak.

Before they recovered, she went on, "I am naught but a prisoner—me, a princess. I shall tell the king so when he comes."

"Weel now!" MacNabh drew himself up and his eyes narrowed to slits.

Roisin snapped, "Ye are no' a prisoner, stupid wench, but a wild thing. Must no' wild things be kept carefully?"

"Shut yer trap," MacNabh told her. His gaze, still narrowed, remained fixed on Darlei. "Ye think to ruin my good favor wi' the king?"

Darlei pressed her lips together.

"Well, ye canna. The king and I were comrades in arms long ago and fought together against yer kind. I doubt much ye can turn him against me."

"He did not intend for you to keep me pent up captive. For you to starve me."

"We ha' no' starved ye, wretched bitch!" Roisin burst forth. "There has been food ye refuse to eat."

"I am sick for lack of the sky," Darlei said. "For the open air." For sight of the man she thought she'd glimpsed.

"By God." MacNabh put down his own knife. "I rue the day I e'er had a letter fro' the king. Woman, this is a workin' house wi' much activity in readiness for His Majesty's visit. I ha' no garden where ye can stroll."

"Allow me, then, out into the yard." She had thought about it much. Estimated the angle from whence the man with his barrow had come.

"Too dangerous. There are men repairing the walls. Moving stone."

The old woman babbled again. "Let her come down here part o' each day. Out o' the room."

MacNabh sighed. "I suppose that will be all right. Though someone will ha' to watch her closely." He pointed at Roisin. "Ye."

"Och, is it no' enough I ha' to sacrifice one o' my dresses as well as sew on it for her?"

"Ye will do as ye're told, if ye want to keep my bed."

Darlei shuddered.

"Now ye've had yer way," MacNabh told her, "eat."

She'd not had her way. Time spent here in the hall did not give her access to the busy yard where she might catch more than sunlight. And it would force her into proximity with these people she abhorred.

But from here she might at least see the main doors. Should they stand open…

It was better, anyway, than a cruel slit of a window.

Determinedly, and with her stomach protesting, she addressed herself to her plate.

"I WILL TAK' ye on." The man who spoke was tall and dark-haired with a look of MacNabh about him. Young enough to be a by-blow, perhaps.

Deathan had caught sight of MacNabh when the man came out to direct those repairing the walls, or inspect their finished work. An aging warrior, comfortable enough in his status and as unappealing as a man could be.

The very idea of him touching Darlei fair had Deathan's blood turning cold.

"Ye sure about that?" he asked the young man.

"Aye so. I fancy my chances."

Did he? Young and green and no doubt nearing the end of his

training. Deathan would hate to kill him.

The fellow already had his sword in hand, though, a third-rate weapon that looked like a castoff.

"Ye will ha' to ask Master Ardroch's permission," Deathan told the boy.

The lad went pelting off without a word. The other men in the yard left off their work as if at an inaudible signal and began to drift up.

"That is young Tighe," one of them said. "He's a canny lad and good wi' a sword."

"MacNabh's son?" Deathan asked.

The man looked surprised. "Got on a serving lass." He grinned, showing gapped teeth. "Roisin fair killed him. That was when the mistress was still alive, and himself had Roisin on the side."

"If MacNabh values him, then I'd best no' take off his head."

"Wha' makes ye think himself values the lad?"

Tighe came running back with Ardroch striding behind him.

"Wha' is all this? An excuse to stop working?" Ardroch asked.

"The lad challenged me," Deathan told him. "Wha' is a man to do?"

Ardroch rolled his eyes. "Go and get yer sword."

A hum had started up by the time Deathan returned, and another circle formed. Men eager for diversion. He tried to loosen the muscles of his shoulders. He'd been laboring since dawn and certainly was not at his best.

Think of Darlei. A step closer to her, mayhap.

Nielan, the man Deathan had defeated last time, stood at the forefront of the circle, his gaze skeptical.

Tighe, though, had stars in his pale-blue eyes.

He was younger than Nielan, aye, and younger than Deathan himself. Quicker too, as Deathan found out when they engaged.

But clumsy. Unpracticed at controlling the power of his blows. A bit impetuous with his slashes.

Deathan circled in a half crouch, happy to let the lad expend his energy. And the old knowledge stirred within him, ran out through his limbs and banished his weariness.

He did not know from whence this knowledge, this warrior skill came. But by all the powers, he began to rely upon it.

He blocked the lad's hasty blows and ignored opportunities that would have allowed him to remove Tighe's head. The men wanted a show, and that was what he needed to provide. He backed and backed, luring Tighe to think he had the advantage before dancing forward again.

Like training a youngster, this was. Surely he had done that long ago.

Only, he had not.

His muscles remembered. As did something in his head. His heart.

Round and round he half lured his opponent while the men, becoming invested in the contest, called encouragement.

Not till the lad began to tire did Deathan press his attack, like a turning of the tide, letting the skill that filled him burst forth. He made the strikes delicate so the boy could catch them before setting up for the finishing blow.

It connected, and the lad's sword broke, clanging in two separate pieces at his feet.

Deathan withdrew immediately and stood back on his heels, breathing hard.

Tighe stared at the hilt of his sword still in his hands while the men all exclaimed in amazement.

"Ye ha' some ability," Deathan told the lad. "Ye need a better sword."

The lad raised dazed eyes to Deathan's face, and thence to his weapon. "Yours is magnificent. May I see it?"

Deathan passed it over, hilt first. As a second son, he did not possess Murtray's finest, but it was a far cry from what was dealt out here.

"Aye so," Ardroch said. "The lad has some ability. I will see can I find him a better weapon."

Deathan nodded and accepted the return of his blade from Tighe. With the remnants of the battle knowledge still running through him, he found he did not want to return meekly to work.

He wanted to storm the house. And take what belonged to him by right of love.

CHAPTER FIFTY

"So ye ha' aspirations, d'ye, to be a fine warrior?" Deathan asked Tighe.

The two of them sat together on a portion of half-built wall in the sunshine. Deathan had progressed from mucking out the stable and providing care to the ponies to helping with the building. And, he thought ruefully, his hands showed it.

To his surprise, Tighe had sought him out when they all paused to take what passed for a rest. The lad apparently felt no resentment over yesterday's defeat.

"Wha' are...aspirations?" he asked with a frown. "The same as wishes?"

"Wishes. Hopes, aye."

"I do. I was born here and—and though I ha' no claim, I can think o' little better than to tak' Ardroch's place as head o' the guard. After he steps down, that is."

"Aye so." The lad knew he was MacNabh's by-blow. The chief doubtless knew it also. Yet Tighe lived in ignominy.

Tighe stole a look at Deathan. "D'ye think I ha' the makings o' a great warrior? I respect wha' ye say. I ha' never seen anyone fight the way ye do."

"I think ye can mak' a fine warrior and a good head o' the guard here, if ye work to hone your skills. It takes work, ye ken."

"Is that how ye got so good?"

Deathan supposed it was. He, like Rohr, had worked with a sword since he was twelve or thirteen. And yet that did not account for the skill he felt rise within him. That which came unbidden and felt very much like something learned on a turn of the wheel.

He suspected, so he did, from whence that came.

"Aye, and there are generations o' warriors behind me."

"Me, also." Tighe looked half proud and half ashamed. His heritage must go unacknowledged. Shyly he asked, "Would ye work wi' me? In our spare time, that is."

Deathan snorted. They had no such thing as spare time.

"I ken fine," Tighe said, "ye may no' be staying long. So Ardroch says."

"That is wha' Ardroch says, is it?"

"Aye. He figures ye are lying low. Hiding out, mayhap. He says ye ha' been a mercenary and may be again."

That was the story and could come true, Deathan supposed, if he and Darlei had to go on the run—after he killed her husband. A favorite of the king.

"Let us just say I am here catching my breath." And working himself to the bone.

Could this young man, though, be his way inside the house?

"I will work wi' ye," he told Tighe. "As Master Ardroch allows."

"I will talk him into it." A big grin spread across Tighe's face before he went pelting off, presumably to do so.

Ardroch came to Deathan not long after. "Did ye agree to train young Tighe? So he says."

"No' to train him but to work wi' him, show him a few tricks." Deathan smiled. "If ye can find him a decent sword."

"I might do." Ardroch frowned. "Once this business o' the king's visit is o'er, I can tak' on training him myself. He is a good lad."

"I can see that, aye."

"I believe"—Ardroch hesitated—"he seeks to bring himself to his father's attention."

"Ah." That weighted Deathan's heart. Tighe wanted Mac-

Nabh to notice him. Deathan wanted MacNabh dead. It scarcely seemed fair.

"I do no' think," Ardroch added morosely, "he will be successful. Now that himself has a new wife upon which to get a son—"

"I will work wi' the lad. We shall see what we shall see."

Work with Tighe he did, Ardroch having sought him a sword. The lad came looking for Deathan whenever they had even a suggestion of a breather or after work was done for the day, which meant they often worked in the dark, lit by flaring torches. Despite Deathan's weariness and his fear over what was befalling Darlei, he enjoyed the sessions. He liked using his muscles for a finer purpose than moving a barrow or hefting stone.

It felt familiar and right.

At night, he should have been weary enough to sleep as if dead. Instead, he had strange dreams, flickers of light and darkness that, when he woke, hinted of memory. He fought in battles. He defended a settlement alive with flame. He trained a squad of women. He engaged in perilous combat and took a man's head.

Memory, or imagining?

MacNabh's men, guards and farmers and grooms pulled from their regular duties to prepare for the king's visit, began to gather round while Tighe trained, curious to watch. Ardroch tried to discourage it, presumably not wanting MacNabh to find out what they were doing, but it proved impossible. As easy to discourage wasps from a pot of honey.

Deathan went easy on the lad, because he wanted to encourage him. Some sword masters slapped their students down at every opportunity, but he went lightly, only tapping the lad with his blade when he made a mistake and telling him, "I could have had ye then."

Tighe always grinned good-naturedly.

One afternoon when it rained lightly and the men took it as

an excuse to suspend work, Deathan noticed a woman had joined the onlookers. She stood solemn, her eyes wide, and her hands clasped tightly. Slight and diminutive, her sandy hair had turned mostly gray.

"My mam," Tighe said when he saw Deathan glancing at her.

"Och, aye."

The woman's gaze was fierce. Protective.

After Ardroch called a halt to the training and they put up their swords, Deathan crossed the stable floor, where they worked, to the woman's side.

"Mistress."

"Mam," said Tighe, who came at Deathan's back, "this is Master Deathan, who's training me."

Master. He was no one's master here.

The woman directed a look at Deathan, up and down. "Are ye a mercenary, then?"

"Mistress, I ha' been many things." Did she come as a spy for MacNabh?

"Why should ye bother to train my son?"

"Because he asked me, and he has talent. He wishes to be more than he is."

"Ye think I do not know that?" Her gaze seared him. "He should ha' a claim here, by right. Not some babe yet to be born."

Deathan's heart jerked in his chest violently. Did this woman who worked in the house know something he did not? Was Darlei, his Darlei, carrying MacNabh's child?

The very idea made him begin to sweat. It did not matter, though. Any child she bore would be part of her, and so dear to him.

"Tighe will be a fine warrior some day," he told the woman, "and worthy o' any man's notice."

Tighe, still standing beside him, seemed to expand with pride.

"Aye so," said the lad's mother. "But life can be cruel."

"Aye, mistress, so it can."

"I would no' like to see my son disappointed."

She walked away, and Tighe followed with a regretful look or Deathan.

The next morning they were at work on the wall when an unnatural silence fell upon the yard. Deathan, moving stones from a cart, turned to find none other than MacNabh at his elbow.

It was the first close look he'd had of the man. Surely well past two score in years, he stood nearly of a height with Deathan and had black hair heavily streaked with gray. Pale-blue eyes glowered at Deathan from beneath heavy brows. The man did not look pleased.

"Who," he demanded into the sudden silence, "by the devil's beak, are ye?"

Deathan hesitated, not wanting to give his true name to this man whom he would likely kill.

"Just a worker, Chief MacNabh," he said as respectfully as he could manage for the surge of loathing that filled him. This man had touched Darlei, perhaps forced her.

Deathan's skin crawled.

Ardroch stepped forward. "This man stopped by, Chief Mac-Nabh, looking for work when we needed the help. I took him on—for a few days."

MacNabh switched the icy stare to Ardroch. "Wi'out asking me."

"Well, chief, I thought as we were so hard pressed wi' the king's visit—"

"I mak' the decisions here. He'll ha' to go."

"But chief—"

"I do no' ken him. He could be anyone."

"He is a braw worker, chief, and a dab hand wi' the horses. He's workin' for his keep."

That made those shaggy brows rise. "Is he, now?" MacNabh's gaze returned to Deathan. "And why should a young, strong fellow do such a thing, lest he's hiding fro' something? Nay, he canna be here when the king comes."

Deathan's heart fell. If he were sent away now without even setting eyes on Darlei…

"Pray, Chief MacNabh." It was Tighe who stepped up from somewhere in the crowd of men. "If I may speak—"

Some unidentified emotion flickered in MacNabh's eyes when he looked at Tighe. Aye, he knew right enough who the lad was.

"Wha' is it?" he barked.

"I ask ye let him stay. He is training me at arms. He says I ha' the makings o' a fine warrior."

MacNabh looked his bastard son up and down with a new expression. "Have ye, then?"

"He does, Chief MacNabh," Deathan put in. "An inborn talent, I should say."

"Chief MacNabh," Tighe beseeched, "if ye would allow him to stay but a wee while yet—"

"Perhaps just till the king's visit," Ardroch added.

"And if the stranger be an assassin? If he aims to tak' the life o' the king?"

"I would ne'er do that." Deathan stared the man in the eye. "No' the life o' the king."

"Och, verra well. He can stay a few days. But nay more than that."

❦

CHAPTER FIFTY-ONE

NO ONE HAD heard from the king, though as Darlei learned during her forced suppers with MacNabh and his two dreadful female companions, the chief had sent out a man to try to locate His Majesty's party and estimate his arrival. That man had not yet returned.

Darlei chafed. But nay, that did not describe her state of mind. She felt fairly sure she'd gone at least three parts mad.

She endured rather than lived through the days, dreading—always dreading—every nightfall that MacNabh would come to her. Orle endured with her. They had both lost weight and near suffocated for want of a breath of air.

Though Darlei argued for it often, when she saw MacNabh at supper, he had not agreed to let them out into the yard.

"No' while the repairs are ongoing," he replied again and again. "'Tis nay place for women."

Once, when she lost control and cried that she was naught more than a prisoner, he'd struck her across the face, knocking her right out of her chair.

"Ye'll be silent till I need ye. Do I no' ha' enough women chirping at me?"

He did. Roisin complained endlessly, and the old woman delivered garbled words to his ear.

Darlei returned to her chamber after that meal with a livid bruise on her cheek, and Orle wept over her.

Darlei had not wept. She was too desperate and far too angry.

She'd not caught another glimpse of the man she'd seen out the window, pushing the barrow. But she remained convinced he was Deathan. That somehow, despite every wish of her heart to keep him safe, he was here.

Terrible, it was, to be so conflicted. To long so hard for him while wanting him far away. Back at Murtray.

Safe.

For she was not safe here. She lived her every moment in peril. Her only hope of withstanding her fate lay in trying to believe no danger threatened the man she loved.

So she needed to get out into the yard, to make certain he was not there, even though every part of her heart wished he was.

No wonder she felt mad. No woman could withstand this. No woman who loved as she did.

Over and over again, she relived the moments they'd shared. The walks up the shore. Those moments out in the tiny boat upon the sea. Making love in secret, to the sweet notes of Coll's harp, while a whole hall full of listeners sat beyond the thin wall.

She recalled all he'd said about the wheel of time. Turning inevitably and bringing them together. Taking them apart again.

Just because they may have loved one another in the past and had met to love again did not mean they were destined to be together in this life. Far otherwise, it seemed.

She'd been allowed a glimpse of him in her life, just like out that narrow window. Allowed to touch him, share his kisses, hold him inside her.

That might be all, for this lifetime. And if it were so, at least she'd known him, if only for a brief glimmer in time.

But och, how was she to survive it? Year upon year in this terrible place, subject to MacNabh's will.

Could a woman live on hate? For now, she decided, it would have to remain her strength.

Roisin came to the chamber door and presented her with the twice-altered gown, which she forced Darlei to try on. When

Darlei did, resentfully, Roisin stood studying her and looking proud of her work.

"It will do. Ye look less the wild woman, withal. Though I suppose the king knows ye for a wild woman, since he sent ye here as such."

Darlei formed her hands into fists. She had been a Caledonian princess once. What had become of her spirit—that which made this woman call her wild? Now she—who had been capable with a bow and unbeatable on the back of a pony—cowered here in a wretched state.

Unacceptable.

"We maun do somewhat wi' yer hair," Roisin went on. "Cover it, perhaps. There is fabric left over, so I will mak' a wimple." She eyed Darlei critically. "'Twill be well if that bruise on yer face heals before the king arrives. I told MacNabh he canna go hitting ye again before then. After the king's visit"—the woman sniffed—"he can do as he likes. He can throttle ye, for all I care." Her eyes narrowed in spite. "To be sure, it might be better if he did."

Orle, who usually kept silent in Roisin's presence, stepped forward. "How dare you speak to her that way? Is she not the mistress of this place?"

In truth, Darlei was. In practice, naught but a prisoner.

"Who do you think you are?" Orle said, unwisely. "Show some respect."

"To her? The daughter of some savage king? I will tell ye who I am, wench—the woman who ruled this place before ye came. Who had things in order just the way I wanted them."

"He had not married you, though," Orle objected.

"We were planning the wedding. And 'tis ye, wee peasant, who should show some respect."

She hauled off and struck Orle where she stood. A solid blow it was that had poor Orle sitting down abruptly on the edge of the bed.

Darlei ran to Orle and wrapped her in a protective embrace,

her anger flaring.

"You can take your disappointment out on me, if you like. But not on Orle. She has done naught." Except be a sturdy friend, suffering through this journey of missteps with Darlei, for little reward.

"Och, I will tak' it out on ye, ye may be certain. Once this troublesome visit fro' the king is done, ye can be sure I will. Ye might be MacNabh's wife, but he can soon be a widower. And ye may be certain"—Roisin's eyes flared with malice—"ye will ne'er bear him a mongrel child."

She went out, taking her needle and thread with her. A moment of terrible silence ensued before Darlei stirred herself. She used the sleeve of the fine new gown to dry Orle's tears.

"You should not have risked yourself on my behalf, Orle, or got between her and me."

"She threatened you! You heard her. You are treated worse here than the lowest hound."

"We both are." And that did not look to change.

Unless Darlei herself changed it. She did not quite know how. But if she were still a Caledonian princess of any kind, if she retained the roots of any wildness in her heart, she would call upon it now.

For Orle's sake, if not her own.

"Come now, stop your weeping," she tried to comfort her friend. But Orle could not stop. All the past days had caught up with her, the weariness, the confinement, and the fright.

Darlei held her, and they curled up in the bed while the tears flowed. She whispered comfortingly into Orle's ear, "Do you think I will let her harm me? Or you. I shall find a way to get us free from this terrible place."

"How?"

"They are a wretched, stupid lot. Surely I can find a way to outsmart them. Me, a Caledonian princess and all." She tried to persuade Orle to smile.

The attempt failed. "The door is always watched with a man

outside."

So it was. Orle was allowed out never, and Darlei but seldom.

There would come a day, however, when Darlei would be ushered out wearing her new finery. Perhaps she could make of the king himself her very best weapon.

CHAPTER FIFTY-TWO

THERE CAME THREE straight days of rain that halted all work in the yard and apparently drove MacNabh half to distraction with impatience. He came down to the bailey—such as it was—not once but several times and had intense conversations with Ardroch.

It did not take long to prize the truth of those conversations out of Ardroch, after. The men had become comfortable with Deathan by then. They all stood in a circle inside the stables and heard their captain out.

"The chief's man has returned," he shared with them. "The one he sent out to check on the king's progress. The king is at Dundee and expected to arrive here within a sennight."

That brought muttered exclamations. The yard and, indeed, the house wall were far from repaired or presentable.

"The chief says," Ardroch went on, "if we work in the rain there will be an extra barrel o' ale, and time off once the king is gone."

So they worked in the rain, and a cold rain it was, as autumn had well moved in. And as any fool knew, autumn proved wet in Scotland.

When the rain intensified rather than eased up and it became evident the promised ale was not forthcoming, the men retired to the stables, where Deathan set out to both amuse and beguile them.

He did not consider himself a particularly charming sort of

man. Back home, he'd been all duty, allowing Rohr the flash and glitter, resigning himself to picking up behind his brother.

But these men already favored him for his skill with a sword. They were bored and restless, and feeling let down by their chief. The flame was already lit. Deathan had only to fan it.

He set up a round of contests there in the stable beneath the relentless assault of the rain. Men drew straws to see who would face whom, short straws always paired together. Weapons were traded to keep things fair, and Deathan insisted it all be done in good fun with no blood drawn, save by pure accident.

And since he oversaw it, no one faced him. Yet.

He showed respect to all and encouragement to many, and the men became invested. There were some fine blades among them, especially in MacNabh's guard, and Ardroch himself proved formidable. The winners of the first bouts faced each other in the next. To Deathan's satisfaction, Tighe—with whom he continued to work one on one—remained among them.

The men began to display some loyalty behind the lad. He was one of them, and yet he was something more. Deathan doubted a man there did not know the truth of the lad's parentage.

In all, very little work got done as Deathan brewed a mild form of rebellion, and he was glad of it. Let the king see his old comrade in arms for what he was, when he arrived.

Every day that passed drew the visitation closer. And every day he worried about the vile horrors to which MacNabh might be subjecting Darlei. At night he dreamed of her—her in a trio of guises. But always her. Always the woman who inhabited his heart.

"Wha' in hell is all this?"

The activity in the stable ceased when the call rang out, cutting through the crashing of rain on the roof that nearly drowned out the sounds of swordplay.

Two of MacNabh's guards, half stripped off since they'd been wet when they came in, faced one another in the cleared, hay-strewn space. They had made their way by bout after perilous bout to the elite remaining few.

The ultimate winner of those bouts would face Deathan himself in a final contest, for naught more than the right to boast of it.

Now MacNabh himself stood in the open doorway, glowering hard enough to bring the roof down.

Ardroch whirled, no doubt feeling himself responsible for the activities as head of the guard.

"Chief MacNabh. 'Tis but a bit o' sport to pass the time while it rains."

"A bit o' sport?" MacNabh stepped farther in, and his men melted away on both sides, giving him a straight path to the site of the combat. "'Tis that ye call it when there's work to be done?"

"Chief, the men canna work in rain such as this. They did try. But we had to duck back in a wee while." Indeed, outside the stable door the rain hammered down like a waterfall.

MacNabh stood soaked, his gray-black hair plastered to his head and shoulders.

"Ye eat my food," he said scathingly, "and ye drink my ale." There were a few shuffles at that. "But ye will no' do my work?"

"Chief," Ardroch said, far less certainly this time, "we ha' been working. If ye doubt it, only look at our hands."

True enough. Deathan's own were so battered by handling stone, he could scarce grip his blade.

"Yet ye ha' time and energy to play at champions, is that it?"

"Aye, Chief MacNabh."

"Who has authorized this?" MacNabh snapped. "For I am damned certain I ha' not."

"'Twas my notion, Chief MacNabh." Deathan stepped forward. If he wanted to win the hearts of these men and any part of their loyalty, he must make sure the blame fell on him.

MacNabh swiveled to face him. "Ye, again? Who d'ye think ye are, then? The king o' the fairies? Some legendary warrior, mayhap?"

"Nay, Chief MacNabh. I just thought 'twould serve to lift spirits all around, since the men ha' been working so hard and the ale that was promised did not appear—"

MacNabh moved so swiftly that Deathan barely had time to react. The chief landed a blow that felt as if it had come from a tree limb on Deathan's left cheekbone. It swayed him where he stood, but did not knock him down.

Suddenly Deathan's blade was in his hand. Not a conscious choice, but an instinctive one. He had wanted this confrontation. Longed for it. But it was supposed to take place inside the house, where he might catch a glimpse of Darlei.

Nay matter. He could kill MacNabh here as well as before Darlei's eyes.

Anywhere.

Rage broke across MacNabh's heavy features, a rage Deathan hoped against hope would push him beyond good sense. He needed MacNabh to be the aggressor. He needed to kill him in a fair, witnessed fight.

"Ye dare to draw upon me?" MacNabh seethed. "Yer chief?"

"In truth, ye are no' my chief, are ye? Just a poor excuse for a man, a bully who thinks he has the favor o' the king."

There was a collective gasp, and men stepped away from Deathan.

"Ye insolent upstart," MacNabh spat. "Throw him out!" He tossed the command in Ardroch's direction. "I will ha' him no more on my land."

No one moved. Deathan had a blade in his hand, and they had all seen what he could do with it.

In a low voice, calm and insolent, he said, "Why d'ye no' throw me off yousel', Chief MacNabh, since 'tis your land?"

"Ye fool o' an interloper." MacNabh examined Deathan from his head to his feet—lean and work-hardened, with not a hint of weakness about him. "Why should I soil my hands wi' ye?"

"Well," Deathan said, "if ye be afraid to face a wandering upstart, wha' can be said o' ye? I think I will stay here where I am comfortable till there be a man among ye willing to chase me awa'."

Further gasps and mutters followed the claim. MacNabh's men could scarcely believe what they were hearing.

Neither could MacNabh. His eyes nearly bugged out from his face and an ugly sneer twisted his lips.

"Ye think I canna?" he demanded of Deathan. "Ye suppose I canna best ye, wi' a sword? Why, I was taking men's heads before ye were born."

Deathan raised his blade. "Show me."

$$\sim\!\!\Longleftrightarrow\!\!\sim$$

CHAPTER FIFTY-THREE

D ARLEI POUNDED ON the chamber door so hard the stout oak panel rattled. She used the heels of her hands and her feet, while calling to the man she knew stood on guard outside.

"Help! Ye must let me out. My maid is dying."

No response at first, none at all, and she feared the ruse would fail. She stole a look over her shoulder at Orle, who lay sprawled artfully in the center of the floor, her hair and clothing disarrayed and looking satisfyingly unwell, the picture aided by the livid bruise coloring her cheek.

"Oh, by all the powers, send a healer! Will you be responsible for the death of an innocent young—"

The door rattled harder and Darlei heard the bar lift from outside. The panel swung open to reveal the incredulous face of a guard.

Darlei imagined he spent much of his time bored to the bones, stationed outside a chamber where nothing very much happened. She had never before done this, cried out or made a fuss. He did not look above twenty or so, and at the moment did not appear to know what to do.

"Wha' is it?"

"My maid is ill. I think she is dying. Yon Roisin struck her, and she hit her head when she fell, so. Is there a healer in the house?"

"I dunna ken." The guard stared at Orle, who appeared not only helpless but quite pretty in her distress, her skirts disordered and her dark hair streaming across the floor. "Go back inside," he said, for Darlei had pushed out against him. "I will ask the chief."

Darlei ordered herself to be calm. To appear sane and rational. But the door was open and her inner wild woman had come alive inside her.

"Nay, we must get her to help at once. You carry her."

"Eh?" He looked astounded.

"Pick her up and carry her. We will go in search of help."

"But—"

"I command you."

He danced from one foot to another, staring first at Orle and then at Darlei. Outside the slit window, the rain pounded so hard, Darlei could barely hear her own thoughts.

"Take her to Mistress Roisin," Darlei urged. "She will know what to do."

"Aye so."

He tiptoed into the room, which lay as disordered as the dwelling of two women with very few possessions could be. Gingerly, and with unexpected gentleness, he bent and gathered Orle into his arms.

"Come," Darlei told him, and stepped from the room.

Her thoughts moved madly. It must be nearly time for supper. She would likely have been allowed out for that anyway. But it was not enough for *her* to escape the room—Orle must also be freed. Usually, as Darlei had learned, MacNabh was not in the hall at this time of day. He often only came in to join the women in time for the meal.

The rain might change everything.

Why had she not thought of that? Curse the rain.

She ran down the steps from the upper corridor and into the hall. Her heart leaped sickeningly when she saw that the place was filled mostly with smoke from the eternally ill-burning fire. No other men at arms, no MacNabh. Just his old mother and Roisin.

Both women looked up sharply when Darlei dashed in, waving her arms and with the guard cradling Orle close behind.

"She is dying! You have killed her. You horrible woman." She ran directly at Roisin—who half started up from her bench at the table—planted both hands at the woman's half-bared bosom, and pushed.

Roisin went over backward and confusion immediately reigned. Darlei got in what blows she could before Roisin might struggle up. The old woman instantly began to screech and babble. The guard, behind Darlei, cried out.

"Stop that. Stop it now!"

Where was MacNabh? Not here, and that must do for now. But he could come rushing in at any moment in answer to the old woman's screeching. If he did, Darlei's attempt was done.

Please, she begged of any powers able to lend an ear. *Keep him occupied elsewhere.*

Roisin, who outweighed Darlei by half, fought to push her off.

"Ye wretched savage! Get awa' fro' me."

Savage, was she? Yes, and at this moment she felt every bit of it.

She got in a few more blows before Roisin, completely disheveled, climbed to her feet. Darlei followed.

The old woman, eyes staring and mouth a dark cave, gabbled at Roisin, who shook herself like a wet hound and directed a stare of rage at Darlei.

"Wha' is this?" To the guard she said, "Put her back in her chamber!"

"But—" he began.

Darlei let him get no farther.

"You have near killed my maid," she accused Roisin.

"I did no'—"

"You struck her. Will you deny it?"

"I did, aye, but—"

"She fell."

"She did no'—"

"Struck her face, her head. Only look at her!"

Orle made a convincing picture draped over the arm of the guard, who held her rather tenderly.

"Send for the healer," Darlei demanded of Roisin, who stood trying to catch her breath. "It will be on your head if she dies. And be certain I will tell the king. I will tell him how we have been treated here."

The guard looked alarmed, and Roisin backed off a step. The old woman continued to babble incoherently.

"Let her die, then," Roisin said. "Wha' is one less savage?" But she looked worried. "Where is MacNabh?" she asked the guard.

"Dunna ken, mistress."

"Go and find him. Put her down—there on the bench."

The man did so, with exaggerated care.

The old woman cried another spate of words, from which Darlei caught only "stables" and "stramash."

"What sort o' stramash?" Roisin demanded. And to the guard, "Go and see."

He went, and Darlei drew a breath she hoped would steady her thumping heart. The odds had just got better, in her favor. Yet she did not take Roisin for any but a formidable opponent. And if MacNabh came in…

She must act quickly, no matter her terror. They thought her a savage, did they? She would show them how strong a Caledonian woman could be.

"Sit down!" Roisin ordered her. "There, beside your maid. I will no' ha' ye trying any o' your sly tricks."

Darlei backed toward the fire. She had spotted the only thing in the room she might use as a weapon, an iron spit that had lain there so long it had half rusted away.

She snatched it up, then dropped it with a clang—it was hot. She wrapped her fingers in her skirt, seized it again, and swung it wildly.

"Back. Back!" she told Roisin, who stared in disbelief. "Orle?"

Orle sprang up, which set the old woman to babbling as if she'd seen a spirit.

Darlei screamed. It was a Caledonian yell, one she'd heard her father's men use when at practice with one another. One she'd even heard the king employ a time or two. It burst from her lips even as she swung the spit and took Roisin in the shoulder, knocking the woman back over the bench once again.

Orle shoved the old woman. Given, it did not take much to knock the wizened creature down. She went squawking and screeching in a manner that might almost have been humorous if it were not so terrifying.

"Come, come!" Darlei snatched Orle's hand, and they dashed out, Darlei still clutching the spit. Out of the hall, through the arched stone opening, and into the rain.

Bless the rain.

It came down so hard she could scarcely see across the bailey, which was not wide. Beyond stood the gate and freedom. She did not know how they would get past the guard stationed there. First they needed ponies—or at least one.

What had the old woman said about the stables?

Darlei drew Orle up against the wall of the house so they could not be seen from above. Plenty of litter here—piles of stone left from repairs, barrels, and the like. Instantly wet to the skin, she tried to keep hold of Orle's hand, which slid in hers.

There would be ponies in the stables. But as soon as she rounded the end of the house, she could hear that—yes, something was happening there across the yard. Many raised voices. Shouts that could be heard even above the rain.

Not *there*, by the gods. They would have to go on foot. How far would they get?

"There!" Orle said, and pointed.

Darlei raised her head and narrowed her eyes. In a field just past the stable were several ponies that, to their misfortune, had been left to graze. And forgotten?

MacNabh's habitual carelessness just might cost him now.

"Come," she bade Orle again. "While they are occupied within."

They ran.

CHAPTER FIFTY-FOUR

"SOMEBODY GI' ME a sword. A good one." MacNabh growled the words, never taking his eyes from Deathan. "I shall, aye, teach this upstart a lesson. And when I am done wi' him, ye will tak' his bloody carcass and leave it on the border o' my land."

His men did not look so certain. But he was their chief, after all, and there were loyal hearts among them.

Ardroch stepped up. "Here, chief, use mine."

MacNabh weighed the sword in his hand with unconscious canniness, never taking his gaze from Deathan. Aye, the man had been a warrior once—likely a good one, given what Tighe had inherited from him.

And still, it did not matter. The old knowledge, that which Deathan had determined lived deep in his bones, or perhaps in his soul, now simmered inside him, ready to flare.

He grimaced at MacNabh. "And when I kill ye? Wha' then? Shall your son"—he jerked his head at Tighe, who stood by, eyes wide—"inherit your lands?"

MacNabh's pale eyes flicked to Tighe also, and an odd look came to them. "Aye so, why not? But ye will no' kill me yet."

They would see about that.

Deathan raised his sword just in time to meet MacNabh's blade, which came crashing in upon him. The man had strength, aye, and he also had some skill, but if he swung his sword like a woodsman felling trees, he would soon tire himself. Whereas the knowledge flooding up through Deathan felt patient and near bottomless.

He did not know what warrior dwelt within him, but it was a gifted, clever one.

He danced, stepping light on the strawy floor. MacNabh remained rooted where he stood, heavy as the rain outside the door. An elemental sort of battle it became, a meeting of opposites with death as the prize.

Deathan's vision narrowed, as did his thoughts. Even Darlei was thrust to the back of his mind as, two-handed, he caught MacNabh's tremendous blows. He saw only MacNabh's face with its pale-blue eyes and the sweat starting to flow.

I must end it. I must take him now.

He got in a blow, a kiss of his blade at MacNabh's right shoulder. The chief reacted like a bull stung by a wasp, reared back, shook his head, and then ignored the wound. But now he moved, turned, and swiveled. Even as the onlookers gasped, his feet tapped the stones in a desperate answer to Deathan's dance.

Did he know he was beaten?

Another sting, this time to MacNabh's left cheek, and the blood began to flow. The onlookers murmured. Would they respect the outcome of this battle when Deathan felled their chief?

One more blow, Deathan decided. Not a sting but a thrust. And not to MacNabh's heart but his throat.

Deathan's feet quickened. He raised his blade and began to whirl.

"Chief MacNabh! Chief MacNabh! 'Tis the Caledonian woman! She is dyin'."

The guard who burst in through the stable door was very young and soaking wet. Face pale and eyes wide, he seemed to fail at grasping what took place in the center of the crowded stable.

At his words, the battle halted, and MacNabh bellowed, "Wha'?"

Nay, Deathan thought at the same instant. *Nay, and nay.*

The lad, out of breath, centered his attention on his chief. His words came out in a garbled stream. "They pounded on the door and said she was ill—dyin'! They are usually so quiet, chief, I didna know what to do. The one said Mistress Roisin had knocked the other down and broke her head. She did look all battered, so I carried her. Carried her down to the hall. I went to find the old healer and sent him there, then I came straight to ye."

"Curse it all!" MacNabh, blood trickling down his face and from his shoulder, lowered his borrowed sword. "Where is the woman now?"

"Still in the hall, chief. I sent the healer thence—"

"Unguarded?"

"Wi' Mistress Roisin and Mistress MacNabh."

MacNabh gave a roar. Without awaiting further information, he brushed past the lad and ran out into the yard, sword still in hand.

Deathan followed him.

Nothing on earth could have held him back, though he could hear Ardroch giving orders behind him, and he sensed the young guard followed.

Then he was in the rain and could hear nothing at all save the drops crashing all around him. Had it ever rained so? No matter. Only one thing meant aught to him now. If something had happened to Darlei…

How would he go on? Face the rest of his life?

MacNabh rushed in through the house door, which stood open and unguarded. With his foot on the threshold, Deathan hesitated. This one step and what he found within could change everything. For on this turn of the wheel—in this life—he might have lost her.

Which meant he would have to search for her again, in the next.

He went in to find the hall full of smoke and in confusion.

Servants, a couple of girls and an old man, milled about. A blowsy woman whom MacNabh addressed as Roisin, who was bleeding profusely from the head, teetered on a bench. An old woman—little more than a bundle of bones and clothing—lay stretched out on the floor, moaning.

No sign of Darlei, living or dead.

MacNabh planted himself in the middle of the floor and roared, "Wha' goes on here? Roisin? Mother?"

He looked to the old woman, who, with the help of an equally aged man who must be the aforementioned healer, sat up and began babbling at him. She had very few teeth and was difficult to understand, but MacNabh must have managed, for he listened and then barked at her, "Where is she now?"

Roisin got to her feet. Formidable and large breasted, she faced MacNabh with a burning gaze. "Gone!" She gestured to the open door. "The both o' them."

Both? *Orle.*

"Did ye no' go after them?"

"How? They pushed yer mam down. And me. As soon as Angus had gone for the healer, they stopped wi' playing at being ill and leaped up. Attacked us. Yer princess had the spit fro' the fire. Look, she has burned me!"

Just like a wild woman, Deathan thought on a bound of the heart. Even as he'd fought for her, she'd been fighting for herself.

He turned his gaze to the door, to the crashing rain. Gone, but where?

"After them!" MacNabh yelled, ignoring Roisin's complaints. "Someone fetch my horse." He turned and glared at Deathan before letting his gaze slide past him. "Ardroch!" he called. "They canna get far on foot, no' in this weather."

Ardroch came running in, fresh from the stables with a number of the other men behind him.

"Fetch my horse!" MacNabh barked at him. "And quick." He turned to Roisin. "Ye fool o' a woman. How could ye let her go? She maun be here when the king arrives."

No other thought than that possessed him, or so it seemed. Gone were all thoughts of combat with Deathan. Not waiting for the woman's feeble protests, he ran outside again.

Deathan once more followed. And wondered—how *could* anyone get away in this weather? The world was gray, a cacophony of pounding rain, and as wet as the bottom of the sea. How could anyone follow the women in this? Equally impossible.

One of the guards went streaking away to the stables. To fetch MacNabh's horse, presumably. But the outer gate stood open and unguarded.

Had she got away? Deathan's heart rose and then plummeted sickeningly. If she had, where might she go? Not home, surely. It would be the first place MacNabh would look. And as Deathan well knew, MacNabh had a right to drag her back here again, alive or otherwise.

She might disappear into the wild. She no doubt knew and understood Scotland's heart far better than he, who'd lived his life beside the sea. He might never see her again.

But he would never stop looking. And at least she would be free.

He jerked to life as a lad came round from the yard leading MacNabh's horse, and two others with their own mounts. He cursed himself—he should have gone at once and fetched his pony. Now he would have to follow on foot.

It did not matter. He *would* follow.

MacNabh climbed a bit stiffly onto his mount and went out through the unguarded gate, his two men in attendance.

Deathan pelted off after, through the driving rain.

CHAPTER FIFTY-FIVE

I T TOOK DARLEI three tries to snag the pony's mane and convince him to stand. He did not know her, so was skittish, and wore no bridle or lead, so she had no way to hold him.

She would never catch a second of the beasts, the others having scattered. She swiftly decided the one would have to do both her and Orle.

She vaulted onto the animal's back and reached down for Orle. "Come up. Behind me."

She did not know if Orle could hear her through the pounding rain. With a panicked look and a shake of the head, the maid mouthed, *I cannot!*

Orle, not the rider Darlei was, might well be afraid. But there was no time to waste. They might be discovered, and would not be able to hear any pursuit.

"Come!" She seized Orle's arm and yanked with desperate strength. Her maid came up behind her onto the bare, sopping-wet pony's hide. "Hold on."

Darlei had been riding from the age of two, and though this was not her own Bradh, and though the beast balked a little, she soon had him in line. She made for the main gate, the paddock where the ponies were located being surrounded by a wall. She did not know if some unfortunate guard stood there, but intended to ride him down if he did.

They had very little time.

Something had been happening in the stables, some disturbance that, thank all the powers, must have called MacNabh away. But the young guard would send the healer and it would be discovered they were gone, and then—

She could think it through no farther.

The main gate stood open and empty. The miracle of it hurtled toward Darlei as they rode through unhindered by anything but the rain. Her pony's hooves tore up the turf and they rode blind and headlong, not knowing where, save away.

She could not let this pony stumble, as she had Bradh back at the beginning of this journey. Before she'd ever met Deathan.

Deathan.

Her thoughts darted to the glimpse she'd had of the man pushing the barrow, out her chamber window. Had it been him? Her heart argued so. But if he was there at MacNabh, that meant she had just left him behind.

And it might have been no more than a fancy. A longing. She thought about him so much, dreamed of him so often, she might have imagined what was not there. For she had not seen the man's face.

And yet…

"Darlei, I am falling!" Orle's panicked plea in her ear had Darlei slowing their hectic pace. Open land lay all around MacNabh's stronghold, now curtained with rain. They needed to head for cover before the chief mounted a pursuit.

"Here. Push up closer behind me," she gasped to Orle. "Hug the pony with your knees. Hold to me, tighter."

She moved off, though not as swiftly, toward a line of trees on the northern horizon. How far off was their cover? She could not tell, with everything blurred and gray. Farther, mayhap, than it looked. The rain might help obscure their tracks. Then again, the pony's hooves might leave deep marks anywhere he trod in mud.

Naught to be done about it.

The pony seemed to have settled to her will, and Orle clutched her fiercely. Darlei increased the pace a little, doubt and hope warring inside her. If they did manage to elude any pursuit…

They had nothing. Not so much as a cloak between them. No food. No flask for water. Not even a flint.

Nowhere to go.

Her heart bade her to head for Murtray. Find Deathan. He would help her. But could he, with MacNabh being her husband?

Mayhap not. She would have to look after herself. And Orle. But oh, it would break her heart if never she saw him again.

THE BREATH SURGED in Deathan's lungs and he cursed himself again for failing to fetch his pony. But he would run forever, if it meant finding Darlei. He had soon lost sight of MacNabh and his party, falling behind. And the world seemed a mad place, devoid of direction.

How did MacNabh know which way to head?

The party had originally ridden roughly northward, after studying the ground. Deathan followed the trail left by Mac-Nabh's ponies. But he was alone, stranded in a world that contained naught but sodden turf, bracken, and wet. Rivulets ran in all directions, the water tumbling down from higher ground. Streams where none had been before. He leaped them, wondering what he would do if he caught up to MacNabh. To MacNabh and Darlei.

He wanted to kill the man.

But he could not, not in front of MacNabh's men. Not unless he could convince MacNabh to finish the fight they'd begun back in the stables. A fair fight.

His sodden hair slapped against his back with every step. His boots were heavy with wet, and the rain ran down his face like tears, but he loped on. How much of a head start had Darlei got?

If she made it away from MacNabh, he would find her. Find

her even if it took him the rest of his life. They would live wild as vagabonds if they must. So long as they were together.

He gave a fleeting thought to his mother, whom he might nevermore see alive. *Mam.* Those bonds were strong.

Was it true that they met with the same people, the same souls, life after life? If so, he might hope to meet with his mam again.

She'd been so ill when he left. By all that was holy, he hoped he would meet her in some other life, if not this one. Would feel the love and comfort of her presence.

It seemed, as he ran along that trail toward either failure or his future, that he could feel his life—his lives—stretching behind him, the places he had been and the deeds he had done reaching back and back, as night extended past the mist of morning. He ran a line connecting the long-ago with the future. He must believe. If he failed to reach Darlei now, the wheel would turn and they would, aye, meet again. He must hold that as his reality.

But och, he wanted her now.

Ahead, he thought he caught a hint of movement and paused, his lungs working like bellows. Through the rain he could just glimpse a row of trees, dark through the gray. Was that where Darlei had gone? If so, she might have a chance, once under cover.

He blinked furiously and thought he saw three blurry forms hesitating there. The grass ahead was thick. Perhaps MacNabh and his men sought to determine which way the women had gone.

He must be there, if and when MacNabh found them. He must be in position to draw his sword and challenge the man, end it once and for all.

He drew breath and ran on.

CHAPTER FIFTY-SIX

Dark gathered beneath the trees, a dense stand of fir, but the higher branches shut out some of the rain that had hit Darlei's skin so hard it felt fit to flay her. Perhaps, she thought a bit frantically, it merely began to grow dark.

How would they see to ride when dark did fall? Oh, but their situation proved perilous. MacNabh followed them. That was, *someone* followed. She'd stolen a glance over her shoulder at one point and seen blurry shapes behind. She could not tell who it was. But it would be MacNabh or his men.

"Can we stop?" Orle begged in Darlei's ear. "I do not think I can hold on." Her arms, tight around Darlei's body, trembled with strain.

"Nay." Darlei could say no more.

A soft sob broke from Orle's throat. What would MacNabh do to the maid, if he got them back? Darlei had a pretty fair idea what he would do to *her*. Confinement would be the least of it. But a disobedient servant?

He would likely separate them so they could not scheme again. He might beat Orle, this gentle soul who had proved to be so constant a friend, with none to stop him, if they retreated to his stronghold.

Urgency enveloped Darlei, making her start to sweat. They had to move slowly here, or risk injuring the pony as she'd injured Bradh, back when all this began.

She might never see her dear pony again. Silent tears slipped down her face. Or her mother, or father, or anyone back home. She might never see Deathan—

She stopped herself there, for the longing was too bright. She could not think on it. It would steal her strength.

They crossed a shallow stream, and she tried to look behind, through the dark boles of the trees.

Movement.

She turned her pony's head and…

A piercing whistle came through the woodland.

Darlei cursed, then urged the pony on with her knees and her hands in his mane.

The beast stopped and stood with his head turned, looking back just as she had.

Darlei sobbed at him, a plea. "Go!" He did not move, for he'd been trained to stand at a whistle.

"What is it?" Orle asked. "What?"

"Stay there." Darlei slid down onto her feet. Her legs threatened to go out beneath her, and she very nearly fell.

Strength, she ordered herself.

The rain now sounded at a distance, high up in the boughs of the trees. She could see two—nay, three forms on horseback, approaching. She could hear them, so close were they.

She had no weapon. No way to defend Orle and herself. She had only what MacNabh wanted.

She turned on the pony, thrust her face into his mane. "Go," she beseeched him. And to Orle, more loudly, "Go! It is me he wants. Not you."

Orle stared at her in horror. "But I can barely ride—"

"You will manage. You are strong. Ride for help. Go home— it is north and east of here. Tell Father all that has transpired."

The approaching riders were now so close, Darlei heard the hooves of the ponies on the fallen branches.

Orle reached for her. "I cannot—"

"You must. I am counting upon you." Darlei gave the pony a hard swat on the rump. It went against everything within her to cause an animal pain. She had one glimpse of Orle sliding up to grasp the beast's mane before the pony took off across the rivulets ahead and on northward.

Would MacNabh whistle for him again?

He did not. Instead he quickened his pace toward Darlei, who stood, her heart beating so hard in her chest that it made her lightheaded.

She watched him come, a big, dim shape on his pony. The three riders surrounded her, so close she could clearly see the rage in MacNabh's eyes.

"Do no' try to run. If ye do, I will ride ye down."

She believed him. Fury flared in his eyes. She had rarely seen a man so angry. If she ran, the next thing she would feel would be his pony's hooves on her back.

"Chief, should we go after the other lass?"

"Dunna bother. She is but a servant. Though I hate to lose a fine pony, 'tis good riddance to the woman."

He slid down off his horse and stepped up to Darlei, looming oversized in the gloom. "Ye ha' cost me a great deal o' trouble."

The words were accompanied by a blow, one Darlei only half saw coming. The shock of it kept her from feeling immediate pain, but rocked her on her feet. "Cost me a good pony." The second blow did knock her down. The pine-needle-strewn forest floor rushed up at her. Blood started at one corner of her mouth.

The place Deathan had so often kissed.

She could fight. She was a Caledonian princess. But if she fought, he just might beat her to death.

Mayhap better dead. Better than what would come.

MacNabh seized her bodily and, with a grunt, threw her up onto the back of his pony. He mounted behind her and spoke into her ear.

"Run fro' me again and I will mak' ye regret it."

Again, she believed him.

DEATHAN HEARD THE whistle just as he entered the woodland. He had run as far as he could and now paced quickly, following the sounds of the party ahead.

Why would MacNabh whistle?

The way through the trees was mercifully clear. Boughs and fir needles lay underfoot. His sodden boots made nothing of them.

Ahead lay a stream. On the other side of it, a clutch of figures. How many? Three ponies. Men on foot. Another, smaller form.

He halted, drawing his sword from the loop at his belt.

If he had to fight for Darlei, so be it. If he had to fight three of them, he would. If he had to die for her…

Before that happened, he must make certain he freed her.

He stepped forward just in time to hear an angry voice. To see the smaller figure fall to the ground.

He leaped the stream. He could see two of MacNabh's guards, still mounted. The man himself on his feet. He watched MacNabh grab a woman—Darlei—up from the ground and toss her onto his horse.

Och, by the gods, by all the gods, he had to—

MacNabh mounted and turned his pony. Deathan drew breath to call out. To challenge the man. They would finish what had started in the stable.

He stepped out in front of MacNabh's pony, his sword raised. The man's horse reared and MacNabh drew it around with a cruel hand. He stared at Deathan as at a ghost before crying to his mount and charging by.

Darlei, clutched hard in MacNabh's grasp, saw him.

She saw him.

A world of communication lay in her gaze, as if she'd cried aloud to him. Caution. Fear. Love.

Do not come after me. Do not try to fight for me. Do not risk yourself for me.

How could he do anything else? He lived for her. Breathed for her. In this life and any other.

MacNabh's two guards passed him with startled looks. He thrust his sword back into the loop at his belt and followed after them.

CHAPTER FIFTY-SEVEN

ACNABH DRAGGED DARLEI into his house by the hair, much as he might drag an errant hound by the scruff of the neck. Her knees hit each of the stone stairs, and when he threw her down in the hall, the flagstones come up to meet her with force.

She lay there face down for a moment, wondering if she had the strength to rise. To face what must come.

The women were both still there in the hall. MacNabh's mother started screeching as soon as she saw them.

Roisin saved her words for when MacNabh dragged Darlei up again by one arm. She looked disheveled, and blood stained her hair.

"So ye caught the wee bitch! I want her beaten, beaten soundly. Battered for wha' she did to me."

"Nay fear," MacNabh grunted. "She will get in full wha' she deserves."

The servants had gathered. They crowded the edges of the room, all staring. They would no doubt speak of this for years.

Roisin said, quite shockingly, "I want to watch. I want to see ye discipline her."

"Get awa' fro' me, woman!" MacNabh elbowed her aside viciously before hoisting Darlei up in his arms.

She struggled. She fought as best she might, kicking and flailing, but she could feel his rage, a ferocious fire, could feel how her struggling served to fuel it.

A voice sounded in her head. *Keep it up and he will kill you.*

That must be the voice of sanity breaking through the terror. She'd been half mad since all this began. The only spot of beauty, of calm, since she'd left home had been Deathan.

Deathan. Had he truly been there in the forest?

I will find ye, always, she thought she heard him say.

But nay. She did not want him here, risking his life. She would save herself or perish.

How was she to save herself?

MacNabh bore her from the hall and on a determined slog up to her chamber. The very place from whence she'd escaped.

Thought she had escaped.

He tossed her not onto the bed but on the floor, and kicked the door shut.

"Get up, bitch."

She still did not know if she could. She could feel all her hurts now, the blows and the scrapes. Worse was to come.

And was this to be her life? At this man's mercy always? Beyond alone, here in this prison?

Somehow she gained her feet and faced MacNabh. "If you beat me, the king will see the bruises. When he comes, he will see what you have done to me. You cannot beat me."

"When the king does come, he will see I ha' applied the discipline that was required. I ha' been too soft wi' ye, by half."

He took a step toward her.

She stepped back, which took her up against the bed.

Another step—he stalked her now—and he unfastened the belt he wore over his kilt. Tossed it, as before, onto the bed.

"I shall breed ye as was meant. I do no' think ye are good enough to carry my sons, but since that is wha' the king intends, so it shall be. Ye may expect me to ride ye every night till the deed be done."

"Nay." It was the only word Darlei could force through her lips.

"And if ye say nay"—he delivered a blow that knocked Darlei onto the bed—"this is wha' ye will earn."

Anger gathered inside Darlei. A desire fully born. With no one here to save her, she *must* save herself.

He came down toward her like a mountain falling. Panic rose inside her, swift and fierce. She could not let it hamper her, such terror. Not now.

His long knife sat thrust through a loop in his leather belt. The belt that now lay beside her. She never later remembered seizing it with her left hand, gripping the pommel against her palm as tightly as she could. But she would remember till her dying day how it felt when she thrust it into his chest even as he came down upon her. Thrust and, with what strength remained to her, twisted.

A look of stark surprise came to his face even as he collapsed to one side. With speed born of loathing, Darlei slid out from under his weight, leaving the knife where it was. His blood warm on her hands, holding her breath, she eyed him there, half tumbled onto his side on the bed.

Waiting. Waiting for him to rise again.

She waited long. MacNabh did not stir. At length she found the strength to tiptoe close enough that she saw his eyes were open, staring sightlessly.

A breath huffed between her teeth.

She washed her hands in the basin, turning the water red, then gathered up her few belongings. Her cloak, some dry clothing which she made into a bundle. Her hands trembled so violently, she could scarcely accomplish the task.

Then she went back out, leaving her chamber door open behind her.

Half the clan, or so it seemed, had gathered in the hall. Many were MacNabh's men, but there were also a number of women present, including Roisin, now back on her feet.

What might they do to her?

She raised her head high, lifted her chin. Met Roisin's stare.

"MacNabh is dead," she said loudly and clearly. "He fell on his own knife while attacking me. When the king comes, you will tell him I married MacNabh as he ordered. I am his widow now."

Roisin gave a cry, and the old woman, MacNabh's mother, moaned. The men stared. No one moved to block her way as, head still high, Darlei walked from the place.

A few of the guards and servants followed her. She could hear that much. Outside, the rain had slackened and night resided deep all around, the pure autumn night. Scotland spread her dark skirt, mayhap to hide Darlei, her daughter, as she went.

Behind her, she could hear Roisin wailing. Ahead of her—

There in the gloom, she saw a man.

He stepped out into the light of the torches that had been lit, no doubt at nightfall, to either side of the doorway. Soaked to the skin he was, his light brown hair slicked like the fur of an otter. His chest rose and fell violently, and he looked…

He looked like the best thing she'd ever seen.

"MacNabh is dead," she said.

"Aye so." The words strained past his lips.

Clan's folk came out through the open doorway behind Darlei. Did they follow Roisin's orders? Would they try to stop her?

Deathan looked at one of them. "Ye ken wha' to do. Mac-Nabh named his heir. In the stables, he did."

"Aye," the man agreed. "When the king comes, I will tell him."

"I will need my pony."

Someone already came around the side of the house, leading it. A tall young fellow it was, with black hair and MacNabh's pale-blue eyes.

"The gods go wi' ye," the young man said to Deathan.

"And wi' ye. Yer father is dead, lad."

"I heard."

"He named ye chief after him, and everyone heard it. Lead yer people well."

Deathan boosted Darlei onto the back of his pony, his hands at her waist a caress.

"Are ye bad hurt?" he whispered.

"I am well, now."

He swung up behind her, drew her to rest against his chest.

She turned her head and his lips traced her cheek. "I thought I saw you there in the forest."

"Aye. Did I no' tell ye I would find ye always?"

Silence envelops Murtray's hall, save for a sweet scattering of notes, pure from Finlay's harp strings. Caught fast in his tale, the assembled clansfolk barely breathe.

He smiles. Chases a flutter of notes up and down the strings in a minor key. Then a happier one.

"So the tale o' our princess ends. Or does it?" A bright shimmer of triumphant notes. "She and her Deathan returned here—to Murtray— having found her woman in the forest on the way, for lovely Orle had not got far on her own. Here at Murtray, Deathan wed Darlei, and she a widow in truth. But a small ceremony it was, witnessed by his mother, for did it not take place in her very bedchamber?" The words come accompanied by another bright, victorious burst of notes.

"In the years after, Deathan was content to be a second son, to tend the keep he loved, look after the land he loved, wi' the woman he loved.

"But the princess..." He runs his fingers down the strings and his gaze focuses on one face there among his listeners. "She made hersel' a promise, that the man she loved need never risk himsel' for her sake again.

"She has kept that promise to this very day."

THE END

ABOUT THE AUTHOR

Laura Strickland delights in time traveling to the past and weaving deliciously romantic stories for her readers. Her first love has always been Scottish Historical Romance, and her work has garnered her several awards including a RONE. At home in Western New York, she's been privileged to mother a number of very special rescue dogs. Her lifelong interest in Celtic history, magic, and music, along with her mantra of *Lore, Legend, Love* are all reflected in her writing.

Visit Laura at www.laurastricklandbooks.com